PASSENGER LIST

PASSENGER LIST

A Novel

J.S. Dryden
with Mark Chadbourn

First published in Great Britain in 2021 by Trapeze,
an imprint of The Orion Publishing Group Ltd
Carmelite House, 50 Victoria Embankment,
London EC4Y 0DZ

An Hachette UK company

1 3 5 7 9 10 8 6 4 2

A CIP catalogue record for this book is
available from the British Library.

ISBN (Paperback) 978 1 3987 0451 0
ISBN (eBook) 978 1 3987 0452 7

Typeset by Born Group
Printed and bound in Great Britain by Clays Ltd, Elcograf S.p.A.

PART ONE

ATLANTIC AIRLINES FLIGHT TO NEW YORK VANISHES

Rescue teams are searching ocean waters south of Greenland after the disappearance of Atlantic Airlines Flight 702 on a journey from London Heathrow with 256 passengers on board.

Contact with the plane was lost at 22.15 local time (18.15 ET), a statement from the airline said. Pilots hadn't reported any problem with the flight's systems, although the course had been adjusted to avoid a storm over the mid-Atlantic.

No wreckage has been discovered. Canada, Greenland and Iceland have despatched air and sea search teams, which are currently sweeping the last known location of the plane.

Distraught families have gathered at JFK and London Heathrow Airport, anxiously awaiting news of their missing relatives.

A spokesperson for Atlantic Airlines said: 'As yet, we have no information on what might have happened to Flight 702. Our investigations continue. As soon as we've verified intelligence, we'll inform both families and the media.'

Statement from Atlantic Airlines CEO Robert Culpeper

Our exhaustive investigation into the disappearance of Flight 702 has now terminated. In the absence of black box information and any wreckage from the plane, we've relied on the evidence of remote system monitoring. These have shown no sign of malfunction in any part of the plane. The last message received from the pilot was a calm sign-off.

The only untoward aspect of the flight was a bird-strike during ascent and we must now conclude that this caused critical damage that manifested in a sudden and rapid deterioration of the plane's systems.

Our thoughts and sympathies are, as ever, with the families of the passengers of Flight 702 at this time.

1

The woman drifted among the trees like a ghost. Dragonflies darted around her, glittering in shafts of Indian summer sun punching through the amber-and-gold canopy over Casperkill Creek. In the distance, the Poughkeepsie traffic throbbed, but the creek was a haven of peace. Birdsong echoed, along with occasional peals of laughter from students sweltering in the shade, swathed in clouds of weed smoke. Kaitlin Le took in none of it. She was haunting the life she used to know.

As she picked her way along the trail, her thoughts flew across forests and rivers and cities to where her brother was being laid to rest. His memory at least. There was no body to bury. Her mother, Mai, would be wailing and her father, Kien, silent, his face like an open grave, with the extended clan of aunts and uncles and cousins twice removed, family friends and vague acquaintances united in grief.

Only she would be missing.

'If you don't come to Conor's memorial, what will people say? You are now our only child,' her mother had pleaded on the phone, her voice thick with the accent of the old country that she steadfastly refused to let go as she guilt-tripped Kaitlin. That was her last resort. Kaitlin didn't want to break her mother's heart, but to attend that memorial service would be an admission that everything she believed about Flight 702 was wrong. And she wouldn't – couldn't – do that.

As she moved out of the shade, she was jolted from her reverie. Here was the life she had planned for herself: Vassar College and ahead, the pink-bricked Blodgett Hall where she'd spent so many hours chewing through the theories of Keynes and Friedman before deciding to shift her focus to structuralism, utilitarianism and what she hoped would be slightly less of a grind.

Who was that woman? she wondered.

A cooling breeze was blowing down the Hudson Valley, hinting at the fact that autumn would be here before too long. Kaitlin trudged on, turning over the new sets of theories that held far greater importance than her studies now.

She'd almost reached the entrance to her student halls when she felt something scrabbling at her concentration. Someone was calling her name, she realised.

Kaitlin turned to see her room-mate hurrying towards her, waving. Amelia was an international student, a Brit, all perfectly formed vowels, sunny outlook and a staggering tolerance for beer.

'Mate,' Amelia gasped as she bounded up. 'What's wrong with you? I've been calling your name for half a mile.'

'Sorry. Distracted.'

'Yeah. That's the problem.' Amelia glanced round to check they weren't being overheard and whispered, 'The dean's office is gunning for you. They sent the Stasi round earlier to haul you in for a show trial.'

Amelia liked her drama.

'Don't worry. It's all under control.'

'Is it, though? Is it really? Mate, you've barely been to class for weeks. You've got to start taking this seriously. They're going to throw you out. For real.'

'I've—'

'Look, I know you've got good reasons. But talk to them, all right? You've got to. People are queuing up to get in this place. The dean's office isn't going to see a space taken by someone who isn't committed. Regardless of . . . what they're going through.'

Kaitlin wanted to shrug and say, 'Whatever.' There were more important things in life, she'd discovered. But her family would be devastated if she got thrown out of college and they were shouldering enough of a burden already.

'I'll do something to keep the dean's office sweet. OK?'

'Finally! Smartest person I know and only now do you start using that big brain.' Amelia tugged her arm. 'Come on. I've bought some brownies, those vegan ones you like. We can pig out and bitch about everyone we hate.'

Back in the room, as Amelia dumped the brownies on a plate, Kaitlin stood by her bed and let her attention drift over the maps and flight plans and witness statements she'd stuck to the walls. Her eyes wandered over the piles of aviation technical manuals and volumes on ocean currents and air disasters, each one flowering an abundance of multicoloured tags to highlight pages of interest. She *would* find the answer to what really happened to Flight 702. Whatever it took.

She pulled out her phone and stared at it for a long moment before calling the mailbox she'd set up. It was a ritual that was performed ten times a day, sometimes twenty, depending on how anxious she was feeling. Everyone who visited the apartment teased her for her constant phone usage. They stopped laughing when she told them why she did it and their faces twisted from a smile into that familiar sickening look of pity. They didn't understand. How could they?

The only calls she'd received to the hotline so far were from conspiracy theorists who were working through their psychological issues and had nothing of substance to add to her hunt for the truth. She wasn't deterred.

One day, there would be a message waiting that would change everything.

The converted townhouse reeked of damp. The walls of the meeting room at the back had been painted a sickly ochre and the carpet was such a dark brown, it sucked all light from the space. The few framed prints were pastels of nondescript subjects, designed to elicit no response whatsoever. Probably for the best. Nobody came here for a good time.

Kaitlin looked around the circle of drawn faces and felt an involuntary clawing in the pit of her stomach. This was her third meeting and they weren't getting any better. *Why was she putting herself through this? These people weren't like her.* But this was the price she had to pay to convince the dean she was getting back on her feet.

'Don't be afraid to let your emotions out. Holding it in is a sin against yourself.' That was Jack, group leader and the King of Platitudes. He lounged in his plastic chair, studiedly languid. His long strawlike hair, thinning on the crown, irritated her, as did his lips. Too thick, too perfectly shaped in an expression of compassion. She felt like a bitch for thinking it, but everything seemed to annoy her these days.

'It's a curse, isn't it?' Marie looked like a yoga teacher who'd been left out in the sun. She waved a hand and ten thousand hoop bracelets jangled on her wrist.

'Tell us what you mean, Marie,' Jack said.

'Grief. A curse. Some cultures think it's a supernatural force, don't they? You summon it in and it sits there on your shoulders. A demon. Maybe—'

Jack nodded. 'It possesses you.'

'Yes, that's it exactly. And you have to have an exorcism. Or something. Drive it out.'

'That's a very good analogy.'

Marie pouted. She clearly didn't think it was an analogy at all. Kaitlin imagined a big boot stamping down from the heavens and squashing Marie flat.

'You know what the answer is? Heavy drinking! Got to be done!' Carlos, one of the others, guffawed.

He was a construction worker, broad-shouldered, big-bellied. Kaitlin liked him but also felt deeply sorry for him. Carlos grinned all the time, every single moment, but his eyes were always screaming.

'No, Carlos.' Jack wagged his finger.

'No, of course not. No. But . . . yes?'

Jack caught his breath, then decided not to pursue. He turned his lamps on Kaitlin and her heart sank.

'Kaitlin. You haven't said anything for the last two sessions.'

'Nothing to say.'

'That can't be true. Why are you here if you don't want to unburden yourself? Keeping it in—'

'Is a sin against yourself,' all the other sheep chanted.

'Why am I here?'

'Yes.'

Because it's the only way I can shut my mother up and keep the dean's office from throwing me out.

Jack leaned forwards. He was determined not to let this go. 'Your twin brother was on Flight 702.'

'Conor, yes.'

'Do you want to talk about him and what he meant to you? It's good to remember the essence of the people we've lost as a way of beginning to cope with their absence.'

'Conor was great. Funny. Kind. We butted heads from time to time, but what brother and sister doesn't?'

'Ah.' Jack raised a finger as if he'd caught her out on the witness stand. 'The way you chose to end your statement on that point . . . Is there something you'd like to say to Conor now, if you had the chance?'

Kaitlin feigned a moment's thought, then shook her head.

'Are you sure?'

That fight. That brutal, stupid fight.

'You're such an idiot, Conor. Do you have any *feelings? Don't you care about anything but yourself?'*

'We hadn't seen each other for a few months . . .' *Or spoken.* 'So no unfinished business,' she lied to Jack.

'It's hard to come to terms with the death of a loved one when it appears so random. Purposeless,' Jack preached, holding his hands wide. 'Our brains crave explanations and without them, the universe appears . . . cruel. Someone you love, snatched away. For no reason.'

'What do you mean, random?'

'Flight 702 was brought down by a bird-strike. An accident. A terrible accident.'

'That's one theory.'

Jack frowned. 'That's what the official investigation said happened.'

'But there's no evidence for that conclusion.'

'I thought—'

'No evidence.' Kaitlin swallowed the edge in her voice. 'All families of the disappeared want answers,' she added, keeping her voice calm. 'That's fair, isn't it? That's what we're owed. Not some lazy resolution designed to wrap things up quickly. For commercial reasons or . . .'

Jack was staring at her with a patronising look of compassion.

'What?' she snapped.

'That's exactly the point I was making. We seek out conspiracies when the universe no longer makes sense. We try to impose order on the messiness of life. I understand how you're feeling, Kaitlin. I think we all do.' Jack looked around the circle of faces and everyone was nodding and smiling sadly. 'But you must move on from these fantasies. You'll never put your grief to rest until you have acceptance.'

Kaitlin stood, trying to maintain control, but she could feel herself shaking in spite of herself. 'What I'll accept is the truth. And until I have that, there's no way I'm moving on.'

She turned and walked out. She wouldn't be back.

As she walked back from town to Vassar, Kaitlin's phone buzzed – a message from her mother:

As you couldn't be at Conor's memorial, here's a video of the service. It was beautiful. So many kind words. I thought you'd like to see it.

Kaitlin pressed Play, but only managed to make it through a few seconds before it all became too much. She knew her mom meant well, but she didn't want to see this now.

Pocketing her phone, she trudged away from the lights. Her steps were a steady, soothing beat and gradually, she felt memories surface. Here was the real Conor, the way she wanted to remember him. That sweet smile, that open, sensitive face. Despite being twins, nobody really thought they looked alike – he was taller than her, with a wiry athleticism that wasn't bad for a nerd. But there were times when she felt they were like the same person.

13

He knew her better than anyone, and there were times when it was almost as if he could read her thoughts and she could read his.

It was their fifteenth birthday. They'd had their presents and cake and the usual family celebration. But later, when the house was quiet, they'd crept out into the night and watched the fireflies glow in the dark as they'd talked about their hopes and dreams for the years ahead.

She'd teased him for wanting to be a code monkey, preferring numbers to people, and he'd teased her back about the guy at school who she had a crush on. They'd laughed and talked for hours. It felt as though nothing would ever come between them. What a great night.

God, she missed him so much.

The full moon glowed just above the treetops along the creek. A chill breeze whined through the branches and Kaitlin shivered inside the blanket draped over her shoulders.

'This'll warm you up,' Amelia said, slopping red wine into a plastic cup.

This had been their Friday night tradition ever since they'd rolled up at Vassar: sharing a bottle of Valpolicella while they put the world to rights, outside when the weather was warm enough, in their room on colder nights. Sometimes they were joined by other girls from their dorm, or they'd be in someone else's room, getting ready for a night of dancing. The last few weeks had just been Kaitlin and Amelia, though. And this would probably be the last al fresco drink for a while.

As Kaitlin reached for the cup, she noticed her hand trembling. *Why did she care so much what some idiot at grief counselling said?*

Amelia smiled at her kindly. 'OK, so where are you at with the investigation?'

Amelia was a good friend. She didn't need to hear any more about this obsession – she'd been assailed by it often enough – but no doubt she sensed Kaitlin wasn't in the best headspace tonight.

The fog that had descended on Kaitlin that night six months ago briefly shifted and for a moment, Kaitlin felt something other than anger and sadness and guilt. A wave of warmth washed through her for Amelia, who had stood by her side through all this. Kaitlin bit off the desire to thank her friend or hug her, for fear it would release such a torrent of pent-up emotion she'd drown in it. All she could do was smile and nod. Even then, Amelia seemed to understand.

'I just wish I had something new,' Kaitlin sighed. 'I feel like I've hit a wall, you know? There's something, I know it. I just need one break.'

'If anyone can crack it, babe, it's you.'

'I don't even know why Conor was on that flight coming back home.'

Amelia showed a concerned face. 'You hadn't spoken to him for a while, right?'

'A few months.' Kaitlin winced inwardly. She'd never spoken to anyone about what had happened between her and her brother. But Amelia had been so kind over the last few months and she deserved the truth. 'We had a fight – a huge fight,' she began. 'He came round to see me that night he got his fifteen minutes in the limelight.'

'Oh, yeah. That was pretty cool. Stopping that dangerous malware all on his own.'

'Well, at the very least, it placated my dad, as much as Dad can ever be placated, anyway. He was never happy about Conor dropping out of school to do cyber security.' Kaitlin flopped onto the edge of the bed. 'I was so proud of him, you know. All of his dreams had come true. But then he told me what really happened.'

'What really happened? Sounds ominous.' Amelia took another swig of wine.

'He stopped the malware because he was involved in creating it in the first place.'

'Whoa.' Amelia's eyes widened.

'Thomas, you know—'

'Boyfriend.'

'Yeah. He's a hacktivist. Part of some secret group of keyboard warriors challenging governments, big businesses and the like. There were some crazies involved. Extremists. When Conor and Thomas found out exactly *how* extreme, they tried to distance themselves, but it was too late. They were in too deep.'

'So those crazies built the malware.'

'To attack world banks. Conor didn't approve of their methods, I'll give him that. But he thought banks were an OK target. A victimless crime, supposedly. According to Conor, the banks are all insured for loss, so he thought, why not? His cybersecurity job at the bank made it easy. Slip the malware into the system, stand back and watch the money drain away, out of the pockets of the rich and powerful and into some good causes.'

'Twenty-first-century Robin Hood.'

'In his head, I'm sure that's how he saw it. But the malware was more corrosive than he realised. It started to eat its way through entire systems, so Conor pulled back.'

'He told you all this that night?'

'Yeah. I mean, at this point, I was still sympathetic. Conor's always been so passionate about the 99 per cent and the 1 per cent. The world's a mess, right? We all know that. He felt it *so* strongly. Sometimes idealism like that clouds your judgement. So, I thought I'd give him a break.'

'This is where the "but" comes in.'

'He wasn't upset at all for being involved or for starting it! Zero remorse. OK, he was hitting a bank, but regardless of what he said, this wasn't a victimless crime. That was regular people's money, stolen from their accounts. If you're living hand to mouth, you don't have time to wait for a bank to sort out the chaos and refund you. You suffer. You starve. You get thrown out of your home. But Conor didn't seem to get that. He was more focused on the bigger picture. And once I realised that none of that stuff mattered to him—'

'You blew up. I've seen that temper. Scary.'

Kaitlin sagged. She regretted getting so angry. The things she said, the words she couldn't ever take back, their last conversation playing out night after night in her head, keeping her awake, overshadowing every good memory she'd ever had of her beloved twin.

'Babe,' Amelia murmured.

Amelia could see the hurt in Kaitlin's eyes, of course she could. Every time that night surfaced in her mind, Kaitlin thought she might fall apart.

'I said some terrible things,' she breathed. 'And I blamed Thomas. Really went for him. And that upset Conor even more. He stormed out, I brooded. Refused to call him, like some . . . like some stupid, whiny brat. The next thing I know, Mom is telling me he's flown to London to get away from everything.'

To get away from me.

'And still I didn't call him. What a bitch. What a fucking horrible bitch. Too proud. Too . . . too arrogant.' She

17

choked back a juddering sob. 'And then he got on Flight 702 and that . . . was that.'

The silence seemed to surround them and Kaitlin felt she might drown in it. Finally, Amelia spoke.

'I'm so sorry, hun.'

Kaitlin scrubbed the back of her hand across her eyes.

'It's all so insane,' Amelia sighed. 'Why didn't you tell me before?'

Kaitlin shrugged. 'I couldn't . . . still can't . . . process it.' She swallowed her sadness and kindled the defiance that had carried her through so much. 'I'm going to find out what really happened to that plane,' she said, her voice hardening. 'If there's been a cover-up, I'll do whatever it takes to bring it into the light.'

'Babe,' Amelia said, worried.

Kaitlin flashed back to that feeling of plunging down a never-ending well when she'd first heard Atlantic Airlines Flight 702 had vanished midway between London and New York with her brother, Conor, on board. At first there had been that debilitating feeling of queasy shock, then disbelief. She remembered those long days and sleepless nights at JFK with their mother and father, surrounded by other desperate families, all of them hoping, waiting for news – any news.

Conor was gone, there could be no doubt of that. Deep down, Kaitlin knew that it was futile to hold on to any hope that her brother and the other passengers of Flight 702 were still alive. And yet, Conor wasn't gone. He lived on in her head in among all the maybes and the what ifs. The longer she hovered in that weird twilight zone without any answers, the more the questions piled up. That was the dam that kept the flood of her grief at bay.

She needed to understand what really happened. That was the only thing that would help her to put Conor to rest.

The facts were bald. The pilots reported a bird-strike as the flight climbed out of Heathrow. The recordings of their conversation with Air Traffic Control showed they weren't remotely concerned by the incident. Once they reached 33,000 feet, they headed west under fine weather conditions. Mid-Atlantic, the satellite link showed a squall blowing up and the pilots decided to reroute slightly around the area of worst turbulence. Even then, there was still no sense of anxiety, nor even the faintest hint of unease. They had negotiated with oceanic control for a change of track and persevered. The co-pilot even cracked a joke and said 'Goodnight.'

That was the last confirmed communication.

Kaitlin shivered, and not from the chill. That was the moment when everything changed and the mystery of Atlantic Airlines Flight 702 began to burn bright. The flight switched direction, from west to north, and headed towards Greenland. A radar station in Iceland tracked the baffling move. Could it have been to avoid the storm? It seemed unlikely that seasoned pilots would take such drastic action. The plane also descended to 20,000 feet. Another inexplicable decision.

Why? Why? Why?

And then came the garbled radio transmission. Kaitlin felt her stomach knot as sickening scenarios played out in her head. The message was recorded by air traffic control in Gander, Newfoundland, its incomprehensible nature only serving to make it more terrifying. Among the fragments of words and crackling static, one thing was clear: panic. Those experienced pilots were gripped by dread.

And then Flight 702 was gone.

No debris was found. The marine search teams swept across a wide area of the North Atlantic, tracked currents, followed the last known path, scanned with radar. Nothing. Not the slightest trace of the plane and all of those people on board.

No sign of Conor.

It was almost as though Flight 702 had never existed.

Kaitlin felt her unease shift to a cold, hard anger. If there's one thing the authorities hate in a situation like that, it's a vacuum. All that space for conspiracists to pour in their theories – wild ideas that could only destabilise the already struggling aviation industry. Share value under threat, jobs on the line.

The scramble to find an easily understandable explanation was almost unseemly. That and the desire to give closure to those suffering families, of course.

The Federal Aviation Authority investigation had concluded that the plane went down due to complications from the bird-strike. Other investigators said the flight had struck a flock of birds with high-altitude migration patterns. All this without a shred of evidence to back it up. Mere supposition. Apparently, that was good enough for some people. Her parents had accepted it blindly, even though she knew it had destroyed them to accept that their only son was dead.

But it wasn't enough for Kaitlin.

The bizarre change to a northwards course; the descent to a lower flight path; the lack of any debris – all ignored.

She wasn't a conspiracy theorist. She wasn't clutching at straws. She was thinking rationally, sifting evidence, as she'd once done every day in class.

She wasn't being driven by grief.

There was a truth waiting to be discovered and she wouldn't rest until she found it.

Kaitlin felt her defiance burn bright and that accompanying surge of energy that had carried her through the last six months.

'Let's head back,' she said to Amelia. 'There are a few things I need to check.'

The thump of bass thrummed from one of the nearby rooms as they made their way along the corridor.

'You want to bounce any ideas off me, I'm here,' Amelia slurred. She'd finished the rest of the wine on the way over.

'You FaceTime your folks,' Kaitlin said. 'I'm just going to review the Greenland data again. Maybe there was some other reason why the plane was heading that way.'

'Don't pull another all-nighter, Kaitlin, all right? I'm worried about you. You're going to burn out.' Amelia turned the key and swung open the door.

In the dark of the room, Kaitlin hovered. She held her breath and wished.

'Go on, check the messages,' Amelia told her. 'If there's another of those conspiracy nutters, we can have a laugh about their latest "theory". There's still an opening for "Bigfoot Did It".'

Steeling herself, Kaitlin pulled out her phone and thumbed the number for her mailbox. There was one message waiting:

Hi. I'm . . . I'm calling for the Flight 702 hotline?

A long pause, but when the caller spoke again, any hesitancy had vanished.

OK. My name's Dylan. That's all you need to know.

Kaitlin felt her neck prickle. She sensed something in that strong, confident voice that she couldn't quite put her finger on. The rolling accent made her think of Texan wide open spaces.

You're doing a good job. Challenging the lies they're trying to feed us. But there's a lot you don't know and the truth is, you're not going to get there on your own.

There was another pause, as if the caller were choosing his words with undue caution. Kaitlin felt her stomach knot with anticipation.

I'm willing to point you in the right direction. But if you carry on down this path, you need to know one thing: you might not be coming back.

2

The laptop screen glowed in the dark. Kaitlin hunched over it, her fingers tapping impatiently on her thigh, tense with anticipation. She'd lost track of the time, but Amelia had fallen asleep hours ago, her breathing steady, and a peaceful silence lay over the dorm.

Dylan's phone message had been terse. Nothing in the words set him apart from the scores of other timewasters who had contacted her, but she'd felt there was something new here. Instinct, she told herself. Or perhaps, today, the day of Conor's memorial service, she'd simply wanted some hope.

The mysterious caller had directed her to the Facebook group she'd set up alongside the hotline for anyone who might have information about Flight 702. For the most part, it was clogged with more useless theories and messages from trolls. Dylan had told her to await a direct message from him there.

So, she waited.

Just when she'd started to reach the conclusion that she'd allowed herself to be led up another dead end, the laptop dinged.

Dylan's message contained a link and said simply:

This will take you to an encrypted app. Download it, then we can talk.

After years of lecturing from Conor about how easy it was to hack into a computer, Kaitlin knew better than to simply click on a link from an unknown sender. She checked the account he was using to message her, but there was nothing; only the anonymous grey outline for a profile picture. No personal details, no photographs. Her fingers fluttered over the keys.

You think I'm crazy? Downloading something that could be spyware or malware?

The response flashed back:

You don't have a choice.

How do I know I can trust you?

You don't.

Kaitlin leaned back. This felt dangerous. Dylan was luring her in. He clearly understood psychology well, knew how much she needed this; how little effort it would take to push her in whatever direction he wanted her to go in. The sensible option would have been to back off.

But Dylan was right. She didn't have a choice.

Kaitlin clicked on the link and downloaded the app.

A few moments later, Dylan's first message flashed:

You made the right decision.

So, tell me who you are.

The less you know about me, the better for both of us.

You sound paranoid.

Just pragmatic.

Kaitlin winced. She still wasn't wholly sure she could trust this contact. Hints of shadowy threats could just be another way to control her.

'Why are you helping me?' she typed.

I want to know the truth as much as you do.

Then why aren't you following these leads yourself?

I'm being watched.

Kaitlin felt her chest tighten as she stared at those words.

OK. Now you're freaking me out.

Good. You should be. Here.

A phone number flashed up in a message bubble.

That's for emergencies only. Get a burner, then send me the number. I'll contact you if anything comes up out of the blue and we need a rapid response.

OK.

Now, I'm going to send you some files. The passenger manifest. Some basic intel.

Kaitlin felt a shiver of glee. She'd been trying to get hold of the passenger manifest from day one. If Dylan had it, he must be legit. Maybe.

The main lead I have right now is a kid abandoned at Heathrow. A Bulgarian. His mother flew from JFK with

him, was supposed to get a connecting flight to Sofia, but she left the kid and flew back to New York alone.

Weird.

Exactly. There's got to be something in that. One of those files names the mother's sister in NYC. You should check it out.

Kaitlin sprawled on the bed, staring at the ceiling. Sleep wasn't going to come easily, she knew that. Dylan's information was good, but was it too good to be true? Her father would call her naive. Her mother would give her that look that sat somewhere between sad, stern and disappointed.

Was *she being stupid?*

Slipping in her AirPods, she scrolled through her playlists until she found one that was calm enough to keep the world at bay but wouldn't disrupt her thoughts. In the dark, she conjured up images of Conor, happier times, kicking sand at each other at Delray Beach in Florida, sitting beside the firepit watching the stars and telling ghost stories at Halloween. Singing stupid songs in harmony. Sharing a stolen beer.

She felt her heart ache for what she'd lost. She'd do anything to put that right. That was the danger.

Kaitlin tapped her foot in frustration as she waited in the annexe to the dean's office. A full half an hour had passed before she was summoned to the desk of the student well-being officer, an elegant woman in her late fifties with a soothing voice.

'How are you doing, Kaitlin?' she asked in a tone that suggested she already knew the answer.

'I just wanted to let you know I've been going to my therapy sessions. As requested.' Kaitlin slid the form across the desk that Jack had signed. There was no need to mention she wouldn't be going again.

'The request was for your benefit, Kaitlin.' The woman scanned the form. 'OK. That all looks good to me. I'm glad you're finally getting some support after your loss.'

'Does this mean you're not going to kick me out?'

'We're not hard-hearted. We take the well-being of our students very seriously and we'll do everything we can to support you.'

No matter what she said, though, the fact was that there were minimum class attendance requirements and Kaitlin had long been failing to meet them. She wondered how long she could skate the edges of the rules before things got serious again.

On the way back to the dorm, she braced herself and checked her bank balance on her phone. *How was she going to fund following Dylan's leads?* The numbers on the screen weren't much of a surprise, but she still felt the familiar sinking dread she always felt when it came to money.

She stressed about it all the way back to her room, but after running numerous calculations through her head and factoring in as few meals as possible, she decided she could probably eke out what little she had. So long as this didn't turn into a never-ending wild goose chase, she should be able to survive.

'If this Dylan guy asks to meet up, don't go alone,' Amelia cautioned. Still in her pyjamas, she eyed Kaitlin over the rim of her coffee mug.

'I'm not an idiot, Amelia.'

'Well, you did download an app sent to you by someone you don't know.'

'This is true,' Kaitlin conceded, shoving underwear into one of the pockets of her backpack.

The rosy dawn light gleamed at the window. She'd been up all night, reading the material Dylan had sent, but she didn't feel remotely tired. In fact, she was buzzing with the possibilities of what could lie ahead.

'You need to text me every day. Twice a . . .'

Kaitlin glanced up from her packing at Amelia's pause. 'What?'

Amelia slammed down her mug and ransacked a drawer, eventually pulling out a key, which she tossed onto Kaitlin's bed.

'What's that?'

'You know my dad's got an apartment in NYC that he uses when he's over here on business?'

'The one he said you could stay at if you were ever out in the city and it was too late to get back here?'

'That's the one. You can stay there.'

Kaitlin frowned. 'I couldn't—'

'You can. And you will. You're going to be there a while, on and off, if you're following all those leads. And, bluntly, you have zero funds to spend on hotels right now. Unless you're planning to sleep rough, which I couldn't possibly allow.'

'Thank you.' Kaitlin felt another wave of warmth for her best friend.

'Don't get me wrong; it's not a penthouse on the Upper East Side or anything, just some basic rooms in the East Village. But there's a bed and a kitchen. I'll text you the address.'

Amelia turned away. Kaitlin knew she was trying to hide the worry she was feeling.

'I'll let you know how I'm getting on.' As much as she could, anyway. After all the warnings Dylan had given, she wasn't about to tell Amelia anything that might put her in danger, too.

'I really hope this works out for you, hun.' Amelia strode over and hugged her. 'I know how much Conor meant . . . means . . . meant . . .'

'It's OK.' Kaitlin squeezed her friend back briefly before easing herself free from the embrace. 'I never know which tense to use, either. Which is right at the bottom of the list of things I don't know.'

3

In Tompkins Square Park in New York, shaven-headed priests in saffron robes chanted Hare Krishna in the pool of shadows under the spreading elm. The sun slipped down over New Jersey, turning the cross streets into rivers of ruddy light. Kaitlin breathed in that stew of traffic fumes and spicy food scents as she hurried under the street lights flickering into life. Her new burner phone was in her backpack. She was ready.

Amelia's family's apartment was on Avenue A, three storeys up above a bagel shop with a fire escape overlooking the park. Inside, Kaitlin's nose wrinkled at the smell of stale air. It was clear that nobody had been here for a while, but it was as functional as Amelia promised. After a quick shower to wash the grime of the bus journey from her skin, Kaitlin tossed her backpack on the bed, pulled out her laptop and got to work.

A message from Dylan was waiting:

Done some digging. The kid abandoned at Heathrow – looks like his mother is Maria Elian, Bulgarian immigrant. Had a place in Queens. See what you can do with that. The usual warning: tread carefully. Don't try to draw attention. Always think there's somebody on to you. That's the best way.

Kaitlin felt a shiver of unease at Dylan's warning. She tapped in a reply with the number of her new cell and then began her search. A couple of hours later, she'd learned Maria Elian's sister, Ana Dragov, also lived in Queens, on Salerno Avenue. Once she had the number, Kaitlin punched it into her burner and listened to the ring.

A woman answered promptly with a thick European accent.

'Hi, is this Ana Dragov?'

'Who is this?'

'I'm sorry – you don't know me. My name is Kaitlin Le. My brother was on 702.'

A pause, then: 'Yes?'

'Your sister was on the plane as well. That's right, isn't it? I was hoping that we could—'

'I can't help you.'

The line clicked dead.

Kaitlin stirred in the dark before dawn, showered and then gnawed on the bagel she'd picked up the previous night. Ana Dragov didn't want to talk. That wasn't going to stop her. She waited until a thin silvery light began seeping through the window, then she ordered an Uber.

Salerno Avenue was just south of Cunningham Park. Big houses, lots of trees, some money there. Kaitlin asked the driver to drop her off a little down the street from Ana Dragov's house and she walked up through swirls of golden leaves, keeping her head down. As she drew nearer, she eyed the place without looking up. No point drawing attention if anyone was watching from the windows. She wanted the element of surprise.

The house loomed up, white SUV in the drive. Kaitlin sucked in a few deep breaths and steeled herself. The last thing she ever expected to do was confront someone on their doorstep. She hoped she was up to it.

After swinging onto the property, she raced up the steps before she lost her nerve, yanked open the screen door and knocked. She tensed as footsteps approached and then the door swung open to reveal a thin woman with jet-black hair and pale skin. No doubt this was Ana Dragov.

'Who are you?' the woman demanded.

'I'm . . . Kaitlin Le – I called you—'

'Get out of here. I have nothing to say.'

Ana swung the door. Kaitlin slammed her palm against it to try to keep it open.

'Ana, please! Just . . . just wait a second.'

The door banged shut.

'I lost my brother,' Kaitlin shouted. 'And you lost your sister. What the authorities are saying, it doesn't add up. All of us, we're in the same boat. We all want answers and I-I think we can help each other. Just give me fifteen minutes. Please . . .'

Kaitlin held her breath, but there was no response. She hammered on the door again.

Don't go crazy. She'll call the cops. That's the last thing you need.

Taking a deep breath, Kaitlin pressed her face close to the wood and lowered her voice. 'Ana, listen. Bratva – he's your nephew, right? Bratva? I know where they took him.'

After a long moment, the door clicked open. Ana's bloodless face appeared in the gap.

'Where they take him?'

'Can I come in?'

'We can't talk here – my parents . . . they get upset. There is Starbucks on 188th. We meet there.'

The door slammed shut again.

Kaitlin settled at a table in one corner, where she could see the whole of the Starbucks. She was getting as paranoid as Dylan. She sipped on a tall latte, tracking every customer who came and went. Finally, Ana walked in. She was wearing a black belted coat, her hair scraped back into a ponytail. She glanced around, saw Kaitlin and marched over as if she were going to arrest her.

Kaitlin smiled, hoping she appeared disarming. 'Can I get you a coffee?'

'Where is Bratva? Address. You give now.'

'I need to ask you about your sister first.'

Ana shook her head. 'I cannot. If you won't tell me what I need to know, I leave.' She turned.

Kaitlin thought she looked scared. That unnerved her even more.

'Ana,' she pleaded, reaching out. 'Ana. I promise you, you can trust me. I'm not a reporter or anything. I'm just . . . I'm trying to put all the pieces together.'

Ana glared. 'I no believe you.'

Kaitlin snatched out her student ID and thrust it forwards. 'See?'

Ana leaned in to examine the card, her eyes narrowing as if this were some trick.

'That's me. Kaitlin Le. My brother is Conor Le. He's a computer scientist, one of the best, and he . . .' Show a human side to put Ana at her ease, that's what she'd told herself, but she could hear the words tumbling out too fast as her emotions surfaced. 'He lives with his boyfriend, Thomas, and a cat named Tova. We used to sneak out just so we could drive around and listen to Willie Nelson on the stereo. He'd stay up late to teach me how to program in JavaScript. He's my favourite person in the entire world . . . *was* my favourite person . . . and I want him back more than anything.'

Ana stared at her with those unreadable eyes. After a moment, she dragged out a chair and sat down. Kaitlin felt a rush of relief.

'I'm sorry for your brother.' Ana's voice had softened, though her face hadn't.

'Thanks.'

'Where you from?'

'Kansas. Missouri.'

'That's a long way.'

'That ID. I'm a student here. Just outside the city.'

Ana nodded. 'You said you had information about my nephew.'

'I do. I've been doing some research. And the official explanation – the bird-strike – it just doesn't make sense.'

Ana continued to stare. Kaitlin shifted, felt herself start to babble, unable to contain it.

'So, first of all, there's no physical evidence that the plane even crashed. There's no wreckage from the flight, no black box, the final transmissions all seemed normal.'

'Spaceship.'

'What?'

'Spaceship came and took them away.'

'That's not—'

'Or it was Russians. North Korea. Lost world of Atlantis,' Ana sneered. 'I don't care. Tell me about my nephew.'

Kaitlin nodded. Recalling the information Dylan had sent over, she replied, 'At the moment, the case is still in the hands of the British social services. I imagine they let you know that already, being the next of kin and everything.'

'Yes, but we only get official letters. They want us to provide so much information. And my husband is away, so . . . it's difficult for me.'

'I understand.' Kaitlin smiled, but she could hear something in the other woman's voice. A hint of a secret, perhaps. 'Where's your husband?'

A moment of silence as Ana considered her response. Then: 'Away.'

'Away where?'

'Business.'

'What does he do?'

'He does . . . business.'

'What kind of business?'

'You ask too many questions,' Ana snapped. 'And you still haven't told me—'

'OK, OK,' Kaitlin jumped in. This woman seemed like she was permanently balanced on a knife edge. 'Bratva – he's been taken to a home in Oxfordshire. About ninety minutes north-west of London. The court's appointed an official guardian.'

'I know all this.'

'Yes, but I've got the address.'

'You give to me.'

Ana swallowed. The first flicker of some emotion crossed that hard face.

'I was like his mother. He stayed with us. Maria was never there. I was with him all the time. When he woke up crying in the night . . . it was me . . . it was . . .' She choked back a sob, fixed that unwavering stare again.

It was a front, Kaitlin understood that now. It was a tactic she was all too familiar with.

'Where was Maria?'

'Parties, rich men, I don't know. And then she came one day and just took him away.'

Kaitlin pushed aside her latte and reached across the table. 'Why would a mother leave her son at the airport? Why would she get on a plane unless there was—'

'Unless she was going to blow up that plane?' Ana's voice dripped with contempt.

'No, that's not what I'm saying. I just . . . Maybe she knew something was going to happen and so she—'

Ana smacked her palm on the tabletop and Kaitlin jumped. All around the Starbucks, heads swivelled towards them.

'Look, you tell me nothing, I tell you nothing. I have to go.' Ana stood up.

'No! Listen, I have the address. The house where they're keeping Bratva. I have it.'

'So, give it to me.'

Kaitlin bit her lip. 'I don't have it with me.'

Ana sneered again. 'This is fucking joke. Goodbye.'

Kaitlin jumped up. Everyone was still staring, but she found she didn't care.

'Ana, please! Please. I need you. We need each other.'

Ana turned to leave.

'Come on,' Kaitlin pleaded. 'I'm just trying to put all this together and find the facts! No one's telling us anything. If we help each other, we can figure out—'

Ana whirled, her eyes blazing. 'Figure what? Listen, in Kansas you have tornadoes, yes? You have big wind and storm. It comes down from sky and smack! Your house: gone. Your whole life: ruined. What is reason?'

'I . . . it's . . .'

'Exactly. You don't know. And you will never know. It just . . . happens. No reason. Just like plane. That plane is gone. My sister. Gone. Your brother. What is reason? I go on Facebook, I join support group. Everybody want to say they know secret, they know what happened. But they don't! No one does. No one will ever know.' She pressed a hand against her chest to calm herself. 'You love your brother?'

'Yes.'

'You remember that. Forget the rest.'

Ana marched away. Kaitlin slumped back in her seat. She'd failed.

Kaitlin slipped out of the Starbucks into the chill, grey late morning. The last of the late summer was fading fast. As she marched away, she felt her determination rekindling. Ana was her best lead right now. She couldn't give up on her. As she turned over all the scenarios of why a mother could possibly abandon her son, she paused at a crosswalk and glanced back along the street.

Her instinct prickled. A woman was walking towards her, late twenties maybe, hood pulled over her ash blonde hair, head bowed, sharp features, hands shoved into her hoodie pockets. Kaitlin had seen her sitting in the Starbucks. The woman stopped to look into a store window, but her body language suggested she was feigning interest, Kaitlin thought.

You're paranoid. Dylan has got into your head.

When the Walk sign blinked on, Kaitlin hurried across the street. On the other side, she looked back. The woman was crossing, too.

Kaitlin's heart thumped faster. Picking up her step, she weaved among the flow of bodies. The blonde woman increased her pace. There was no doubt now.

Snatching out her phone, Kaitlin ordered an Uber with a collection point further along the street ahead. When she saw the car arriving, she threw herself into a run and dived in the back.

As the car pulled away, she locked eyes with her pursuer. The woman watched her pass, easing down her hood, and she continued to stare as the car rumbled off into traffic.

4

Night came down hard. Kaitlin crouched by a chain-link fence among the yellowing grass and beer cans. She looked past the pool of light surrounding the street lamp to the shadows cloaking the warehouse. This part of Queens was deserted after business hours. Empty lots, storage units and crumbling factories waiting for redevelopment, the air heavy with diesel fumes. Sirens whined in the distance, but silence lay heavy in that place. Not somewhere she wanted to be caught out.

She shivered in the chill. Her fingers were already going numb. After her disastrous meeting with Ana, and the strange blonde pursuer, Kaitlin had retreated back to the apartment, feeling defeated. But as she stared at the wall and wondered whether or not it was time to accept defeat and head back to Vassar, a wave of determination flooded through her. She owed it to Conor to broach Ana one more time, even if she got a slap across the face for her efforts.

As her Uber had pulled up on Salerno Avenue for the second time that day, the white SUV in Ana's drive had reversed out at speed and raced away. Kaitlin had ordered the Uber to follow it, in return for a good tip. They'd ended up here.

The SUV was parked further up the street. Ana was still inside and had been for an age. Every now and then, the interior flared – the light from her phone as she made calls.

What was Ana hoping to do here? She had no idea.

Kaitlin's hands were growing numb and her limbs were starting to cramp after so long crouching in the cold. She thought longingly of her dorm room, covered in fairy lights, and for a moment she wished that she was back at Vassar, getting ready for a night out with Amelia. Maybe she should jump on the subway and head back to the apartment. But before she could weigh up her options, another SUV screamed up, black this time, and four heavyset men climbed out, casting furtive glances around. Ana clambered out of her car and began to jabber at the men in a language Kaitlin didn't recognise, probably Bulgarian.

After a moment, one of the men unlocked a padlock on the door of the warehouse and they all went inside.

Kaitlin hesitated for a moment. No one knew where she was right now and she could hear Amelia's voice in the back of her mind telling her not to take any risks. This was too suspicious to ignore, though. She crept along the fence and eased through a ragged gap onto an area of broken bricks alongside the towering building. There was no way that she was getting in through the front entrance, but there might be a window down here where she could spy on whatever was going on inside.

The only windows that she could reach were all dark and caked with dust, but halfway along the wall, broken steps led to a basement door daubed with graffiti. Empty nitrous oxide cartridges rattled around her feet as she ventured down. Another padlock and chain hung from the door to a loop on the jamb, brown with rust.

Kaitlin sighed. She wasn't getting in that way. This was futile. But as she turned to go, she was startled to hear sobbing echoing from inside. Kaitlin pressed her ear against the blistered wood. A woman was crying, low and constant and heavy with despair.

She felt a wave a nausea flood her stomach. She wished she was better at this, but she already felt way out of her depth. Her father would exhort her to leave, admonishing her that this wasn't her business and it was better not to get involved. But she couldn't leave someone in such distress without checking.

Perhaps she could call the police. But to say what? She rattled the rusty chain and noticed the metal securing loop in the jamb was loose. The wood was rotten. Gripping the chain with both hands, she wrenched it hard and the loop popped out of the wood. For a moment, she paused, waiting to see if anyone had heard.

Her blood pounded in her ears so loudly that she could no longer hear the crying. She put her shoulder to the door and pushed hard. As it ground open, a sliver of light carved across the steps.

Kaitlin peeked through the gap and her breath caught in her throat. A bare light bulb shone across a brick basement that had been divided into what could only be described as a cage. Behind a row of bars, eight women huddled. They all looked to be around Kaitlin's own age, in their late teens or early twenties. Filthy mattresses lay on the cold flags and a bucket sat in one corner.

When they saw Kaitlin, the women launched into a cacophony of desperate pleas in that same language she'd heard before. Clutching hands reached through the bars. One of them, a hollow-cheeked woman with dyed blonde hair, wrenched a couple of the others back and hissed, flapping her hands to indicate they should be quiet.

As they fell silent, Kaitlin heard the rustle of voices somewhere above them.

The blonde woman jabbed a finger towards a blistered, paint-spattered desk against one wall. 'Please,' she said in faltering English. 'Keys. Save us.'

Kaitlin's head spun. She couldn't begin to process what she was seeing here. But she threw herself to the desk where the woman was pointing, rattling through beer cans and pizza boxes scattered on the top.

'No! Inside,' the woman urged.

Yanking open drawer after drawer, Kaitlin finally glimpsed a bunch of keys. She stabbed one after another into the lock on the cage door as the sound of movement above continued and the women grew more anxious. Eventually, one slid in and turned.

As the door swung open, the women piled out, screeching and howling and falling over each other. They scrambled past Kaitlin, fighting to get out of the door and up the stairs.

The buzz of voices from upstairs thundered into cries of alarm.

Shit, Kaitlin thought. *I've done it now.*

She hurled herself after the freed women. Still sobbing, they scattered across the waste ground beside the warehouse. Kaitlin raced back across the bricks the way she'd come. Bestial roars erupted at her back as those thuggish men she'd seen earlier flooded out of the basement in pursuit.

Blinking away tears of fear, Kaitlin clawed her way through the gap in the chain-link fence. One of the wires raked the back of her hand and blood spattered the ground.

She stumbled, sprawled across the sidewalk, ripping her jeans, but she heaved herself up, ignoring the throbbing pain spreading through her left knee as she sprinted on.

As she ran past the edge of the wasteland in front of another row of warehouses, a figure loomed out of a doorway and grabbed her. Kaitlin shrieked. A hand clamped across her mouth, the other hand dragging her into the dark.

'Keep your mouth shut,' a woman's voice hissed. 'Make any noise and you're dead.'

Kaitlin struggled, but the grip on her tightened.

'Relax,' she breathed in Kaitlin's ear. 'I'm a friend.'

The hunting men's call and response echoed through the night as they pounded along the street. Kaitlin relaxed her body and pressed back against her captor. Right then, it seemed like the only option available to her. She could feel the woman's heart pounding against her back – she was scared, too.

From the shouts, some of the men turned back, no doubt searching for the women who had escaped whatever terrible fate their captors had had planned for them. One set of footsteps cracked past the doorway, but it didn't cease, continuing past them.

When the sounds of pursuit had ebbed away, the woman eased Kaitlin out of their hiding place. It was the woman who had followed her out of Starbucks earlier that day. The woman glanced up and down the street to be sure, then thrust Kaitlin towards a beat-up Honda.

'Who are you?' Kaitlin whispered, her eyes wide.

'Not here. They're not stupid. They'll retrace their steps searching for you. Get in the back and keep down.'

Kaitlin ripped open the rear door and sprawled across the back seat. The woman pulled away with a screech of tyres.

'Who were those women? What was all that?' Kaitlin gasped.

'Later.'

'We have to call the cops. They need help.'

'Call the cops right now and everything that was happening there will move to another location, one we don't know about. Be patient. I'll tell you everything you need to know soon enough.'

Twenty minutes later they were seated at a table with a bottle of Budweiser each, in a low-rent bar filled with the vinegar stench of stale beer. The lights were dim, the music loud and the only clientele were a row of men hunched along the counter who looked like they'd given up on life.

'I need some answers,' Kaitlin demanded. 'What *was* that back there?'

'You'll get them.' The woman pulled back her hood and shook out her hair. 'Name's Valarie Vennix. I work on investigations for *New York Magazine*.'

'A journalist.'

'Allegedly.' Valarie swilled back a mouthful of beer.

Kaitlin noticed she always kept one eye on the door.

'You could have got yourself killed back there. What were you thinking?'

Good question. What had she been thinking?

'I'm trying to find—'

'I know what you're doing.' Valarie dipped into her backpack, pulled out a tan envelope and slid it across the table.

'How? What's that?'

'You can try to guess or take a look. I'll wait.' Valarie lounged back in her chair.

Kaitlin tore open the envelope. Sheafs of paper slid out; it appeared to be a collection of transcripts and some photos. She looked up with a quizzical expression.

'Left for you at my reception by a mysterious benefactor who wanted to get them to you quickly. Presumably didn't know where you were hiding out.'

'And how did you find me?' Kaitlin asked, raising her eyebrow.

'We're following the same leads, for different reasons. I know Ana. I've staked out her place. But to answer your question, I know you through our mutual friend.'

'The mysterious benefactor?'

'Well, "friend" is a strong word.' Valarie smiled. 'How are you getting your contacts?'

'I don't know what you mean.' Kaitlin feigned dumb. She didn't want to give too much away, had no idea how much she could trust this woman.

'Good answer. So, no one told you about Ana Dragov? These crime families take their privacy very seriously.'

'Crime family?' Kaitlin felt a pang of unease. If she'd known that going in, she might not have been quite so cavalier. 'OK. I got a message pointing me in the right direction.'

'Who gave you the tip?'

'It was anonymous.'

Now Valarie grinned. 'This is a great dance. I'm loving it. Shall we call him Dylan? Just . . . you know . . . for no reason.'

Kaitlin couldn't hide her surprise.

'You know him?'

'About as much as you do, I bet. The only thing I'm 100 per cent sure is that that's not his real name. You're not the only one he's been helping.' Valarie sipped another mouthful of beer. 'It's good to have someone on the inside, though, isn't it?'

'On the inside?'

'Someone with access to . . . stuff. Take a closer look at those photographs.'

Kaitlin flipped through the glossy prints, all of them images that seemed to have been taken from a security camera.

'Th-that's Maria and Bratva getting off the plane in London.' She remembered their faces from her online search. 'Who would have access to an airport security camera?'

'Dylan seems to.'

Kaitlin skimmed the rest of the photographs.

'So here, they're walking through the terminal. That's Maria kneeling beside the boy, kissing him.' Kaitlin frowned. 'Walking away, on her own. Wait . . . who's that man she's talking to?'

'Dimo Dragov.'

'Ana's husband?'

'Right. I've been investigating him for a while and hounding his wife for months. But Ana Dragov won't talk to anyone. Except, apparently, to you.'

'I guess that's because I kind of blackmailed her. I told her I knew where her nephew is.'

'Wish I'd thought of that. Did she tell you where her husband was?'

'Away. On business,' Kaitlin replied sardonically.

'He's disappeared. Most likely to Europe. Probably in Bulgaria.'

'You think he has something to do with Flight 702?'

'I don't know. What I do know, though I can't prove it beyond all doubt, is . . . Well, you tell me. Do you know what Dragov does?'

'Well, to some extent. "Business", according to his wife.'

'He's a trafficker. Young women, mostly, from Bulgaria. He brings them over on tourist visas with the promise of work or marriage and then, when they get here, they just . . . disappear.'

Kaitlin flashed back to the faces of those caged, terrified prisoners in the warehouse basement. She felt queasy.

'They get drugged, forced into prostitution, then passed around his network of "businesses associates",' Valarie continued, her voice growing cold. 'Washington DC mainly. Playthings for powerful people.'

45

'Jesus.'

Valarie's face hardened. This wasn't just a story to her.

'I'm going to nail him. I'm pretty close now. I've got quotes from his top lieutenants. Women who told me he interviewed them for jobs as quote, unquote "personal secretaries". Just a few more pieces of the puzzle and I'll have him.'

'I hope you get him, I really do. But what does all this have to do with 702?'

'How do you think I found out about this whole Bulgarian sex trafficking operation in the first place?'

'Beats me. How does anyone find out about something like that?'

'You don't, unless you're a customer. Or . . . unless someone rats them out.'

'Maria.'

'Clever girl. Maria was going to whistle-blow to me and share everything she knew about Dragov and his sick little empire.'

Kaitlin let this information settle on her. Suddenly, she could see all sorts of possibilities that she hadn't considered before.

'You think Dragov had something to do with the plane going down?'

Valarie's eyes flickered towards the door again. Now, Kaitlin could understand the journalist's permanent state of unease. Criminals like Dragov would go to any length to prevent their secrets from being exposed.

'I haven't got any proof of that. But in those photos Maria looked terrified before she left to get on that plane. And she left her kid behind. I mean, that doesn't sound like someone who feels completely safe to me. My theory? Dragov found out that Maria had betrayed the family and sent someone after her to take care of it in the way that these people take care of snitches. I'll leave you to speculate on what that has to do with the flight.'

Kaitlin was already speculating about the numerous ways a crime family could bring down a plane. But one other thought was niggling.

'Why would Dylan choose me to get involved with all this?'

Valarie swilled down the last of her beer. 'Maybe he saw something in you. Or maybe he just sees you as cannon fodder for whatever he's trying to achieve. You get cut down by gunfire. Someone smarter and better gets through while the people behind this are distracted.'

What was Dylan's real agenda? *Had she been too naive? Was she putting herself in real danger by following his guidance?*

Valarie slammed her glass down on the table and smiled without humour. 'The bottom line: in the end, we're all on our own.'

As Kaitlin pondered the dismal message, Valarie stood up.

'Come on. I'll drive you back. Where to?'

'The East Village.'

'EV it is.'

In the car, Kaitlin watched the lights flash by, but her thoughts were running with those frightened women. She probably wouldn't be able to sleep tonight for worrying if they'd escaped the men who were pursuing them.

If anything, their plight only strengthened her resolve. Ana had plenty of questions to answer. Kaitlin had to ask them.

Kaitlin looked around the bustling Starbucks, which was just as busy as the last time she was here. Maybe she was still being naive coming back here, but she'd thought long and hard about the information she'd gleaned from Valarie and she'd reached a conclusion, based on logical analysis.

When Ana came in, she marched over to the table and said, 'I come for address. You have with you?'

Kaitlin steeled herself. This was the moment she'd wrestled with all night. But the desire for answers outweighed her own safety.

'I know about Dimo's business.'

Ana showed a blank face. 'I don't know what you're talking about.'

'I met Valarie Vennix. From *New York Magazine*. She told me some interesting stories.'

'So what?' Ana's eyes narrowed.

'Where's your husband?'

'None of your business.'

'He was on Flight 702 with Maria, wasn't he? He was waiting for Maria in London so he could take her right back to New York.'

Not hiding out in Bulgaria. A man like Dragov wouldn't flee at the first sign of trouble. He had a good life here; an established enterprise that made him rich. And he dealt with powerful people in Washington. He wouldn't abandon any of that if he could find another way out.

Ana turned up her nose. 'I don't know what you talk about.'

'Sure you do. I got a handle on Maria's phone records.'
Thank you, Dylan.

'You know who called her just as she landed in London? It was you.'

Ana stared, not backing down.

'Why? Was it to warn her?' Kaitlin leaned across the table. 'What exactly was Dimo's plan for Maria when he got her back to New York? Was he going to punish her for betraying him? Maybe . . . kill her?'

'You seem to have all the information. Why don't you tell me?'

'Maria didn't abandon her son. She was trying to escape with him, wasn't she? To give him a better life. Away from Dimo, away from all this. And then—'

'Listen, stupid girl—'

'No, you listen! She left Bratva in the airport terminal because she knew he'd have a better chance at a good life than if he stayed with her and faced whatever Dimo was going to do to them.'

Ana's eyes blazed. 'You have no idea what you are talking about. My husband was a good man. He took care of his family. My sister was . . . a disgrace. She think everyone in America have it easy. She think she is judge. Look at her – betraying her own family.'

'Don't you care? About what your husband does? That he was going to hurt your own sister?'

About all those poor women?

Kaitlin stood up. 'I'm . . . I'm finished here.'

'Give me the fucking address.'

'I don't think that's a good idea.'

'That's not your decision.'

'No. But it was Maria's.'

'You will regret this, Kaitlin Le.'

And that was probably the only honest thing Ana had said to her.

Outside, in a bitter wind, Kaitlin pulled out her burner and thumbed a number.

'I told you to contact me through the app. Only call if it's an emergency,' Dylan snapped when he answered.

'Right. Um . . .'

He sighed and his voice softened. 'What do you want?'

'To thank you for the photos and the phone records.'

'No need. I hope you find the answers you're looking for. Anything else?'

Kaitlin swallowed, then blurted, 'Who are you?'

Silence.

'Why are you helping me?'

'I'm just someone who wants to find out what really happened.'

'Did you know someone on Flight 702?'

'You don't believe the bird-strike theory, right? Well, neither do I,' he replied, ignoring her question.

'How did you get those CCTV images of Maria?'

'You can't ask me that stuff.'

'Some of this doesn't make sense. Ana seems pretty sure that Dimo Dragov was on the plane. Why wasn't he on the passenger list?'

'Fake passport? It's easy to do, especially for someone with Dragov's background.'

'But Dragov had nothing to do with it,' Kaitlin replied. She'd thought she was so close. 'Unless the members of his own gang decided to take him out. That's a possibility, I suppose.'

'Exactly. We've got to follow every lead. Some of them are going to take us to brick walls. But it's the only way we'll find out the truth. And some might initially seem like nothing and then, as more information comes in, they take on a new relevance. Turn over every stone. Study. Record. Keep trying to see the connections. We'll only know the truth at the end of the line.'

'So what now?'

'I've got another lead. Really interesting. Suggests a strong reason why the plane might have been diverted.

Need to dig deep into it, though, to find out how much is real, how much hearsay. I'll send a recording to the app. Take a look at it.'

Kaitlin felt that familiar unease tug at her. 'How do I know that you're not part of this? A member of Dragov's crime family trying to throw me off the scent?'

'I put you on the scent, remember?' His voice dripped acid. 'You've got to keep thinking clearly, Kaitlin. Don't worry about Dragov's people-trafficking trade. Valarie's like a dog with a bone. She'll shut it down.'

'I'm not sure I can trust you.'

'I don't have time to reassure you. You can either trust my intel or not.'

She had no choice, did she?

'Good,' he said, taking her silence as acceptance. 'The person you should really be looking into is . . .'

Kaitlin heard talking in the background.

'I've got to go. I'll be in touch.'

'No!'

The line went dead. A moment later, her phone rang again. She felt relief that Dylan had called back so quickly.

'Thank you,' she gushed.

A jumble of discordant sounds crashed.

'Dylan? Dylan, is that you?'

Kaitlin shivered. *Was that shouting? People screaming?*

'Hello? Hello?'

The line went dead once more and this time, no one called back.

Later, in her apartment, Kaitlin's phone chirped and she felt a rush of warmth when she saw that it was Amelia calling.

'Babe, just checking in to see how you're doing,' her friend said.

Kaitlin closed her eyes and smiled to herself. She couldn't believe how good it was to hear a friendly voice.

'Living the life. Thanks for the loan of the apartment.'

'So, you gone all Veronica Mars yet?'

Kaitlin filled in Amelia on the meeting with Ana and the encounter at the warehouse.

'Oh my God. Oh. My. God. Kaitlin, what *are* you doing? What if they'd caught you?'

'They didn't.'

'Yeah, but what if? Mate, you're not bulletproof. You can't take risks like that.'

How could she explain to Amelia that she no longer really cared what happened to her, that for a long time now, it had felt like any risk was worth it? She decided against it.

'Yeah, I know. I learned my lesson,' she assured her.

'Wow. I hope those poor women got away. What kind of world are you getting into?'

Kaitlin couldn't answer that either. She shifted the conversation on to more mundane matters, friends' relationship issues, Amelia's pie-in-the-sky plans to get her folks to take her to Barbados for the holidays, schoolwork, anything that took her back to the life she'd once had.

Afterwards, she luxuriated in the commonplace. For the first time, it dawned on her that if she was going to get through all this, she'd need the anchor and the security that Amelia and her family offered. It was time to stop pushing them all away.

NURSE: According to my thermometer, your temperature is almost 38 degrees. And you're feeling well?

AMERICAN WOMAN: Mm–hmm.

AMERICAN MAN: She's fine, yes.

NURSE: Madam?

AMERICAN WOMAN: I'm fine, thank you.

NURSE: Do you have any flulike symptoms at all? Muscle pain, fatigue, headaches?

AMERICAN MAN: She's good.

AMERICAN WOMAN: [sniffs, coughs]

NURSE: Madam, forgive me, but you don't look very well.

AMERICAN WOMAN: It's . . . it's the dry air from the plane.

AMERICAN MAN: Is all of this still necessary?

NURSE: I don't make the rules, sir. I'm just a nurse. But you had to consent to the return screening when you purchased your ticket, as do all the other aid workers who spend time in the region.

AMERICAN MAN: Are they filming us? Shouldn't you have asked to film us?

NURSE: Well, sir, they're not recording a reality show. It's for security reasons. Neither of you left the capital?

AMERICAN MAN: No, no. Our foundation works in education, all in Kinshasa.

NURSE: Madam, you really do look a bit off-colour–

AMERICAN WOMAN: Oh, Jesus Christ! How many more times are you gonna tell me I look like crap? [crying] I'm sorry I don't look so lovely without my make-up on and

53

I'm sorry I'm not good at travelling, but I swear to you, I don't have some godforsaken jungle disease, OK? My God, we've been killing ourselves trying to build schools no one seems to care about, we've been flying for ten hours, I just wanna go home and see my grandchildren.

AMERICAN MAN: Honey, you're doin' the Lord's work.

NURSE: I'm sorry, madam. I didn't mean to cause any offence; I'm just following protocol. So, can I just ask you to confirm that neither of you went to any of the recently infected areas in the past eight weeks?

AMERICAN MAN: No, no, no. We never went upriver. Our work is in the capital.

NURSE: Very well. You're all set. Cheers. Have a safe flight.

AMERICAN WOMAN: [coughing]

AMERICAN MAN: Have a great day.

5

Spoons chinked against mugs and bacon sizzled on the grill. The coffee machine hissed in a cloud of steam and low-level conversation pulsated. The diner's early morning symphony swelled.

As she stepped through the door, Kaitlin breathed in the appetising aroma of fried food and fresh brew. Her stomach rumbled. She'd been skipping meals, trying to eke out what little funds she had until this business was done.

But the recordings Dylan had forwarded had intrigued her enough to move fast. She could see how this one could be important. An evidently sick woman, possibly infected with a virulent strain of something or other, would be a nightmare scenario for any flight. Could a couple returning from the Congo have unleashed a deadly pandemic on board Flight 702, a fast-acting virus that had brought the plane down?

Pausing, she surveyed the diner from under the brim of the New York Jets cap she'd pulled low to hide her face as much as possible. Paranoia was a way of life now; she wasn't taking any chances.

There was the woman she'd come to see, in a booth at the far end. Dolores Grier was African American, mid-fifties, carrying a few extra pounds and looking cornered. Her eyes darted around and her nod to Kaitlin was surreptitious.

After the Flight 702 memorial service attended by the President where the sick woman's daughter had spoken,

Dolores had left a garbled message on the hotline. She sounded frightened. Dolores had been working for Atlantic Airlines and was now back in the US. A direct witness. That was gold dust.

Kaitlin slipped onto the bench opposite her contact. 'Hi. I'm Kaitlin.'

'Dolores.' She continued to look around the diner. 'You weren't followed?'

'No. I'm being super careful.'

Dolores leaned back in her seat, relieved.

'Do you mind if I record this?' Kaitlin asked, sliding her phone across the table.

'S–sure.'

'OK, I don't want to waste your time, so let's get straight into it. You were on the gate for 702, is that right?'

Dolores moistened her mouth. 'Yeah.'

'Tell me what happened.'

'This older couple, the woman – she looked sort of tired. She kept kind of falling asleep. And sneezing. So this kid, he was, uh . . . Latino or Arab. He comes up to me and says "Hey, that lady's sick." Apparently, they'd been in Africa.'

'You didn't tell the FBI?'

'It's not like I decided not to tell them. I just didn't say anything. And the agents had so many questions about the other passengers. They didn't ask about the old couple.'

'What happened after the kid told you they looked sick?'

'I called them over. Wayne and Wendy LaPeer. The man was so friendly – Mr LaPeer. He said his wife was just tired 'cause they'd been travelling ten hours. They'd been doing charity work or something. I didn't know they'd come from somewhere that had been under an infection advisory – the medical screeners who process aid workers dealt with all that. And the woman just . . . looked at me with this, uh . . . sort of gaze. It was kind of hollow. Seemed like standing was taking a lot of energy. I asked her if she was well enough to fly and she just said, "I'm trying to go home." And so, I let her go home.'

'OK, tell me—'

Dolores twitched and leaned across the table. 'I think there's a man staring at us. No, don't look!'

'What man?' Kaitlin felt the heat rise in her neck.

'The guy in the green jacket. Or maybe he's just eating eggs.' Dolores sighed. 'See? This is what my life has become. Wondering if strange men are following me because I couldn't fess up when I should have.'

'You think she was really sick? Sick enough to maybe . . .'

'Have somethin' to do with the plane going down? Yeah. The look she gave me – I can still see it so clearly. Glassy eyes, red eyes. Clammy. Her skin was kinda yellow. But her husband was just . . . smiling so big, as if it were just the most wonderful day. Like a big, happy dope. I thought maybe she was sort of like me. Like a version of me where I didn't get divorced, and me and Jimmy spent a couple of weeks in Kinshasa every year to remember how lucky we were.' Her eyelids batted down for a moment.

'And your bosses, your co-workers – none of them saw the LaPeers?' Kaitlin pressed.

'Don't think so.'

'You didn't speak to them about it after the plane went missing?'

'No, dear, I've just been thinking about it myself.' Dolores played with her coffee spoon. 'I quit Atlantic after the accident. Before I left, though, I-I looked up the LaPeers' ticketing transaction. They bought the tickets the day before the flight. They were in a rush. And then I let them on.'

Dolores dropped the spoon and it clattered in the saucer. She sucked in a deep juddering breath.

Kaitlin felt a rush of compassion at what this woman must be going through. 'Are you doing OK, Dolores?'

Dolores blinked away hot tears. 'Oh God, I'm such a monster. I let a woman with a crazy disease on a plane, and your brother dies and here you are comforting me.' Dolores glanced past Kaitlin's shoulder and her eyes narrowed. 'OK, that guy is definitely looking at us.'

'Dolores . . .' Kaitlin cautioned. Those mood swings weren't good. There was a lot churning away inside this woman.

Dolores drew another ragged breath. 'Hundreds of people dead. A good chance this is all my fault. Unless . . . maybe you know something I don't.'

'I-I don't know much. Yet.'

'Oh. There it is, I suppose.'

'The couple. You said their name was LaPeer?'

'Yeah. They have an Instagram page. It's still up. I look at it sometimes.' She stared deep into her coffee cup, yet another victim of Flight 702.

As she made her way out of the diner, Kaitlin felt her phone vibrate. It was her mother calling. She stared at it, letting it ring until it went to voicemail, and then she felt a bout of guilt.

She couldn't face talking right now. There would be too many questions, endless attempts to get her to return to class, to give up her search.

What a terrible daughter she was. Not so long ago, she'd never have dreamed of ignoring her mom's calls. They were such a close family and she'd always had a particularly tight relationship with her mom. Texting every day, FaceTiming every couple of days. Her mother was so loving, a true matriarch who cared for her brood.

Her father, in contrast, was both stern and strict, though no less loving underneath it all, Kaitlin knew. He carried with him that immigrant drive to work hard, to see his family succeed and not struggle as his own parents had. That focus on discipline sometimes made him seem bad-tempered and aloof, but underneath was a gentle man who just wanted the best for his children.

The loss of Conor had hit both of her parents terribly hard. Her mother had become, if anything, even more effusive, lavishing twice the love and attention on Kaitlin. Kaitlin knew that love had to go somewhere, that her mother was clinging on to her one remaining child out of a deep-seated fear that she might lose her, too. Though it pained her to admit it, carrying the weight of it all sometimes got suffocating.

Her father had retreated into himself, barely talking and disappearing for long stretches to be alone. Kaitlin had caught him drunk on two occasions when she'd visited home. That wasn't like her dad at all. She was worried about him.

If she were really honest with herself, she knew she ought to be there supporting them, and that thought only made her feel worse. She kept telling herself there would be plenty of time to be there for them once the truth about Flight 702 had emerged, when they'd all be able to return to the lives they'd had as best they could.

Was that just a pipe dream, though? She stared at the voicemail notification, then slipped her phone away. She couldn't afford to be distracted right now.

★

Down in Tompkins Square Park, someone was playing a guitar and singing a poor cover of a Taylor Swift song. Kaitlin heaved up the window and leaned on the ledge, looking out over the fall display of gold and amber as she hit the keys on her phone.

A man picked up after a couple of rings, his voice sounding like someone who'd missed his train by a split second. 'Population, Refugees and Migration. This is Dobbs.'

'Hi, I'm looking for Melonie Diaz.'

'Melonie is no longer with us.'

'Oh. I'm sorry.'

'That sounded bad. No, she's not dead. She quit. How can I help?'

'I had some questions about an NGO that your office funded. The LaPeer Schools Network? They were in Kinshasa.'

Dobbs made a strangled note of irritation. 'Where did you say you were calling from?'

'My name's Kaitlin. I'm a friend of their daughter's.' An easy lie. But she needed to know what might have made Wendy LaPeer sick. How virulent was it? Could it have been so bad that it brought the plane down? She needed experts and lying was the only way she could see to gain access to them.

'OK.' His voice softened. 'Tragedy what happened to them. I can only imagine. Both parents . . .'

'I know. She's . . . she's still a wreck.' Kaitlin had no need to fake these feelings; they rolled out of her with ease. 'I know six months may sound like a long time to be grieving, but it's . . . still hard for any of the family to talk about what happened. So, I'm calling on their behalf. Did you know the LaPeers at all?'

'Met them last year when I was visiting our projects in Kinshasa. They ran a good operation. Kept their schools going, and that's the hardest part.'

'It's just that, Mr Dobbs. The reason that I'm actually calling is that the kids are worried Mr and Mrs LaPeer may have been . . . sick, before they got on the plane.' *God. When did she become such a good liar?* It was a good thing the man on the other end of the line couldn't see her face.

'Sick?'

'Yeah. That maybe they had something that . . . might have spread . . .'

'I read that theory. That the LaPeers were infected with the Ebola virus and this somehow spread throughout the plane and had brought it down. It's hokum.'

'How can you be so sure?'

'Three reasons. First, the Ebola outbreak was way upriver. And the only people who go upriver into the jungle are missionaries, and the LaPeers weren't missionaries. Secondly, all staff are quarantined before they leave the DRC.'

'So, the LaPeers would have been quarantined?'

'Absolutely. We do that as a precaution because the signs don't appear for several days.'

'And what are the signs?' She'd done her research. She knew the answer, but it was good to hear it from the expert.

'Fever, headaches and then . . .' Dobbs' voice trailed off.

'Go on.'

'Well, basically, if you develop Ebola, you . . . well, your whole body just starts to melt. But we have to do a health screening for anyone coming out of the DRC,' he added in a hurry, no doubt trying to sweep over the gruesome image. 'They didn't have Ebola.'

'But Mrs LaPeer was sick.'

'Maybe she had a cold.'

'And the third reason?'

'What?'

'You were talking about reasons. You said there were three. What was the third reason?'

'Ebola was eradicated in the DRC over a year ago.'

'But you said that upriver there could be some—'

'I said that's where the Ebola outbreak occurred. But they eradicated it in just forty-two days. The WHO are usually incredibly effective at disease mitigation.'

It was clear that this man had nothing more for her.

After she hung up, Kaitlin clambered out onto the apartment's fire escape and looked out over the city. Dobbs was adamant, but she still wasn't convinced. Maybe it was instinct. Maybe that corrosive paranoia was turning her into one of those crazy conspiracists. *Was this how it happened? A slow march from reason into a swamp that eventually swallowed up everyone who ventured in there?*

There was a cover-up. There had to be a cover-up.

She needed to know more. She grabbed her phone and opened Instagram. It was time to delve into the LaPeers' lives and look for a way to reach their daughter.

6

The offices of Murray & Wexler were on West 42nd Street.
On a good day, they smelled of the bakery downstairs and
on a bad day, they reeked of the garbage barges unloading
at the wharf on the Hudson River. There was nothing Rory
Murray could do about that, short of moving premises, but
this really wasn't the time. One breakthrough, that was
all he needed. One big case and the world would smell a
whole lot sweeter.

And Flight 702 was his path to that.

Rory stretched out his legs on the corner of the desk,
showing off his polished Cuban heels. He was a tall man,
but he liked that extra height they gave him. Imposing.
Good when walking into meetings.

'Law Firm to the Stars. What do you think about that,
Shana?' Rory raised his hands to frame an imaginary bill-
board. He could see it in his mind as clear as day. His
personal assistant seemed to be having trouble, though.

Shana was standing in the doorway to his office, looking
confused. She had a big heart. He liked that. She was a
terrible personal assistant, though.

'Danny Guzman!' he said.

'Danny?'

'Danny Guzman! *Days of Our Lives*. Admittedly it was
only a small role, for . . . three weeks? But he's a star,
right?'

'Oh, yes. You represented him in the—'

'Potentially catastrophic "hot food in the lap" suit, yes. Could have been devastating for Mr Guzman in his line of business. If he'd been scarred . . . Northern Airlines understood that and it's to their credit that they were prepared to settle.'

Shana stared.

'OK, I can see this one isn't catching fire with you. Let me think on it.'

'OK, Mr Murray.' His PA turned to go, then said, 'Don't forget Renee Keffler is coming in.'

Rory frowned. 'That isn't in the calendar.'

Shana showed a sheepish face. She'd forgotten to put it in his diary. Again.

As his PA slipped out, Rory shouted, 'When's she coming, Shana?'

A muffled 'Ten minutes,' floated back.

Rory swallowed his irritation and jumped to his feet. He ran his fingers through his hair in front of the hand mirror he kept in his top drawer, spritzing with aftershave – just a little, he didn't want to smell like a gigolo. Then he practised his smile a couple of times and loaded his brief-case with the documents he'd put together on Flight 702.

Renee Keffler had an imposing intellect, a caustic tongue and a bearing that suggested she always knew more than the person she was talking to, which she usually did. That was exactly why Rory liked to use her as an expert witness whenever he could. She dominated the opposition before she even opened her mouth.

'Renee!' Rory boomed, throwing his arms wide when Shana ushered her through the door. 'Always, *always* a joy to see you.'

'Still working out of this shithole, Rory? When are you going to move up in the world?'

'I've stayed to honour the memory of Karl Wexler, you know that. And yes, maybe I've stayed too long, but you can't put a price on loyalty.'

Renee sighed. She'd always had a low tolerance for his flights of fancy and dazzling wordplay.

Low frequency, Rory, he told himself. *That's the way to go.*

'Let me treat you to lunch. I owe you that.'

'Fine. Anything to stop me breathing in the garbage fumes.'

Rory led Renee to the deli three doors down. It didn't look much from the outside, but the pastrami on rye was so huge, it was a heart attack in waiting.

Once the sandwiches and beer had been delivered, Renee flicked out a paper napkin and asked, 'So, how's the aviation law business, Rory?'

Rory wagged a finger at her. 'Always straight down to the nitty-gritty, Renee. That's what I like about you. Business is good, yes, but it could get a lot better very quickly. If I can nail down what happened with Flight 702.'

'I figured that's what you wanted to talk about.'

Renee had been a top-level executive at three different airlines, climbing the ladder methodically until she shocked everyone by switching to the enemy and becoming an air accident investigator. That put the fear of God in every CEO, because she knew their games inside out.

'I didn't work on 702, you know that, Rory,' she said, opening her sandwich to inspect the contents.

'I know, I know. And I also know that there isn't a single thing that happens in the industry that you're not aware of.'

'This is true.'

Rory took a bite of a pickle. Projecting nonchalance in a situation like this was key. Any hint of desperation always threw you on the back foot and that was the last thing he needed right now. He was in a race against time.

'I'm putting together a class action.' As, no doubt, was just about every other aviation law firm. He needed to lock down his clients fast.

'Against the airline or plane manufacturers?'

'Maybe both. Right now, I'm not sure where culpability lies.'

'There's no indication that it was down to manufacturer error.' Renee paused. 'I've got to say this. This is bigger than anything you've done before. Not even close. Are you sure—'

Rory held his arms wide, the pickle waggling between his fingers. 'Am I sure I'm up to it? Renee! This is me!'

'You're not chasing low-level passenger litigation cases here, Rory. This is the big leagues.'

'I'm ready. I've been building towards this.'

And if he didn't do it now, with the state of his reputation, it was probably game over. The stink of garbage for the rest of his life. He felt his stomach twist at the prospect, but he showed that winning grin without a flicker of doubt.

Renee sighed, unconvinced, but he didn't care. All he needed was a chance to show everyone what he could do.

'Everyone I've spoken to,' she began, 'in the Air Accident Investigation Branch and the National Transportation Safety Board is . . . perplexed, shall we say. Perplexed at the NTSB's official statement – their unprecedented statement – of the bird-strike theory.'

'I knew it!' Rory clapped his left hand down on the table and his plate jumped. 'Sorry. Passion gets the better of me sometimes.'

Renee raised an eyebrow but chose to ignore him.

'It just doesn't add up. On any level.'

'So, you think there's a cover-up?'

'I think there are still a lot of questions to answer. Which, for reasons undiscovered, are not being answered. Or even looked into.'

'Cautious answer, Renee, good. Political, perhaps. That kind of argument works before a judge. But you know that.' Rory chewed on his pickle for a moment, thinking. 'OK. Human error?'

'Possibly.'

'Pilot fatigue?'

Renee twitched her nose, unconvinced.

'Improper procedures?'

'No evidence.'

'Decision errors?' He hesitated, then: 'Or the plane was brought down deliberately by the crew?'

'We know that's happened in the past.'

'That would explain Atlantic's rush to judgement. It's definitely not good for business if your passengers think they might be ditched in the ocean every time they board.'

'I'll tell you what I know.' Renee dissected her sandwich with a careful stroke. 'The captain had a reputation for being erratic. He didn't always follow mandatory pre-flight checks.'

'That hasn't come out!' Rory felt that familiar tingle of excitement in his belly. He knew he'd been right to call Renee.

'The first officer switched out at the last moment. Claimed he was ill, but he had a history of conflict with the captain. And . . .' She paused, deep in thought. 'Not sure I should go here. But, in the spirit of leaving no stone unturned . . . The investigators uncovered a link between the first officer's replacement and a radical Islamic group.'

'I see your point. Cultural bias? Or significant? We can't know for sure unless someone digs into it.'

'There are red flags all over. Why did the captain try to send out a cell phone message minutes before the plane lost contact? It would suggest he no longer had access to the communications system.'

'Renee, you're a lifesaver. There's a lot of red meat here – plenty I can use when I'm persuading the families to join me in this journey.'

'Glad to be of help. All right, Rory. Now, you fill me in on your catastrophic private life. Which ex-wife is going for your jugular this time?' She grasped her sandwich, ready to take a big bite. 'This is better than Netflix.'

Rory swept into his apartment, tossed his briefcase to one side and flicked open his laptop on the coffee table in front of the sofa. The buzz from lunch with Renee still hadn't faded. If anything, he felt more energised than he had done in years. The old Rory was back.

He punched a key and settled back to listen:

Hi, Mr Murray. You've been leaving messages on my phone. Listen, buddy, if you keep phoning someone and they don't pick up, maybe, just maybe, they don't want to talk to you. Just a tip to help you out. I'm not interested in your services. I already have legal representation. Now, fuck the hell off and leave me and my family alone.

'OK. That's a maybe.' Rory scribbled a note on his yellow pad.

The next message played and he sighed when he heard the voice of ex-wife number two, Eloise.

> Rory, the clinic called to say the bill hasn't been settled.
> This is your daughter, Rory, your flesh and blood. And
> you know what? I don't appreciate having to be the one
> who always—

Rory tapped the trackpad and jumped forwards to the next recording. This time it was the voice of his investigator and his shoulders loosened a little.

> I've got something for you, but er . . . You'd better pay
> me this time. And don't be late, or I won't be working
> with you again, OK? So, I have one lead – the bereave-
> ment officer at Atlantic Airlines. Jennifer Wong. Obvi-
> ously, she wasn't talking, but now she's quit her job and
> set up as an independent therapist. Might be more
> open. Here are her details . . .

Rory slipped his digital recorder into his jacket pocket so no one would know it was on. When Jennifer Wong ushered him into the small meeting room in her new office, he exclaimed, 'Hey, Jennifer! Great to meet you face to face, finally. Surprised Atlantic Airlines allowed someone of your experience to get away.'

'The airline cut back on that particular service budget when the investigation into 702 ended. Take a seat.'

Rory pulled up a chair.

'It was time to move on, anyway,' Jennifer continued. 'So, you said you had some questions you wanted to share with me.'

'Yes, indeed.'

'And you are legal counsel for . . . one of the families?'

'For several, yes. We're gathering information.'

'Against the airline? I'm not sure I'm allowed to say anything that—'

'Not against the airline. We're just representing the families' interests, to make sure they get what they're due.'

'Can I ask you which families you represent?'

'You can, but I'm afraid I'm not at liberty to disclose their details at this stage,' he replied with a broad smile.

'I see. How many families?'

'Again—'

'You're not at liberty to say. So, is this evidence-gathering? I just want to be clear on what this is actually about.'

'Well, everything is useful. Anything you can tell me about the conversations between the airline and families.'

'I was there to help with their emotional needs.'

'I know. And from what I hear, you did an amazing job under extremely challenging circumstances.'

'Thank you. Have you ever lost someone, Rory?'

'Yes. Yes, I have.'

'Someone who went before their time?'

'Yes.'

'Then you know yourself. Everyone deals with loss in their own unique way. It's especially hard for people when they hang on to the hope that their loved one might still be alive. But, in the case of Flight 702, we knew within the first few hours that that wasn't the case. There was very little trust. A lot of anger. A lot of theories. But whatever happened on that plane, we knew there were no survivors and my job was to be that bearer of bad news.'

'To the relatives?'

'Yes. To convey that information to them as clearly and compassionately and professionally as I could. That was my job. Details of one-to-one counselling sessions are obviously off-limits.'

'Absolutely.'

'Client confidentiality.'

'You wouldn't be breaking any confidences if you were to introduce me to some of the relatives – as someone they can talk to. In confidence. If they wish. Because, after events like this, people do sometimes disappear.'

'Usually because they don't want to be bothered by lawyers like you.'

'I want to help them.'

'OK. Whatever.'

Rory glanced down at his notepad, taking a moment to gather his thoughts. Jennifer was stonewalling as much as she had when he'd phoned her across the weeks after the plane vanished. But there was a way through, there had to be.

'So, generally speaking, your role was to help the relatives come to terms with—'

'To give them certainty.'

'Yes.'

'The bird-strike theory. Your job was to push that line.'

'That was the information we had at the time.'

Finally. A chink: at the time.

'You're not working for the airline any more. You can—'

'I can't do anything. No.' Jennifer peered into the corner of the room as if she might find something of interest there. 'I don't want to get caught up in this.'

Rory pounced. 'Is that because you think there is something to hide? Did you feel the airline wasn't being honest, Jennifer?'

Jennifer stood. 'I have a meeting at two. If there's nothing else . . .'

Continuing to sit, Rory ignored the therapist's mounting frustration. 'Did the airline use you to get the families to sign an NDA and not talk to the press about their concerns?'

'I really have to go.'

'Do you keep in touch with any of them?' he pressed.

'They have my new details. They know they can come to me whenever they need to.'

'I've tracked a few down. Some are very hard to reach.'

'If you want names, there's a Facebook page. You probably know about it, right? It's run by some woman who's pretty plugged in. Kaitlin Le, a relative of one of the victims. If you want to reach out to any of them, you can try there. I've got to go. Good luck with it all.'

7

The Atlantic wind blasted across the mudflats and stirred the browning rushes in the gleaming wetlands. A storm petrel wheeled across the silver sky, its trilling a warning of bad weather to come. The shore of Long Island Sound had already lost its summer appeal and Kaitlin shivered as she hurried away from the waterfront towards the white-painted clapboard house.

One breakthrough, that was all she needed. Thank God she had Dylan steering her. The Facebook page and the hotline were now jammed with trolls and messages from some ambulance-chasing lawyer, looking to make a fast buck out of the grief of the families. Clearly, it was Dylan or nothing.

As she climbed the steps, the door swung open to reveal a broad-shouldered woman with short blonde hair, one eyebrow cocked and a confident look that suggested she wouldn't take any shit.

'So, you're my good friend who called the State Department for me because I was too grief-stricken?' Beatrice LaPeer asked, her voice dripping with sarcasm.

'I am so sorry, Ms LaPeer. I can explain.'

'Relax, relax. Call me B. Come on in. I guess we have a lot to talk about.'

Kaitlin stepped into the warmth of an airy lounge, the scent of baking cookies drifting from the kitchen. Beatrice waved a hand for Kaitlin to sit on the sofa.

'So, Martin Dobbs called me from the State Department. Said that a young woman was asking about my parents.'

'It was just a white lie,' Kaitlin explained. 'I didn't realise they'd call you to follow up. I guess that was stupid on my part.'

Beatrice folded her arms. 'Don't get me wrong: I was fucking pissed. But then I saw your group online and . . . I guess it made more sense.' Her face softened. 'I'm sorry about your brother.'

'Thanks.'

'You must have been close. To be going to all this trouble.'

'We used to be, yeah. We're . . . he was my twin.'

'Oh my God. That must be even harder.'

'Yeah. We kinda took different paths after high school. I went to college and Conor got a job in London – he was always a bit of a super-brain. And, you know . . . noble.' She felt her words dry up. It was still hard to talk about him.

Beatrice seemed to sense the weight of emotion and moved to the kitchen to give Kaitlin some space. She returned with a coffee pot and two mugs, which she set on a low table in front of the sofa.

'And now you've dropped everything because you don't believe the bird-strike story,' she said, back to a more businesslike approach.

'A woman reached out to me. She was at the airport before 702 departed. She said your mom was sick.'

Beatrice sat in an armchair and poured cream into her coffee.

'My dad called me from Heathrow. I had no idea they were even coming home. I remember thinking, shit, are they gonna want me to pick them up from the airport, 'cause that's, you know, a whole thing. But then he said Mom wasn't feeling very well and they just wanted to get home.'

'Do you know what was wrong with her?'

'No, but I figured she must have been pretty wrecked, 'cause my dad doesn't call me. It's always my mom who calls, then she gives him the phone and we have awkward small talk. He never, ever calls of his own accord. He has much better things to focus his energy on, like being the colonial overlord of the Congo.'

Kaitlin showed a blank face, but she could sense the strain behind Beatrice's comment.

'So, their organisation – they built schools in Kinshasa?'

Beatrice snorted. 'That's one way of describing it. I mean, yes, they definitely built schools. But they went there to convert people.'

'Doesn't the State Department prohibit NGOs from spreading religion?'

Beatrice smiled. 'A lot of volunteers who go over there are religious. They used to pay for the trips with Church bake sales and fundraisers, and then they found out it's a lot easier to get State Department funding and just keep the religion thing on the DL.' Beatrice motioned for Kaitlin not to forget her coffee. 'Lately, the Department has been like a chicken with its head cut off and so it's been a free-for-all. At least that's what my mom said.'

'So, they were doing missionary work in Kinshasa, but no one at the State Department was supposed to know, or they'd lose their funding?' Kaitlin blew on her coffee, but her mind was racing. *If these evangelists were involved in deception from the very beginning, how far would they go to hide things?*

'Basically, yeah, but Kinshasa's all Christian. The Catholics and the Mormons got to them ages ago.'

'Then where did they go?'

'Up the Congo River.'

'Up north? In the jungle?'

Beatrice nodded. 'They'd go with their students, back to their parents' villages. The Jesus sell works a lot better when you have an insider.'

'Do you know anyone they worked with over there?'

Beatrice thought for a moment. 'There was another couple. Unitarians, I think, from Connecticut, but I don't remember their names. I guess I could have asked more about what they were up to. But I don't know, I just never thought . . . I never thought that they could disappear.'

And there was the thing that drew so many disparate people together. 'I know exactly what you mean,' Kaitlin said.

Beatrice showed some photos of her parents and Kaitlin politely listened to a few reminiscences, but she was already running through ways she might be able to track down the couple from Connecticut.

She was back out in that bitter Atlantic breeze fifteen minutes later, skimming through searches on her phone. As she did, she noticed she had a bunch of missed calls and voicemails. Amelia. Her mom, three times. Amelia again.

Everyone was worried about her. She felt bad for ignoring them. They meant well, of course they did, but most of the time she felt she didn't have enough left inside her to give back, to reassure them she was OK. And anyway, that would be a lie, wouldn't it? She wasn't OK. She hadn't been for a long time.

That morning, she'd had a weird sensation when she'd looked in the bathroom mirror and wondered who it was looking back at her. She remembered what it was like when she smiled all the time, when she'd had that carefree nature that gave people an inner glow.

Grief had hollowed her out. The very shape of her features had changed, with the sagging of the muscles and too many nights spent sobbing.

As she made her way back towards the waterfront, she wondered if the old Kaitlin might be gone for good.

Chuck was a big guy with a belly that rippled every time he laughed, which was a lot. Kaitlin couldn't help but grin as she sat opposite him in the neat lounge of his New Haven home in Connecticut. Amid all the hardship, his good humour was infectious and probably what she needed right now.

'How did you find us? We've only been back in the States for two weeks,' Chuck said. He was in his late forties, hair already silvering fast.

'I saw you tagged on the LaPeers' Instagram page. They mentioned they were travelling with a couple from Connecticut.'

'Oh, wow. Miracles of technology.' A woman appeared at the door, scrubbed face, no make-up, also beaming.

'This is my wife, Madge,' Chuck boomed.

'Hello,' Kaitlin said.

'Hi! It's so nice to meet you,' Madge said. 'I'll get us some coffee.'

'That would be great, honey,' Chuck said as she swept out.

Those folks had so much energy, Kaitlin thought. *Where did it all come from?* These days she felt like she was permanently running on empty.

'So, how's Beatrice doing?' Chuck asked.

'I don't know how much the LaPeers told you about their daughter, but she's very tough. She's gonna be OK. But as a congregation, we're still trying to absorb the fact that they won't be coming back.'

Kaitlin's lying skills were getting better by the day. 'Chuck, we were wondering why Wayne and Wendy left the way they did – in such a rush. Beatrice said she thought they were upriver until the day before they left. Do you have any idea where they were?'

'I wish I could help you, but I don't know. The last time I saw them was three weeks before the flight.'

'Where'd you see them?'

Chuck heaved himself up and crossed the floor to a map of the Democratic Republic of Congo that was framed on the wall. He studied it for a second, then tapped a finger on a location.

'Up in Mbandaka. They were on their way down from a visit to a student's family near Makanza.'

'They were leaving the jungle?'

'Yeah.'

'Do you know how often they'd be up there?'

Chuck swayed back and crashed down on his chair. 'Normally, one weekend a month. It's not easy to get up there and it's not especially comfortable. Particularly for Wendy. She preferred Kinshasa. Wayne was the one who liked being upriver.'

'In the infection zone.'

'Technically, yeah, but that whole designation, that's . . . they're overly cautious. And when Western governments draw maps like that, they dehumanise all of the people living there. Someone needs to engage, someone needs to reach out.'

'So, the LaPeers could have visited before they left?' Kaitlin pressed.

Chuck laced his fingers across his belly. 'I dunno. They'd usually tell me when they were coming. I'm always going up and down the river, so we'd take a boat together.' He pushed his head back and looked at her along his nose. 'You seem a little disappointed.'

'I'm just trying to get as accurate a timeline as I can.'

'The LaPeers are still gone and that's a great sadness. Lovely, lovely couple. But there's no way to bring them back. Maybe the best way to move forwards is to thank the Lord for the time you had with them and to thank the universe that the rest of us are still here, with a chance to grow and love. We're still alive.'

But sometimes it doesn't feel that way.

'Well, thank you for seeing me.' Kaitlin stood up. There were still questions to answer here. But she had other leads.

'Oh, uh – would you like to say a prayer together for them before you go?'

'No. But thanks.'

Kaitlin was at the door before Chuck replied, 'Sure.'

When her stomach started to growl, Kaitlin trudged into a convenience store not far from her next stop. There wasn't much on offer beyond junk food, but she was so hungry she no longer cared what she stuffed into her mouth. She grabbed an armful of chips and candy and a microwave burrito and dumped them in front of the checkout guy, a ratty-faced stoner with heavy lids and a lingering stare.

He ran her card, stared at the reader for a long moment, then muttered, 'Declined.'

Kaitlin inwardly sagged. She knew her funds were low, but if she didn't have enough for a cheap pile of additives and preservatives, she was in a bad way. Finally, she scrabbled together enough coins for a bag of chips. It wasn't much, but it would have to do.

Outside, she wrestled with herself for a while, then forced herself to pull out her phone and make a call.

'Hey, Mom, it's me,' she said, feeling disappointed with herself. All those calls she'd ignored and now she was only getting in touch to beg. 'I wondered if you could help me out.'

A few minutes later, Kaitlin had the promise of some cash in her account. She felt hollow having to ask, but it was a mark of how desperate she was becoming.

The New Haven Research Laboratory sprawled across several acres, but the important parts of the complex were buried up to three storeys below ground. It was only a short hop from Chuck's house, had a lucrative government public health contract and drew on the Ivy League expertise of the nearby Yale University. Kaitlin knew all this. She'd done her research. Experts were what she needed now and this place was full of them.

As she eased through the entrance metal detector and the Plexiglass shield slid back, she glimpsed William Schroeder waiting for her, as distinctive as he'd appeared on the laboratory's team web page, with a mop of black hair and glasses that looked a size too large for his face.

'Hello! Kaitlin Le?' he hailed with a wave.

'Hi.'

'Sorry about all the security.'

'No worries. Thank you so much for meeting with me.'

William swept out one hand to guide her towards the elevators. 'My pleasure. Not many people come knocking down my door to ask about this stuff. And they should.' He punched the button to sub-basement three.

'So, are you familiar with the region?'

He grinned. 'All epidemiologists are familiar with Central Africa.'

The doors dinged open and they strode along a corridor.

'This couple, they were in the Democratic Republic of Congo,' Kaitlin said.

'And you think they contracted an infection?'

'I thought so. But then I learned that they hadn't been up in the recently infected areas, by the jungle, for at least three weeks.'

'But the disease could have been incubating without any symptoms. Up to twenty-one days for Ebola, if that's what it was.'

At a door with a thick glass plate in it, William scanned his key card. The lock buzzed and William once again reached out a hand in a show of courtesy.

'This,' he said, 'well, this is where all the magic happens. Come on through.'

Kaitlin glanced around his office and turned up her nose. She thought Amelia was messy, but this looked like several trash cans had been upended. Piles of books and papers, a barely visible desk scattered with assorted junk, including a half-built Lego Death Star, and walls covered with photographs and charts.

William plucked up an open bag of chips and waved it towards her. 'Chip?'

'I'm good, thank you.'

He stuffed a handful of chips in his mouth and crunched them as he brushed off a chair for Kaitlin and then settled into his own chair behind the desk. Kaitlin held out her phone towards him.

'Could you, uh . . . say your name and – and what you do?'

William swallowed, then replied, 'Sure. William Schroeder. I'm an epidemiologist.'

'Thank you.'

'So, Ebola?'

'At first I was thinking Ebola,' she began. 'But then the State Department guy said that there was no more Ebola in the Democratic Republic of Congo at all, so—'

William laughed. 'Who said that?'

'One of the NGO co-ordinators.'

'Why would you ask a secretary about infectious disease?' he said with a frown.

'Because . . . he decides where the Americans go?'

William dipped into the bag of chips again. 'Right. Yeah. Based on where Ebola used to be, and what form the virus last took,' he said, distracted by his snack. 'The thing about these aggressive diseases – things like Ebola, necrotising fasciitis, meningitis, cholera – is that they're not entirely stable. All of our doctors and governments, they're always a few months behind the latest version of the virus or the infection.'

'OK, so let's say Wendy had gotten infected with something. If it was a really aggressive form of disease and then she got on a plane, do you think that . . .?'

'You wanna know if it could turn into a zombie plane?'

'Is that a thing?'

'Are you kidding? It's one of my favourite hypotheticals for a catastrophic outbreak.' He lounged back, staring at the ceiling. 'Planes are breeding grounds for this stuff because of recycled air. You know, there's been several instances of flights having to divert or make emergency landings because the crew were overcome with something.'

Kaitlin stiffened, feeling a ripple of something like dread, mixed with excitement, run through her. 'Oh. I didn't know that.'

'It's never led to a crash – as far as we know. But it's just a matter of time. There are forms of meningitis that can paralyse you in a couple of hours. That could do the trick.'

'And Wendy could have gotten one of those in the jungle?'

'Maybe. I mean, Nigeria's had some bad outbreaks in the past few years. And like I said, you never know how aggressive the new form will be. As soon as you start giving people antivirals and retrovirals, the infections start adapting. All viruses mutate as they move through a community, but the distribution of antivirals and retrovirals can exacerbate this. A lot of these viruses are held in animals – bats, birds, that kind of thing. Just like the plague. And they can pass new versions of the virus among each other. And then when the wrong – or right, depending on which way you look at it – animal comes into contact with someone and boom. You've got an outbreak.'

'Wow.'

'Yeah. Eventually, we'll be totally fucked.' William leaned towards the phone and said, 'Sorry.'

'OK, so, maybe they got a new form of an infection in the jungle.'

'Maybe. But I mean, if she was already showing symptoms, she would have spread it before getting on the plane. There would have been like 50,000 dead people in the DRC within a week. And I don't think I read about that on the news.'

'Wait! I don't understand.'

'With infectious disease, you can incubate for a while, even weeks, without being contagious. Some people can be totally asymptomatic and still spread an infection. And as soon as you show symptoms, you're basically a contagious disease monster. You sure there isn't another reason why they were leaving in a rush? Because it sounds to me like they probably just died in a plane crash. A normal boom. But I love where your head went.'

★

Dolores frowned, looking as miserable as the day Kaitlin had left her. They were both back in the diner, swathed in the aromas of sizzling bacon and brewing coffee.

'OK, what man?' Kaitlin said, trying to keep the edge out of her voice.

Dolores leaned across the table and whispered, 'It's the same man from last time. But this time he's in a blue blazer.'

Cutlery clattered somewhere behind the counter.

'Which one?'

'See? That's him!'

'I didn't look last time, so . . .'

'How are you going to be the detective if you can't even keep track of who's tailing us!'

Kaitlin fought back her exasperation. 'No one's tailing us. It's all in your head. And so is this idea that you're responsible for 702.'

Dolores furrowed her brow. 'You really think so?'

'I'm positive.'

'How do you know that?'

'We have no reason to think the LaPeers are the reason why the plane went down. They didn't have Ebola or any other infection. They were tested for everything before they left.'

Kaitlin wasn't despondent that the Ebola angle hadn't – yet – worked out. Everything was part of a larger puzzle, the useless pieces as well as the ones that might lead to a solution. And who knew when something she thought she'd discarded would come back into play.

'They were?' Dolores said, looking stunned.

'The State Department gave them all the tests and the LaPeers didn't have anything serious. And that – that's what I was coming to tell you.'

Dolores juddered with silent sobs, her hands clasped in prayer. After a moment, she steadied herself. 'Oh, thank you! Thank God! Oh, Kaitlin, you don't know what this means to me. Here I was going crazy when . . .' Dolores stood up. 'Thank you. I feel so much better.'

Kaitlin felt a wave of warmth as she watched Dolores walk away. She'd done some good here. In the absence of answers, that was something.

As she crossed the diner towards the door, Kaitlin's eyes flickered towards the man in the blue jacket Dolores had suspected. Something jangled inside her – recognition, perhaps, instinct – and she paused by his table.

'What do you want?' she said.

'Excuse me?'

'Why are you following me?'

'Don't know what you're talking about. I'm just sitting here, enjoying my coffee.'

'You were watching us. What are you, FBI?' she demanded.

'What? I-I have no idea what you're talking—'

Kaitlin felt that toxic paranoia knot her stomach. 'I saw you outside my apartment yesterday.' *Had she?* She couldn't be sure. But she thought so.

'I think you need to calm down.'

A waitress drifted over and in a calming voice, inquired, 'Hi, are we all doing OK over here?'

'This young woman here seems to be a bit upset.'

'I'm not upset. You've been following me.'

The man looked up at the waitress. 'Hey, I've just been sitting here. I don't know what's happening.'

The waitress' eyes settled on Kaitlin, deciding she was the bad guy here. 'Honey, you're disturbing the other customers. I think that you should—'

Kaitlin forced a smile. 'I'm sorry. It's just a misunderstanding.'

She walked away, but her neck prickled at the sensation of eyes on her back, and that feeling didn't go for the rest of the day.

Kaitlin lounged on her bed, watching the shadows pool in Tompkins Square Park, her burner phone clutched in her hand.

'Hey, listen, I think the Feds are watching me,' she said as soon as the call was answered.

'You sure?' Dylan sounded breathless.

'No. But . . . maybe.'

'It's good to be paranoid. Keep your wits about you. If you're really worried, get out of there.'

'And go where?' Kaitlin shook her head incredulously. 'I don't — Hey! Hey!'

'Dylan? What's happening?'

'Argh.'

'Dylan? Are you there?'

A moment of silence, then Dylan's exasperated voice floated back. 'Yeah. Just some kids kicked a ball at my head.'

'Where are you?'

'Walking through a park. Back to the office.'

'What do you do?'

'Something boring. It was nice, what you did for that lady, telling her it wasn't her fault.'

Changing the subject. Dylan was always on his guard.

'If I can't get rid of my own guilt, I might as well . . . Never mind.'

'What do you have to be guilty about?'

'The usual stuff, I guess. Things I didn't get to say to my brother. Things I wish I hadn't said. Things I wish I'd asked.'

'Like what?'

'You don't want to hear about my family drama, Dylan.'

'Maybe I do.'

'Yeah? Well. Maybe I don't want to tell a complete stranger all of my secrets.' At that moment, she wished Amelia was there, someone she could talk to, be herself around.

'Right.'

'Sorry. I-I didn't mean to sound harsh. You've been really helpful. And I appreciate it. I'm just frustrated.'

'You're not alone there.'

'Wendy LaPeer was definitely sick. But I'm no closer to finding out what she contracted. Or even if she's relevant. The problem is, when you dig deep, *everything* takes on significance. But maybe none of it's important. Just random stuff that creates the illusion of a pattern.'

Dylan paused for so long she thought he'd hung up. Then: 'We may never know for sure what happened. You get that?'

'We will. We'll know the truth,' she insisted. 'I won't give up until I do.'

'So, you're still in?'

'Of course.'

'Good.'

Was he testing her? Manipulating? Kaitlin chewed on a nail, feeling uneasy.

'Because I just got a ping on a credit card that was used to buy a ticket for 702,' Dylan continued. 'A woman who actually boarded the flight.'

'Someone's using a dead woman's credit card?'

'Not someone else. The same woman. Gonna send you a video uploaded to Reddit. Take a look. She got off the plane before it took off. Apparently, she knew it was going to go down.'

Camera Video Uploaded to Reddit, Closed Caption

PASSENGER FILMING: What's this lady doin'?

PSYCHIC WITCH: You don't understand! We have to get everyone off this plane.

PASSENGER FILMING: She's flippin' out!

FLIGHT ATTENDANT: Ma'am, please return to your seat. We're about to push back from the stand.

PSYCHIC WITCH: No, no, no, we can't do that. We need to get off right now.

PASSENGER FILMING: Yo, there's this crazy lady on my plane.

FLIGHT ATTENDANT: Please calm down, ma'am.

PSYCHIC WITCH: Don't touch me! Don't touch me, don't touch me. Let me off this plane!

FLIGHT ATTENDANT: Ma'am, are you feeling OK? Have you . . . have you taken something?

PSYCHIC WITCH: No, I haven't taken anything! This plane—

PASSENGER FILMING: She's drunk.

PSYCHIC WITCH: This plane is going to crash.

FLIGHT ATTENDANT: You're upsetting the other passengers. Please take your seat.

PASSENGER FILMING: Here's security. Game over, crazy woman.

FLIGHT ATTENDANT: That isn't helping.

PSYCHIC WITCH: I need to get off this plane right now!

FLIGHT ATTENDANT: OK. OK. He's going to escort you off.

SECURITY: Ma'am, please calm down.

PSYCHIC WITCH: No, no, don't touch me, don't touch me!

PASSENGER FILMING: Oh, she's going to get . . .

PSYCHIC WITCH: No, no, no, you have to get everyone off this plane! It's going to crash! You have to get everyone off this plane – everybody, get off this plane!

SECURITY: Please come this way, ma'am. We'll remove your bag from the hold.

PSYCHIC WITCH: Everyone, you have to get off now!

PASSENGER FILMING: There she goes!

[applause]

PASSENGER FILMING: Oh, man. That was . . . that was nuts. Hope she's wrong.

8

The sign above the door read 'Psychic Witch' in one of those seventies fonts that looked like the shapes made by a lava lamp. Adding to the sense of times past, a mystical all-seeing eye had been painted in glittering gold in between the two words.

Kaitlin stood on the sidewalk and surveyed the large window on which had been etched 'Your Future Revealed'. Thick crimson drapes hung on either side. It was too shadowed to see much inside. This was the Village. There had always been a lot of weird here.

Kaitlin felt a hint of disgust. She had no time for those who preyed on other people's grief, promising to contact their departed loved ones, telling them what they wanted to hear in order to prise cash out of them. But she had to set all that aside. If this woman had fought to get off the plane, it was because she undoubtedly knew something. You didn't have to be a psychic to see that.

What it was that she knew and how she learned it — that was the mystery. It would take a subtle touch, but Kaitlin felt she was getting better at this. Once she'd got the video footage from Dylan, she'd done enough research to set her trap.

She went down the steps and pushed the door open. A bell jangled. In the gloomy interior, she breathed in the sickly-sweet scent of incense. The woman she'd come to meet glided through curtains from the rear of the store.

The psychic witch was thin, with leathery skin and heavy make-up. She looked much calmer than she'd been when she was scrambling to get off Flight 702.

'Hi, I'm Kaitlin,' Kaitlin announced, trying to keep her voice light.

'Hello, dear. So lovely to see you. You're exactly how I pictured when I heard your voice on the phone.'

The woman held out a hand towards a small table with two chairs. Kaitlin sat.

'I'm sorry for the lateness of the hour,' the psychic said. 'My business has seen quite the uptick in the past few weeks. That video of me got posted to a Reddit something or other and . . . well. Many people have been seeking my services.'

'So, do I call you Psychic Witch? Is that your name?'

'You can call me Mia.'

The woman had a theatrical air, good at performing. It would take a delicate line of questioning to cut through that and get to the truth.

'OK. So, you're the only one who was on that plane who's still here. Who's still alive.'

'Goodness me, yes, I suppose that's true.' Her eyelids fluttered half shut. 'It's strange, I've tried to contact them.'

'Contact who?'

'The passengers. All of those people who were on the flight. I've tried to find them in the other world, but I can't.'

'The other world?'

'The in-between space. When people die, it can be a difficult adjustment. They don't always know that they're dead. They end up lost. Reliving scenes from their lives, creating a comfortable landscape around themselves. Only when they accept that they're dead can they move on. Cross over to the other side.'

Kaitlin nodded, hoping her blank face showed none of her thoughts. 'And until they do, you talk to them?'

'Usually. Manhattan is full of the restless dead. I talk to spirits every day. But the souls on that flight – they haven't crossed over, but they're not here either. They're not anywhere.'

'Maybe they're in the sea.'

Mia wafted a hand over the table. 'Did you know that you have a guardian? We all do, but I can see yours. Right behind you.'

'A guardian?'

'You were close to your brother, weren't you?'

Kaitlin stiffened. She didn't want to go there. 'Yes.'

'You are halves of a whole. Together in birth, but not in death. That isn't good. The universe prefers balance. And now you're unbalanced.'

'I'm not sure I know what you mean.'

'Yes, you do.' Mia closed her eyes. 'But – oh, I see. It was already unbalanced, wasn't it?'

'Excuse me?'

'There was hurt between you. A fresh wound over an old scar. You've always been carrying his burden and now it's even heavier.'

Kaitlin felt her unease harden. 'That's not why I'm here. Why did you want to get off the plane?'

'You've seen the video.'

'Sure. But I'd like to hear it from you.'

Mia leaned across the table and stared. 'I had a feeling. I've learned to trust my feelings. Do you trust your feelings, Kaitlin?'

'I'm not sure I'd be sitting here if I did.'

'You don't believe in what I do?'

'I don't think I understand what you do,' Kaitlin replied,

choosing her words carefully. 'Or what you claim to do, anyway.'

'I read people. Sense their auras, their pasts, their futures. I talk to spirits. Or, rather, they talk to me.'

'And what do they say?'

'The plane wasn't safe.'

'The spirits told you that?'

Mia leaned back, resting the tips of the fingers of one hand on her brow. 'No, no, it wasn't the spirits. It was an intuition. One that settled deep into my bones. It was . . . overwhelming. That ominous feeling.'

Kaitlin forced a neutral face, but she felt sure it looked fake. All of the passengers on 702 were dead and this woman was weaving a ludicrous fantasy.

'You just got on the plane and felt nervous?'

Mia narrowed her eyes. 'Kaitlin, if you don't believe in what I do – which you clearly don't – then why are you here? The video should tell you everything you need to know.'

'I need answers,' Kaitlin said, her voice hardening. 'And I have pieces of the story – more pieces than the official investigation bothered to look at – but I need to put it together.'

'Let me help. I want to help.' Mia put her head back and screwed her eyes shut tight. 'Don't be disturbed. I'm going into a trance. In my mind, I'm going back to that day. Sometimes this brings up details that my conscious mind doesn't recall. Speak softly, if you will. Any negativity dooms the process.'

Kaitlin stifled a sigh.

'It's cold,' Mia began after a long moment. Her voice was lower, almost a growl. 'Cold air blasting from the vent. I try to switch it off. It isn't working.'

'Who is around you?' Kaitlin asked, keeping her voice low. 'Anyone who stands out?'

'The congressman.'

'Congressman Harris?'

'Yes, that's the one. He's in business class. He's come back to talk to someone. I think a journalist. The moment the congressman came down the aisle, the journalist pulled out his phone to record it, but Harris just shook his hand. He's looking very smug. Smiling, glad-handing, but . . . There's something wrong with his aura. A darkness to it.'

Though she was sceptical, Kaitlin felt herself drifting into the spell Mia was weaving.

'There's a couple sitting across the aisle. A man and a woman,' Mia continued. 'She's sweating. It's so cold, why is she sweating? The man is trying to make her comfortable. He's asking the stewardess for water.'

Wendy LaPeer.

'Who is sitting next to you?'

'An Arab gentleman. Charming. He asks if I wouldn't mind moving so his wife could come up and sit next to him. She's white. But she's sitting in a middle seat and I have merinthophobia.'

'What's merinthophobia?'

'The fear of being restrained. Planes these days – the seats are so close together that being in the middle is like being tied up.'

'So, you stay where you are?'

'Yes. The man becomes very icy. He shoots daggers at me – like I'm being inconsiderate for not moving. He calls out, "I'm sorry, Chrissy, but we can't sit together." Very passive-aggressive.' Mia shuddered. 'I feel dread, coming over me like a thick fog. I know in that moment that the plane's heading to disaster. I try to warn them. They won't listen. They won't listen!'

Mia jolted from her trance. She looked around as if she were surprised to find herself back in her store. Kaitlin eyed her, trying to decide how much of this was theatre.

After a moment composing herself, Mia stuttered, 'At least the doctor was probably able to sit next to his wife.'

'The doctor?'

'The man sitting next to me. He was a doctor. Did I not mention that?'

'He told you he was a doctor?'

'He had a folder from the University of Damascus in Syria. I asked him about it and he said he was a doctor conducting research there.'

'What kind of research?'

'Something on immunology. He didn't go into it. That's when he asked me if I'd move.'

Kaitlin felt a twinge. *Was Mia sending out a subtle clue? A doctor. Immunology. Some kind of viral threat.*

'Where did the feeling of dread come from?' Kaitlin asked. 'The doctor? Or the congressman?'

'I've learned not to question these feelings, just to follow them. Everyone on that plane was doomed. I could feel it in my bones.'

'But you said that Congressman Harris had a dark aura about him.'

'Yes. Something insidious. It's possible the feeling came from him. Perhaps he had less than honourable intentions. Or perhaps someone was trying to hurt him.'

'You think it's possible he was being targeted?'

'Anything is possible, dear. But surely there are easier ways to kill a congressman.'

Kaitlin studied Mia's face. She made a good play of sincerity. And she'd flagged up two potential lines of inquiry: an immunology doctor, hinting at disease spread, perhaps, and an attempt on the life of a member of congress.

What does she know?

'I tried. I tried to tell them and no one would listen,' Mia was saying. 'They wrote me off as a nut job. That's not my fault. It's not my fault the plane went down. It's not my fault that no one believed me.'

Time to move this on. She'd given the psychic witch enough rope.

'What were you doing in London, Mia?'

The other woman's nose twitched. 'I see. You suspect I'm involved somehow.'

'Why were you in London?' Kaitlin pressed.

'I was in Europe on a business trip.'

'I'd like to show you something.' Kaitlin pulled out her phone and swiped to a news channel video. She'd become good at this. She'd done her research.

'I don't need to see the plane footage again, Kaitlin. I've seen it far too many times. I lived it.'

'This isn't the plane video.'

Kaitlin pressed play. A scene from the International Criminal Court in The Hague rolled. The judge was saying, 'The court will rise for sentencing.'

'You recognise that man?' Kaitlin pointed to the craggy-faced figure in the dock.

Mia's face darkened.

'Slobodan Begovic, former Croat–Bosnian general – one of six commanders incited for mass war crimes. This is his trial six months ago at the International Tribunal.'

'Mr Begovic. Would you please stand?' the judge said.

'I will not. I do not accept the jurisdiction of this court,' the general growled. 'I reject the ruling of this court. You cannot put me in prison.'

Onscreen, Begovic uncapped a small vial of liquid and threw it back.

'Monsieur, what are you doing?' the judge inquired.

Begovic pushed his chin out with defiance. 'I have taken poison. You will not imprison me.'

Kaitlin studied Mia's face as the sudden commotion in the court played out on the phone.

'Why are you showing me this?' Mia said in a wintry voice.

'You were there, weren't you?'

'And you saw for yourself – I'm not in that video.'

'But you were at The Hague. The general was your client.'

'I'd left by the time Begovic departed this existence.'

'Did you know he was going to do it?'

Mia shook her head with vehemence. 'I'd have warned the court had I known. He may have been a client, but he deserved the sentencing he was given.'

'What were you doing there?'

'Helping Mr Begovic to contact his mother in the next life. He wanted to say goodbye.'

'Right.' *How much more of this could she take?*

'The general was in a great deal of pain. And he wanted to say goodbye to someone whom he loved dearly. He wanted to ask forgiveness. Who am I to deny him that chance? Isn't that what we all want?' Mia continued, passion edging her voice.

'Not all of us have committed genocide.'

'I don't discriminate when it comes to putting a soul to rest. Mr Begovic got closure.'

Kaitlin tugged the phone away. The first time she stumbled across the video, she heard alarm bells. After listening to Mia, they were still there.

'How did you even get involved with someone like that?' Katilin asked incredulously.

'I'm very good at what I do. Word travels fast.'

'How do people know about you at The Hague?' Kaitlin probed. There was something buried here, she was sure of it.

'I wasn't always a psychic by trade, Kaitlin. I used to live and work in Europe.'

'Doing what?'

'If you were able to find out what I was doing before getting on that plane in London, I'm sure you can figure that out for yourself.'

'Trust me, I will. You're hiding something.'

Had the general warned Mia that the plane was in danger? That was her current theory. And Mia had used that warning to bolster her earning potential as a psychic. She put up enough of a show to ensure her performance onboard was recorded and uploaded. If that was even remotely true, Mia was colder and more cynical than Kaitlin had ever imagined. She could have saved them all.

She could have saved Conor.

'All this talk about the congressman and the doctor,' Kaitlin continued, her emotions running away with her. 'You're creating distractions.'

'Distractions from what?'

'From you. You knew the plane was doomed, you work with criminals, or—'

'So that means I must be involved?' Mia sneered. 'You want there to be a reason for why I knew about the plane. For there to be some massive conspiracy. But there isn't. The formal investigation proved that.'

Kaitlin felt her chest tighten. She didn't want to hear this again.

'The investigation was closed too soon. As far as I know, they didn't even look into your work in the Netherlands. There has to be a logical explanation for what happened. A real one.'

'And you think I'm that explanation? That I conspired to bring down a plane, boarded that plane, only to make a spectacle of myself and get taken off? That's your logical explanation?' Her smile broadened. 'Digging into this won't bring your brother back, Kaitlin. You need to accept he's gone and move on with your life.'

Kaitlin snorted. 'Everyone keeps telling me that. Not until I find out the truth.'

Mia leaned across the table, her eyes widening. 'You're afraid to know the truth. Because the truth might involve your brother.'

'What? That's insane. He didn't do anything. He had nothing to do with this.'

'Your brother was Conor Le. I remember seeing his name in the news. Saving the world from what would have been the worst cyberattack in history. That was him, correct?'

Kaitlin felt her simmering annoyance with this fake start to bubble over. 'I've indulged you long enough.'

'Why are you so angry, Kaitlin?'

'Because you're a phony! This entire thing – the news, the investigation – it's all a lie.'

'And you're the one who's going to uncover the truth?' Mia mocked.

'No one else is doing it!'

'And that will help you to put your brother to rest? Purge him from your life?'

'I'm not trying to purge Conor.' The witch was trying to push her buttons, Kaitlin knew that. And she was succeeding. *Why couldn't she stop rising to the bait?*

'You're swallowed in grief and anger. It surrounds you, suffocates everything bright in your aura. If you let it, it'll consume you.'

'You don't know what you're talking about.'

'Don't you have anyone to share this pain with? You can't carry it alone.'

Kaitlin flinched. 'I'm not alone.'

'Excuse me for saying so, but you seem very alone at the moment. Where are your parents? Surely they can help you to carry this burden.'

'They're dealing with their own pain. I have things under control.'

'How about Conor?' Mia interrupted. 'Did he have someone he loved?'

'Yes, but, we don't – we don't talk much. I don't know him that well,' Kaitlin stuttered.

Don't let her get to you.

'Just tell me what you know,' Kaitlin snapped.

'Nothing that I saw or heard will help you. It's the souls you need to worry about, and those souls aren't anywhere to be found. Conor isn't resting yet. I don't know where he is. But you won't be able to find rest until he does.'

She's playing you. Don't fall for it. Why are you such an idiot?

'Come and see me,' Mia urged. 'Perhaps together we can find him in the spirit realm – help both of you to move on.'

'Now you're trying to squeeze money out of me? Yeah, I think it's time to go.'

Kaitlin stood and marched towards the door.

'You have to confront this grief, Kaitlin,' Mia called after her. 'Trying to solve a mystery that isn't there is just a distraction. It won't help Conor's soul be found.'

Kaitlin wanted to press her hands over her ears. Instead, she kept walking.

Nor will paying a crackpot to pretend to talk to spirits.

'Don't go down this path, Kaitlin,' Mia continued. 'If you keep going, I see nothing but darkness in front of you.'

Kaitlin laughed. The bell tinkled as she opened the door.

'This person who was important to Conor. You must talk to them.' Mia was shouting now.

'Don't tell me what to do.'

'I don't need to tell you, Kaitlin. You already know. I think you just needed to hear it.'

As Kaitlin stepped out into the chill, she heard the scrape of a chair and feet pattering towards her. She half turned and saw Mia holding something out.

'Here, take my card.'

'I won't be needing it.'

'Trust me. You will. You will be back.'

9

As she walked away from the store, Kaitlin wrestled with her thoughts. Under the sodium glare of a street light, she punched the keys of her burner and listened to the other end ringing out.

The self-styled psychic witch was a fake, Kaitlin had no doubt about that. And yet Mia's words still played out in her head. Everything the self-professed psychic had said about Conor and Thomas struck so close to those deep-seated feelings of personal guilt. Even so, why was she allowing herself to be sucked in?

The voicemail clicked to life:

Hello, you've reached Thomas. Leave me a message and I'll call back when I can. Cheers.

Conor had loved Thomas. Why didn't Thomas care enough to respond to Kaitlin's calls? She had tried him repeatedly since the news of the plane going missing, but to no avail.

Kaitlin felt her hand trembling as she pressed the cell to her ear.

Thomas, I know you're probably sick of me leaving messages and I guess, as you haven't returned a single call, that I'm the last person you want to talk to, but I need to speak to you. About Conor. He told me some-

thing before – I think it may have something to do with
. . . Just call me back. Please.

Kaitlin hung up.

Please, God, let me be wrong.

Kaitlin pushed her head down, trying to quiet her raging thoughts as she trudged towards the East Village. A couple of blocks had passed when a blue sedan rolled up beside her. A woman with a brown bob and thin lips, dressed in a dark suit, climbed out and thrust a badge towards Kaitlin.

'I'm Agent Gerard and I'm with the FBI. We need to talk.'

Kaitlin's heart hammered. She felt the urge to run, but she knew it would be futile.

'That's Agent Hoxley behind the wheel. Don't worry about him. He doesn't say much. I'm the one you need to pay attention to.'

'W-what is this?' Kaitlin stuttered.

'Kaitlin Le, right? I need to ask you some questions.' Agent Gerard fixed her piercing blue eyes on Kaitlin.

'I haven't broken any laws,' Kaitlin babbled.

Inwardly, she was cursing herself for being so stupid. Dylan had warned her about taking care. Instead, she'd been too thoughtless, she could see that now, too impatient to find the answers she needed. And now she was likely to pay for it.

'Relax. You're not in any trouble,' Gerard said.

Kaitlin pushed her Jets cap back, trying to seem more defiant than she felt. 'Do you really have an agent tailing everyone involved with 702?'

'Excuse me?'

'That guy in the diner?' she said, recalling the man who had freaked out Dolores. 'And I saw him outside my apartment, too. He has a nice little collection of brightly coloured jackets.'

Agent Gerard cocked an eyebrow. 'We haven't been watching you. If you'll forgive me for saying, but you're sounding a little paranoid. I'm part of the team working on the ongoing investigation.'

'What ongoing investigation?' Kaitlin replied, baffled. 'I thought the FBI had everything sewn up?'

'It's still an open case. No wreckage. And that means it's a complex investigation.'

Kaitlin felt her head swim. *The authorities were still looking into 702?* Why didn't she know this? Why didn't Dylan?

'What do you mean, complex?'

Kaitlin felt a deep cold settle on her before she heard the agent's words, almost as if she knew what she was going to say.

'You need to come with me.' Gerard swung open the car door. 'This is about your brother, Conor.'

The Jakob J. Javits Federal Building towered over Foley Square. Only two floors of windows blazed at that hour and they housed the FBI New York field office. Kaitlin trailed from the elevator between the two agents, trying to appear composed. Soon she was sitting opposite Agent Gerard in a bare interview room under a fizzing strip light. Agent Hoxley stood in one corner, observing.

Once Gerard had finished recording the date, location and interview subject in the microphone, Kaitlin asked, 'So why am I here?'

'Your brother, Conor. You were close to him, right?'

'We're twins. We were twins.'

Gerard was nonchalant, but Kaitlin wasn't going to fall for that. There was a game being played here.

'What was he doing in London?'

'He lived there. I mean, he worked there. You guys know everything about him. You know everything about all of the passengers who were on that flight. You investigated them all, the media investigated them.'

'Let's go back to the beginning.'

'I'm not sure what you mean.'

'He worked in cybersecurity.'

'Yeah, he did.'

'Did you know he was under investigation?'

Kaitlin flinched. She couldn't hide that, but maybe it played in her favour. If Gerard could see her honest shock, it wouldn't seem like she was involved.

'No. What for?'

'The police raided his apartment in London the week before the flight. They took his computer. Looks like he was involved with some pretty dangerous people. Embezzlement, malware—'

'You have it wrong. He was the one who *stopped* the malware.'

'Did he?'

'He was in all the newspapers. He was a hero! It could have been devastating and he found the kill switch.'

Gerard smiled. 'I wonder how he knew about it.'

'It was his job to know. He was a cybersecurity expert.'

'Maybe that was just to cover his tracks.'

'Cover? For what? Why would he be . . .' Her voice trailed off. She could feel her heart starting to thump. 'You think . . . You think he had something to do with the plane going down?'

'Conor was involved with creating software that could hack into a plane's controls.'

Kaitlin felt a pang of horror. That couldn't be true.

Could it? After their final argument, she'd wondered what else he might be prepared to do. She'd worried – and she'd pushed it all aside. But no, Conor would never do something like this.

She shook her head. 'What the hell are you talking about? He was on the flight. Even if – even if it were possible, why would he do that?'

'Do you know Thomas Rider?'

'Yeah, he's – well, he was Conor's boyfriend.'

'Have you ever met him?'

'Once. They both came over last summer to see our parents. And that's it.'

'Are you currently in contact with him?'

'Not currently. I wrote him a letter over the summer and he wrote me one back.'

'Did Conor or Mr Rider ever ask you to deliver anything for them, or to contact anybody?'

'No, they didn't. Why don't you just talk to him?'

'He doesn't want to co-operate. He's not American, so we don't have any jurisdiction. Really more MI5's area. Or maybe the Federal Security Service's in Russia.'

'The Russians?' Kaitlin said with incredulity. *Was the agent just trying to get a rise out of her?*

'Your brother never talked to you about these things?'

'I don't hear any "things". Just allegations.'

'We know you're doing your own investigation'—Gerard shrugged, her tone becoming dismissive—'or whatever you like to call them, into what happened to that plane. That's your right. But let me give you some advice: don't get mixed up in this.'

Kaitlin rolled her eyes. 'What, exactly, should I not be getting mixed up in?'

'Money laundering, cybercrime, electoral fraud. We have

reason to believe that your brother was involved with a Russian syndicate.'

'And what reason do you have to believe that?' Kaitlin demanded.

Ignoring her question, Gerard stood. 'A warning. These people don't play games.' She handed over her card. 'If you hear from Thomas, it's in your interest to call me.'

Agent Hoxley swung open the door.

'You're free to go, Kaitlin,' Gerard said.

Outside, Kaitlin bent into the chill breeze as she hurried downtown. Her eyes darting for any sign that she was being watched, she pulled out her burner once more.

Once Thomas' voicemail had played, she said:

Hey, Thomas, it's Kaitlin again. I'm sorry I keep calling, but I just really need to talk to you. It's important. Even more than it was before. Call me back.

Hearing Thomas' English accent in his answerphone message brought back a rush of memories. For a moment she was back in that low-rent bar, breathing in the aroma of stale beer and surrounded by the strains of some country ballad. There was Conor, smiling shyly, as he guided in this tall, good-looking Brit with pale skin, blue eyes and a shock of blond hair. It was the first time she'd met Thomas, but they hit it off in no time, laughing over beers as if they'd been friends for ever.

Conor had made a great choice and she could see from the affection gleaming in her brother's eyes how much this guy with his dry wit meant to him. How she ached for those times.

Maybe she was being stupid to try to make contact after that brush with the Feds. But now a whole new batch of questions was burning in her head and there would be no peace until she knew the truth about her brother.

What was Conor really capable of?

Kaitlin jumped three different subway trains, adding an extra fifty minutes to her journey. She'd specifically set off in the morning rush, hoping she could lose herself in the crowds, choking on the reek of sweat and fresh aftershave in the packed cars. Paranoia was eating away at her. She'd barely slept a wink and in the end, she'd called Amelia just to hear a friendly voice. Amelia was concerned, firing questions until she was certain Kaitlin was all right.

Even that brief moment of normality did little to calm the torrent of disturbing thoughts rushing through her head. She felt haunted by the accusations Gerard had made. When the agent had spoken about Conor and his life, Kaitlin couldn't escape the feeling that she was hearing about a stranger. She and Conor had always been so close, knowing each other's thoughts, finishing each other's sentences. *Could it really be possible that she didn't know her twin brother at all?*

The financial district swelled with too many suits and she looked more out of place even than the tourists taking snaps of the New York Stock Exchange. Soon, though, she was hurrying away from the sights and into the sprawl of functional blocks that provided the life-support system for the moneymakers.

After a short wait in the fifth-floor reception of Munio Inc. – a start-up that her research had told her was making waves – her contact swept out to greet her with a grin and a cheery wave. He looked barely older than her, close-cropped hair, dressed casually.

Once they'd settled into an office, Kaitlin slid her phone across the table and said, 'We're recording. Do you want to tell me your name and what you do?'

'Oh, OK,' he replied, unfazed. 'I'm Sam Haddad, cyber-security specialist.'

'My brother used to work in your field. Kind of.'

'I was going to ask! Conor Le, right?' Sam gushed.

Kaitlin nodded.

'Wow. He was something special, wasn't he?'

'Yeah. He was.'

Sam winced. 'Sorry. I always speak before I think. It really was awful, what happened. A tragedy, really. I had a lot of respect for him, what with preventing the Koschei malware attack and everything.'

Kaitlin forced a smile, but she wasn't in the mood for small talk. 'Look, anyway, sorry, my questions are just about planes. Do you think it would be possible to hack into a plane's controls?'

'A few years ago, someone did manage to hack into the ground control system at . . . I think it was Paris, but Air Traffic Control figured out what was going on almost immediately. And since then, they've really closed the loopholes.'

'But it could be done?'

'Possibly. But very unlikely. Actually, no. I'd say it's impossible. There are too many safeguards in place.'

Kaitlin felt a wave of relief and picked up her phone. 'That's great, thank you.'

'But you could hack a plane from inside the aircraft,' Sam noted.

Kaitlin lowered herself back down.

'Wanna guess how?' Sam grinned, clearly in his element. 'The in-flight entertainment system. People want to do more and more through the in-flight entertainment and that makes it a potential security risk.'

Kaitlin slid the phone back. 'Go on.'

'You could get tons of information that way. Names, credit card numbers . . .'

'Could you hack the controls?'

'Like the cockpit controls? It would be harder.' Sam stared into the middle distance, thinking. 'If you're trying to make the autopilot do something, it could be easily overridden by the pilot.'

'But it's possible, right? It could be done?'

'Sure. There have been a few papers on this. Definitely something the airlines are looking into.'

Sam pushed his hands behind his head and leaned back. He was enjoying the conversation.

Kaitlin felt like she was about to be sick.

'I mean, let's not go overboard. I'd say a hack of the in-flight entertainment system would cause a minor disturbance, at best. The hackers could spoof flight information, map routes, maybe, or speed statistics, altitude values, that kind of thing. But if what you're asking is . . .' He leaned forwards, growing awkward now he could see where this was going. 'It wouldn't be a very effective way to . . . You know . . . If someone wanted to . . .'

'To bring the plane down.'

'Right.' Sam eyed her. 'You don't think your brother—'

'No. No, of course not. He wouldn't. But, I don't know, he could have been trying to do something else. Maybe.'

'Like, maybe he was trying to help. Like, if there was something else going on.'

Kaitlin locked eyes with Sam for a long moment and she watched that familiar pity rise up.

'I don't think this is what did it,' he said in a gentle voice. 'And I'm sorry if I've been insensitive about this, or awkward. I get excited about things. Probably too much. Even my wife says I'm a nerd, and she's an accountant.'

'It's fine. And thank you for your time.'

As she walked back to the elevator, Kaitlin tried to feel reassured by Sam's final words. *But why was Conor even on that flight?*

Why hadn't he let her know he was coming home?

Kaitlin kicked through the golden leaves in Tompkins Square Park as she spoke to Dylan. She'd started to worry that maybe her apartment was bugged.

'I'm totally freaked out. What if Conor *did* have something to do with it?' She glanced around, scrutinising the couple making out on the bench. 'I mean, the FBI certainly seems to think so. And now they're trying to get Thomas. And he won't even return my phone calls and now I learn Thomas has Russian friends. I just . . . I want to know what he and Conor were doing.'

'You really think the Russians could have been involved?'

'I don't know. I don't know anything any more. Yeah, if they had sketchy Russian hacker friends.' She sighed. 'It's just that I feel more alone than ever. With Conor gone, I have no one.'

'You have me.'

'Right. I don't even know your real name.'

'*Mir tesen.*'

'What?'

'"Small world" in Russian. Literally translates to "the world is crowded".'

'You're not helping, Dylan.'

'Back in ancient history, there was a lot of hope that the online world would bring everyone together. Beyond nations and cultures. Cyberspace as a global village.'

'Conor used to talk about cyber-utopianism all the time. He was so passionate about it. He was part of this group – the Elysians? All about uniting the world. I used to tease him. How could people still believe that was possible? But Conor always was an idealist.'

Kaitlin watched the whorls of leaves in the fall breeze. She'd been so close to Conor. *But how much did she really know about him?*

That night, she lay in the dark, unable to sleep again. It seemed to have become a regular thing, her mind running away with itself, chasing answers and turning over thoughts that only got darker the deeper into the night she went.

She missed her old life so much, the mundane things as much as anything. She yearned for college, even those long, boring lectures where she had to fight to keep her eyes open in the sticky warmth of a late summer afternoon, still fighting the after-effects of one too many drinks at a frat party.

That feeling of her intellect being challenged had felt so good after so long feeling stuck in high school. She missed the rapid back and forth in class with clever people, all the wild new ideas she'd taken in, firing her up and driving her to want to learn more and more.

Now, all that was gone. These days, her brain felt like it was sinking down in a swamp most of the time.

In the darkest of moments, she wondered if she'd lost her future completely. *Had she traded away those dreams she'd always had of doing great things?* She'd hoped to write a book one day, maybe use her brain and her voice to change things, big things, like motivating people to tackle the climate emergency. Her father had always accused her of being too idealistic. She was like Conor that way, and she didn't take it as an insult.

But now it all seemed to be drifting away from her. *What if she'd lost them by chasing ghosts? What if there was no answer to the mystery of Flight 702?*

10

Rory Murray brushed the pretzel crumbs off his lapel, adjusted his tie and watched the young woman in the Jets hat staring at her cell as she huddled on a bench in Tompkins Square Park. She looked like a little storm cloud. But what did he expect? Her life had been consumed by the loss of her brother on 702, to the degree that it seemed like she'd all but dropped out of school and given up on a glittering future.

Still, she was key to pinning down many of the passengers' families for the class-action suit, he was sure of it. But for someone so central to keeping the victims' cases alive, she was certainly hard to track down. At one point, his investigator had almost been forced to give up.

Rory tried on a few expressions, finally settling on one he hoped was serious but hopeful, and then he walked over.

'Kaitlin Le?'

Her head jerked up and she scrutinised him as if he were about to attack her.

Rory threw up his hands. 'I'm a friend. Rory Murray. I'm—'

'The lawyer.' Kaitlin's face was one of disgust.

'That's right. I've—'

'You've been spamming the Facebook group with posts about your business.'

'Hey, don't see them as business posts! They're offers of help. You're doing a real great job keeping the candle alight. But you need a champion. A knight in shining armour, with a sword that can cut through all the red tape and bureaucratic shenanigans.' This time he held his arms wide as if to say: that's me!

'I don't need any help.'

'No, you seem a very capable person. Very capable. But think of all the other families. Don't deny them. And isn't it true that we all need help at some time? A problem shared and all that.'

Kaitlin slid her phone away and stood up. 'I'll say this in the politest possible way: leave me alone.'

'I told you, I'm a friend.'

'You really think I'm that stupid?' Her eyes blazed. 'You're a lawyer. You don't do charity. This is all about hard cash for you.'

'Yes, there are obviously some financial benefits here. But that doesn't mean I can't feel for the families as well. The authorities have clearly covered up what happened to Flight 702. There's a yawning mystery at the heart of that disappearance and no one involved is going to get any closure until the truth is found out. Let me help.'

'You're good at talking.'

'And that's exactly why you need me in any court of law.'

'But if there's one thing I've learned over the last few months, it's how to recognise bullshit,' Kaitlin snapped. 'You want in on this for yourself. I don't want anyone like that at my back. I can't trust them.' She turned and marched away, her voice floating back, 'Don't bother me again.'

Rory grabbed a coffee and sipped on it as he walked back towards his apartment. The caffeine helped him to focus. That was certainly a frustrating encounter, but you didn't get anywhere in the law by giving up easily. He'd come back to Kaitlin Le when she'd had time to calm down and see reason. He couldn't afford to let this class action slip through his fingers. He needed this more than anything he'd needed in his life.

His cell rang and he answered.

'Dad?'

'Zara? What time is it there? Everything OK?'

'No, actually, it's not. It's horrible here. I don't like it. Can I come back?'

'What, to New York?'

'Yeah. I just want to get away, Dad. It's awful.'

Rory sucked on his teeth. 'You remember what happened last time.'

'I can't stay here, Dad.' Her voice crackled with a stifled sob.

'Darling, you need to hang on in there. Get everything right. Get back to who you were before all the . . . issues. Then come back.'

'Can't I be in a clinic in New York?'

'Your mother wants to be close to you, you know that.'

'I don't believe that, Dad. It's you who doesn't want to be close to me.'

'That's not true. Why would you say something . . .' Rory bit down on his words. Getting irritated was counterproductive. Zara hadn't been thinking straight ever since her addictions had taken hold.

'I want to come back. I want to come back. Please, Dad. Talk to Mom. I can't handle it here. We're not allowed to go out. It's like a prison. There are cameras everywhere.'

'It will get better. You'll get better. You'll see. It'll be OK.'

'No, Dad, it won't.'

The line died. Zara had hung up.

Rory trudged back to his apartment. He wasn't going to let the varied and numerous problems of his domestic life knock him off course. He felt for Zara, he really did. But she was in the right place. Knowing that didn't wipe out the pain he'd heard in her voice, though.

He ordered in pizza, then propped himself up in bed with his laptop, alternating between bites and tapping keys.

When the MacBook pinged with an incoming call from a familiar name, he instantly hit Answer. This wasn't one he wanted to miss.

'*Hola*,' he said, swallowing his mouthful.

'Hello . . . Señor Murray?'

'*Sí. Gracias por responder a mi publicación.*' He'd given up expecting Eva to respond to him after three messages into a void.

'*Tu hablas español?*'

'*Un poco.* My first wife . . . *Mi primera esposa era de Venezuela, así que yo* . . . My Spanish is a bit . . . *fuera de práctica. Lo siento.*'

'It's OK, we can speak English.'

'I read about your situation. Thank you for returning my—'

'Jennifer said it was OK.'

'Jennifer? The family liaison counsellor from—'

'The airline, *sí*. She said you were a good man, that we could trust you.'

Rory raised his eyebrows. *Well, that was unexpected. Not going to look a gift horse in the mouth.* 'OK! All good! As I said in my message, I'm representing a number of relatives and . . . er . . . Monika was cabin crew, right?'

'*Sí.*'

'So, first, I need you to know that whatever the airline may have offered you, and I have no reason to know if they did or didn't, whatever they may have made you sign isn't important. If they're found to have been negligent, the payout we can get you by pursuing this in a court of law will be far in excess of—'

'My daughter is alive.'

'I'm sorry?'

'She called me.'

'What! When?'

'I want to invite you to our group, Mr Murray.'

'Wait a minute, are you saying Monika wasn't on Flight 702?'

'No, she was. And I need you to help me find her.'

The rich aroma of baked goods drifted from the church hall. Rory breathed it in the moment he jumped out of the cab; the only positive to an evening visit to this part of Brooklyn. Eva was waiting for him under the light over the door, a big woman with a face that fell into easy smiles.

He hailed her and they exchanged pleasantries before she said, 'We've been looking for someone who'll take us seriously, someone who can help us. Come . . .' She ushered him into the warm atmosphere.

Rory tried to suppress his desire to launch straight in, but curiosity got the better of him.

'When you say you had a call from Monika, what did she say?' he inquired. Testing the water. *Was this woman crazy, grief-stricken or both?*

'She said she was healthy and OK, but that she couldn't come home just yet.'

'Why? Was she being held somewhere?'

'No, but she said there was something she needed to do. She couldn't tell me. Through here . . .'

'Did you record the call? Do you have any—'

'Proof? I thought about that a lot. I guess I was so shocked. It was late at night when she called. Obviously, I wasn't expecting it. I even wondered afterwards if . . .' Eva paused, thinking.

'You imagined it?'

'I can see you're thinking the same thing, Mr Murray.'

'No, it's just . . . well, yes.'

Eva smiled. 'But then I met the others.'

She swung open the door to the meeting place, where three men and two women chatted in the centre of a circle of chairs.

'This is Mr Murray,' Eva announced. 'The lawyer I was telling you about.'

Everyone nodded. A couple raised their hands in greeting. As he pulled up a chair, Rory read the faces: one was suspicious, three were hopeful, the other he couldn't tell.

'We meet here in the church once a week,' Eva said. 'We've all been contacted.'

'Why have you come to see us, Mr Murray?' a beefy guy in a plaid shirt asked.

'My firm, Murray & Wexler.' Rory handed out his business card. 'Please, take my card. We're representing a number of relatives of passengers on board Flight 702 and we're building a case against the airline, the plane manufacturer and its associated companies. And the more families who join us . . .' He glanced around those faces again. 'I'll be honest, though, I'm a little confused. I mean, you seem to be saying you've had contact with passengers on Flight 702.'

'We have,' one of the other men said.

'But the plane crashed into the Atlantic.'

'We don't believe that. That's why we need your help.'

A woman with long grey hair leaned forwards. 'We think the plane was diverted to a secret location. Our loved ones were coerced into carrying out some secret work for the government, that's what we believe.'

Belief.

Rory smiled and nodded.

'Let me show you something,' the man in the plaid shirt said, pulling out his phone. 'This is my son, Lucas. He'd been on a vacation in France with his mom. She's French. They were both coming home on 702.'

Rory watched as a video rolled of a child reciting a poem:

> The Moon comes every night to peep.
> Through the window where I lie:
> But I pretend to be asleep;
> And watch the Moon go slowly by.

'What a cute kid,' Rory gushed. 'I'm sorry for your loss.'

The man wafted a hand, dismissing his sympathy. 'Lucas had an extra toe on his left foot. Before his mother took him away, we talked about having it removed. Not that it was a problem, but just growing up, we didn't want him to have any insecurities about being different. We didn't want him to spend the rest of his life having to buy different size shoes. So, look closely.'

He played the video again.

'What am I looking for?' Rory asked.

'He has five toes on his left foot. The sixth has been removed.'

'Is it possible his mother had it done when she took him to France?'

'It takes at least six weeks to recover from that kind of operation. His foot would be bandaged or in plaster for at least six weeks. But look: no scar even. I've had doctors examine this and they say that Lucas was operated on at least two months before this video was taken. At least.'

'So?'

'He was operated on *after* Flight 702 disappeared.'

Rory nodded, keeping his eyes on the frozen image on the video so he didn't reveal what he was really thinking.

'All of us here have been contacted,' Eva said. 'Emails, calls . . .'

Rory looked to the man in the plaid shirt. 'And you were sent this, when?'

'I found it. Online. I've spent the last six months scouring the internet looking for him.'

'Your son, Lucas,' Rory mused. 'What's his surname?'

'James.'

'There were six minors on Flight 702. I don't recall a Lucas James on the passenger manifest.'

'His mother was travelling on a different name.'

'What name was in his passport?'

'I don't know. She was trying to stop me from seeing him. I think she changed his name when she left the family home.'

'Wait. She took your son to France?'

'We were going through a difficult patch. We needed time apart. But then we spoke and we decided we wanted to be together again. And they were coming back.'

Rory smiled. He didn't know what to say. But as he looked around those faces again, he saw the desperation lodged just beneath the surface. They wanted everything made right, the world put back as it had been when life made sense. He felt a pang of compassion for these poor souls. It was a long time since something like this had happened. He pushed the feeling down. He didn't like it. It was too destabilising, too much of a distraction from his aims.

'Have you had contact from the airline?' he asked.

'They don't accept that my son was on the flight. That's why we need you.'

'Look, I really appreciate you inviting me here, but unfortunately, I'm late for another meeting,' Rory said, standing. There wasn't much here that would help his case. In fact, some of them might damage it.

'But you'll help us, right?' the man in the plaid shirt pressed, looking pained.

Rory smiled weakly as he stood from his chair.

As Rory stepped out into the night, one of the other men hurried down the church hall steps. He had an expensive haircut and had the look of those guys from high-powered legal firms who always made Rory feel small.

'Mr Murray. I'm Jim Travis,' he said, holding out his hand. 'I run this group. I just wanted to say that not everyone here is imagining things. People do that, sure. But some of us are real. I lost my dad.'

'I'm sorry for your loss.'

'Don't say that. I'm serious. I just want to honour his memory by helping all of the other grieving relatives. They need support. We don't ask too many questions of those who come. We don't want to judge. Sure, we get a lot of . . . well, you know what I mean, but that's OK. This is a safe place where I hope people can find some peace in the world. That's all we want. All I want.'

He lowered his eyes, his face flooding with emotion. Rory felt another one of those annoying bouts of compassion.

'Anyway, if you want names, addresses, telephone numbers, there's a girl who lost her brother. She was going round visiting lots of relatives, collecting stuff, maybe you should talk to her.'

'Kaitlin? Kaitlin Le?'

'Yes, Kaitlin, that's right.'

'You've spoken to her?'

'A few weeks ago. Actually, she was supposed to come to one of our meetings. But she never turned up.' Jim smiled. 'She's pretty intense. Driven, maybe. But she's got a big heart. That counts for a lot.'

'Thank you,' Rory said. 'Kaitlin is definitely someone I need to speak to.'

Back in his apartment, Rory lounged on his bed, trying to put out of his mind all the faces of those people in the support group. He flicked on *The Tonight Show* and let it drone in the background, hoping it would distract him, when his cell rang.

Rory frowned at the name that flashed up and then answered. 'Petra?'

'OK, I'm authorised to send through the airline's proposal.' Brusque, no-nonsense, but that was Petra. He'd never got a minute of small talk out of her during all the months they'd been in contact.

'Proposal?'

'We're putting together a settlement. I'm contacting all of the lawyers representing families.'

Rory muted the TV. 'The airline wants to settle? Why now? It's a bomb, that's what they're saying. So, what's going on?'

'Come on, Rory, beggars can't be choosers. Read it and we'll get together.'

'You don't understand. This isn't about the money, Petra. My clients want the truth.' Even as the words fell out of his mouth, he was surprised to realise for the first time that they were true.

'You're quite the crusader, aren't you, Rory?' Petra's voice dripped with acid. 'You need to look at this seriously and get back to me if you don't want your clients to miss out. Everyone else is on board with it. What's your problem? You need the money. Everyone in the business knows that.'

'What's *my* problem? My clients want to know what happened. If it was a bomb, how did it get on board? They want an apology, an admission of culpability. That's how they'll get peace. That's how they'll begin to rebuild their broken lives. They want the truth and then we can talk about compensation.'

'So, do you want it or not?'

'What?'

'The proposal. I'm just giving it to you ahead of the meeting as a professional courtesy.'

'Send it over.'

'There you go.'

Rory's laptop dinged.

'See you at the meeting on Thursday.' Petra hung up as abruptly as she'd called.

Once they'd hung up, Rory opened the file and began to read, but his mind kept returning to what he'd said to Petra. *Who was he?* He didn't recognise himself any more.

11

The hotel bar was low-lit with plenty of shadowed corners for off-book business meetings or illicit assignations. More importantly, it had a door directly off the street. Kaitlin slipped into the drone of low conversation and the chinks of ice falling into glass then looked around.

A familiar face hovered in the half-light in a corner booth where all entrances were visible. The man's hand flickered in barely perceptible greeting.

'So, you *are* FBI. I knew it,' Kaitlin said when she took her seat.

The craggy-faced man opposite was the man with the coloured jackets who'd unnerved Dolores both times they'd met in the diner.

'Agent Dennison,' he said. 'Thank you for meeting with me. Can I get you a drink?' He raised a glass of Scotch to her.

Kaitlin ignored the offer. 'You made me look like I was delusional thinking that I was being followed.'

'My apologies. I was working undercover. It was necessary—'

'To be an ass?'

Dennison shrugged. 'Yeah. Goes with the territory sometimes.'

'So, what are you doing here? Conducting interviews in bars isn't standard FBI procedure, as I now know very well.'

'I'm not here in any official capacity. Like I said on the phone, my employer isn't exactly happy with me. But you're right, we shouldn't stay here. It's too public.'

'No offence, but I'm not going anywhere with you. I don't care that you're FBI.'

'I'm not. Not really. Not any more.'

Kaitlin eyed him.

'I was fired. Officially, put on suspension, which is the Bureau's way of trying to get rid of me and keep me quiet at the same time.'

'Why would they want to keep you quiet?'

'Because I know too much. Listen, you're smart to be distrustful, but we can't talk about this here. I've been working out of a storage unit, cash only, so the Bureau can't track my cards.'

Kaitlin shook her head. 'No way. I'm not going.'

'I know you've been working on your own investigation and we might each have a missing piece that the other one needs.'

'I'm not going to help you to carry out whatever revenge you want to get on your former employer. That's insane.'

Was this some kind of set-up? Kaitlin couldn't be sure. She couldn't really be sure of anything at all these days.

'No, no, no, that's not what this is about. I was suspended *because* I was investigating. They didn't want me to keep digging.'

'I thought that was the whole point of the Federal Bureau of Investigation to, you know, investigate?'

'I wasn't officially on the 702 case.' Dennison stared into his Scotch for a moment. 'My daughter was on that flight. FBI protocol. You don't investigate cases where you have a personal connection. Gets in the way of objective thinking.'

Kaitlin looked at Dennison in a new light. She could see it now – that hidden corruption of grief in the flicker of the eyes, the sag of the facial muscles, like a mist settling on the features.

'I'm sorry,' she said simply, knowing there was nothing else to say.

'She was about your age. Her twenty-second birthday was seven weeks ago.'

'Emily. That was her name, right?' Kaitlin said, realising. Dennison nodded.

'I should have put it together before. Emily Dennison – I've read over the passenger list, like, thousands of times. She was one of those people who . . .' She hesitated, then continued. 'I didn't think she was worth digging into. She was just a student.'

'Yeah. Art history.' Dennison sucked in a steadying breath. 'She was studying abroad. Rome. She'd had such a great time. She couldn't wait to show her mom and me all of her photos. She liked shooting on film.'

'I'm so sorry.'

Dennison jerked, throwing off his grief, refocusing. 'Listen, I don't buy the bird excuse either. I think there's something much, much bigger at play here. But both of us are already being watched closely by the Bureau and who knows who else. So, we can't talk about this in public.'

Kaitlin studied him as she made her calculation. After a moment, she nodded her assent.

The storage unit was on that endless dismal strip of feature-less industrial sprawl and the lowest of low-rent motels between JFK and the Queens-Midtown Tunnel. Dennison killed the engine of his sedan and led the way through a maze of units in the reek of spilled oil and vehicle fumes.

Stay sharp, Kaitlin told herself. *Get ready to run.*

Dennison heaved up the roll-top door of his space and ushered her inside before wrenching it down again. A strip light shone across piles of documents and walls covered with newspaper clippings, maps and photographs.

'Apologies for the mess,' the agent muttered.

'No different to my dorm,' Kaitlin replied.

She eyed a chart with lots of strings going back and forth between images and scrawled notes. It was ten times more complicated than the pieces of background information she'd stuck to her own wall in the dorm.

Dennison noticed. 'There's a reason TV uses the whole—'

'Murder board thing?'

'Whatever you want to call it. It's a helpful way to organise your thoughts.'

'Heard of computers?'

'You millennials,' Dennison sighed.

Kaitlin allowed herself a smile. Maybe he was OK.

Dennison shuffled through a handful of files. 'Let me catch you up on where I am.' He handed one of the files over. 'Here's a report from the National Transportation Safety Board from three weeks *after* the crash.'

Kaitlin flicked through the pages. 'I don't see anything about 702 in here.'

'I know. I think that's why it's been overlooked. But it does mention a civil aviation accident team that was sent out to Kuala Lumpur on the fourth of May. But there were no crashes in Malaysia that year. So why were they there? And then, this.' Dennison thrust another file into her hand. 'One of the investigators on the Kuala Lumpur team attended a private lecture on . . . OK . . . "viral attacks on aircrafts". And the Kuala Lumpur team came through Heathrow, which is, yeh know – interesting, to say the least.'

Kaitlin felt a flicker of unease. Dennison had grown increasingly manic, almost babbling, his hands trembling.

'What exactly is your theory?' Kaitlin couldn't help but feel that this was getting a little out of hand.

'I don't think the plane crashed. I think it was diverted. I think this is all a massive government cover-up.'

'A cover-up of what?'

Dennison turned away, searching another heap of files as if he hadn't heard her. 'If we can find where the plane is, then we can expose it all.'

'Expose what?'

'There was a doctor on the plane, from the University of Damascus. Dr Mohammad Aziz.'

Kaitlin steadied herself. OK, this was something. She thought back to her interview with the psychic witch and her account of the doctor wanting his wife to sit next to him.

'Aziz. The one studying immunology,' she said.

'I think he brought a virus on board.'

'What are you saying? Biological warfare?'

'It's a serious national security concern.'

'I looked into that, but there wasn't any concrete evidence. And then your colleague got in my way before I could find anything more.'

'Who? Agent Gerard? She just spouts the company line. She's not dedicated to finding out the truth.'

Dennison's eyes blazed. Kaitlin felt her unease grow.

'The FBI, they're all part of this,' he gushed. 'And they want to keep me quiet, but they won't. They don't know about this storage unit yet. But it's all here. The answers are all here. I just need to find them.'

Kaitlin looked from his face to the jumbled room. Obsession seemed to be the norm for everyone who got sucked into the Flight 702 orbit, herself included, but Dennison seemed further gone than most.

'Look at this,' he continued, waving a paper at her. 'This formula was in one of Dr Aziz's research papers. It's all theoretical, supposedly. A worst-case scenario hypothesis.'

She backed towards the door. 'I'm sorry, Agent Dennison, but I really need to get out of—'

'But what if there actually is a disease that's capable of 7h:100c:95f?'

Kaitlin stared. 'What did you just say?'

'It's a formula: 7h:100c:95f. How scientists describe the spread of disease.' Dennison ranged around the unit, scrubbing one hand through his hair.

'What do you mean?'

'Take Ebola, say. One of the deadliest viruses in the world today. That has a spread formula of 74d:100c:56f.'

'Meaning what?'

'A person infected with Ebola would lead to a hundred more cases in seventy-four days. Out of those hundred cases, fifty-six will be fatal.'

'OK, so, then 7h:100c:95f is—'

Dennison waved a hand at her. 'Right! Seven hours, one hundred cases and ninety-five deaths. From each infected person. Can you imagine how fast a disease like that would spread in a city like New York?'

Kaitlin felt a jolt of panic. Yes, Dennison seemed off-kilter. *But what if he was right?*

'Do you think this new disease could be real?' she demanded.

'I think Dr Aziz was developing it in Iran and I think he was bringing it here.'

'Why would he want to do that?'

'Plenty of reasons. Maybe he'd been radicalised, maybe he needed a facility to study it in, maybe he just wanted to sell it to the highest bidder. The why doesn't matter. I think the government knew what was happening. And so, they diverted the plane. There's a shadow.' He rustled through his files until he found the one that he was looking for. 'There's a shadow in a satellite photo over Greenland. It doesn't look like much, but I think it's proof that the plane landed there.'

'A shadow?'

Dennison tapped his finger on the image. 'Yeah, see? It's slight but irregular. There are no clouds there, no structures. What else could it be?'

Kaitlin felt the world spinning around her. She was so deep into all this now, it was hard not to lose perspective. *What was real, what wasn't real?*

'Why would the government keep it there?' Dennison asked. 'Why? That's another thing. I think the pilot tried to make a call out. Why else would her phone suddenly turn on? The captain was going to call out to tell the world what was happening on the plane, so the co-pilot had to kill the captain and take over.' He stopped and jabbed a finger at her. 'You need to go to Atlanta.'

Kaitlin reeled at the sudden shift, barely able to keep up.

'There's a medical conference there. Some of Dr Aziz's colleagues are attending. I can't go. The FBI is watching me too closely, but you need to talk to them. Find out more about Aziz's research.'

'I can't just go to Atlanta!'

'Why not? Are you telling me you haven't followed up leads with less than that?'

How could she tell him she didn't trust his judgement enough to throw everything down and head to Georgia?

131

'One of the scientists Dr Aziz worked with, Professor Marshal, he and Aziz met when they worked on a study together at the Centers for Disease Control and Prevention. The work they did together was classified, but it was included in the Bureau's file on Dr Aziz.'

'What kind of study was it?'

'That wasn't in the file. Not even the FBI knew. Go to Atlanta and ask Dr Marshal about what the CDC was paying him to do. Hell, if you can, go to the CDC itself. See what you can find out.'

'Why would they tell me anything?'

'You're a smart girl, Kaitlin. You've made it this far. You'll come up with something. Don't you want to know what happened? Don't you want to know if something this deadly exists?'

Back in her apartment, Kaitlin sat on her bed, lulled by the drone of traffic from the street below. *Could she trust Dennison? Or was he just sending her way off course like Flight 702?*

There was also a more practical problem. How could she afford to get to Atlanta when money was increasingly tight? She couldn't ask her parents for any more cash. She'd felt guilty enough the first time, and she knew that she'd have to tell them what the money was for. They'd just swamp her in a lecture about what a wreck she was making of her life, and maybe they were right.

She also wasn't sure that she could trust Dennison's judgement, not by a long way, but there was a niggling voice at the back of her head that kept taunting her: *what if he's right?* If it was a lead, she couldn't afford to ignore it.

After half an hour wrestling with her guilt, she realised she only had one choice. She pulled out her phone and called Amelia.

12

Kaitlin leaned against the wall in the deserted corridor, listening to the applause rumbling through the closed doors of the lecture hall. Atlanta was warmer than NYC at this time of year; a balmy seventy-five degrees but unpleasantly sticky with it. She'd never visited Georgia before, wasn't sure she wanted to this time.

She felt so grateful for Amelia. Her friend's family was loaded, but Kaitlin knew that she'd have loaned her the cash for the flight even if Amelia was down to her last few bucks. She was endlessly generous and despite the huge amounts of money Amelia had grown up with, she was the most grounded, down-to-earth person Kaitlin had ever met, making friends with anyone who crossed her path, regardless of their status or background.

The applause drained away and a low voice began to speak, tearing Kaitlin's thoughts away from her friend and back to the task in hand. She drew herself up and was ready when the door opened and a man in his mid-fifties stepped out after completing his talk. This was the guy Dennison suggested might be a good contact. Marshal was slim and bald, with silver-framed glasses that had no doubt once been fashionable.

'Professor Marshal?' She showed what she hoped was a disarming smile. She'd become pretty good at them since she'd started on this path.

'Yes. Do I know you?'

'No, I'm sorry. My name is Kaitlin Le. Do you have a minute to talk?'

'A minute. Are you attending the conference?'

No doubt he was curious about her young age. Understandable. She ignored him. 'I actually want to talk about Dr Aziz.'

'Really? Why?'

'I'm studying biology at Georgia Tech and I was really interested in Dr Aziz's work. I'm so sorry to hear that he was on Flight 702.'

'It's a huge loss. He was an excellent scientist.'

'Do you know why he was coming to America?'

'For a conference – one that I was chairing, actually. On immunology. He was to be a keynote speaker.'

'That's fascinating. Do you happen to know what his speech was going to be about?'

'As you're aware, Dr Aziz's expertise was in human resistance to biological attacks. His experiences in Damascus . . . well, he was very motivated. Seeing all the suffering from those chemical attacks, he feared that there were plenty more coming. Something worse.'

'What do you mean?' *Don't push too hard. Play dumb.*

'Chemical attacks are hard to escape, but you typically know they're happening and they're not always deadly. It's not the same for biological attacks. Mohammad's fear about biological weapons was that by the time we noticed a population suffering, it would be too late to reverse. He wanted to get ahead of it.' Marshal showed a wan smile. 'He'd always been a bit doomsday about things, to be frank. And looking at the situation in Syria, well . . . who was to say he was wrong?

'The problem is, if you look at a chemical attack, you know how it's going to work. You know how long it'll be effective. What the range is, the likely casualties and so forth. With biological strains, it's a whole different story. You don't know how things are going to work. How the virus may spread and mutate.

'Viruses are very strange things, neither quite living nor exactly dead. They need to invade living organisms to replicate. You simply can't control them once they're released.' He paused. 'At least, not with any certainty.'

'So, was this the area that you and Dr Aziz collaborated on?'

'Collaborated? Not really. Let's say our interests often overlapped.'

The lecture droned on through the door.

'How so?' Kaitlin pressed.

'Mohammad was very dedicated to public health, clearly, and I'm a microbiologist. Even without weaponised viruses, one of the greatest threats to public health is bacteria and how well a country's infrastructure is equipped to handle that bacteria.'

'Oh, interesting.' Kaitlin turned her practised smile on the professor. He lit up, enjoying the attention. 'So, you and Dr Aziz would . . .'

'Mohammad would cover the human side and I'd cover the micro side. I'd look at specific bacteria or a virus, what it was capable of, and Mohammad would focus on how the human immune system would respond.'

'And weren't you involved with a grant that he received?' Marshal frowned.

'The two of you did a study at the CDC, right?'

'How do you know that? That study never went public.'

'Why is that?'

Marshal's face darkened. He was suspicious now. Maybe she'd punched the right button.

'That was years ago. I can't imagine it would be relevant to anything you're studying in school.'

'Why? Was the study unsuccessful?'

'Just because something was successful doesn't mean it stays current.'

'So, it *did* work?'

The conference hall door swung open and a woman poked her head out.

'Professor Marshal? You've got a few questions, if you're happy to take them.'

'Fine. Thank you.' He turned back to Kaitlin. 'I'm sorry, I'll have to bring this conversation to an end.'

'Was Dr Aziz developing biological weapons?' Kaitlin blurted. It wasn't elegant, but it might be her only chance.

Marshal's face reddened with simmering anger. 'That's not an accusation you can just throw around, especially not here.'

'Please, Professor Marshal. This is important.'

'Mohammad was studying the effect of different viruses and bacteria on the human immune system. He was *not* weaponising science. He'd never do that.'

'Do you know that? For sure?'

'What are you implying?'

'We think we know who someone is, but that isn't always . . .' Kaitlin gathered herself. 'People have secrets.'

'Yes, I believe they do. And it's clear to me now that you yourself are keeping several.'

Marshal spun away from her, back into the lecture hall.

As she stepped out into the hot sun, she checked her phone and saw she had a missed call from her dad. She felt a sudden wave of panic. Her father never called her. It was always her mom who made contact on behalf of both of them.

Fumbling, she rushed to return the call. Her heart was in her throat. Surely something couldn't have happened to her mom?

The second she heard it connect, she babbled, 'Dad, is everything OK?'

There was a long period of silence that made her heart pound even faster before, at long last, her father replied, 'Kaitlin. How are you?'

His voice sounded so awfully flat, drained of any emotion, like he'd been drugged. 'Dad, I was worried. Are you OK? You called.'

'I just wanted to hear your voice, my daughter. It's been so long.'

She heard a faint slur in his words. *Was he drunk? During the day?*

'I'm sorry I haven't called much, Dad. I—'

'Yes, yes, I know, you have your life now. You don't need us any more.'

She felt stung by that, though she knew he didn't mean it. 'Dad, are you OK?'

'We're worried about you, Kaitlin, your mother and I,' he went on as if he hadn't heard her. 'You were so close to Conor. And now . . . and now he's left such a space in your life.'

The words drained away and Kaitlin heard a stifled sobbing. A moment later, the line went dead.

Feeling sick at the buried suffering she'd sensed, she hurried to call her mother's number.

'Mom. I just had a strange call from Dad. He seems so . . . I mean, not like himself. How's he doing?'

The brief silence that followed told her all she needed to know. Her mother was usually quick to fill every space with words.

'Your father is finding things . . . difficult at the moment. He keeps a lot bottled up and then . . . well, it's not good for him.'

'Have you talked it through with him?'

'You know how he is. He won't admit to anything.' She paused, then added hopefully, 'You could come home for a while. He'd love to have you around.'

Kaitlin felt her heart sink. 'Mom, I can't.'

'OK. Not to worry. Your father's a strong man. He just needs time to come to terms with this.'

'Look, just . . . Just let me know if there's any change, or anything . . . anything . . . You know.'

'Of course.'

'I love you, Mom.'

As she hung up, Kaitlin felt a dull ache seeping deep into her. She was worried about her dad. She was worried about her mom. She was worried about all of them.

If she found answers, perhaps that would heal some of the pain. She had to focus on that. It was all she had.

Dust motes danced in the sunlight slanting through the window of the Atlanta motel room. Kaitlin sat cross-legged on the bed and called Agent Dennison.

'The moment I mentioned the CDC, he went from a professor geeking out to sketchy scientist protecting state secrets,' she said.

'And he said specifically that Dr Aziz was working on biological weapons, not chemical ones?'

'Right. Could that have brought the plane down? I mean, if he'd had some sort of virus or nerve agent on board.'

'Certainly. If he'd found a way to get the agent into the air recirculation system, disabled the filters, it could have incapacitated everyone in minutes. But I don't think the plane was brought down.'

'Why not?'

'The shadow, Kaitlin! That plane is safe and sound somewhere. If Dr Aziz had found a virus that was truly 7h:100c:95f and was planning on releasing it or selling it, that's plenty of reason to ground a plane.'

Kaitlin swallowed. Her mouth was too dry. She didn't know if she could cope with this line of inquiry. She'd spent so long convincing herself that Conor was dead, she didn't want to reignite all the feelings with false hope.

'Who do you think he'd have been selling it to?' she asked, forcing herself to be businesslike.

'Anyone. The bioweapon black market is massive and global. He may have been smuggling something from Russia, or his own lab. I imagine there would be a buyer for it back home, but maybe he got a better offer here.'

Her cell buzzed with another incoming call. 'Gotta go. I'll be in touch.' She switched to the new call. It was her mother again. 'Mom?' she said. 'Is everything OK?'

'Is everything OK with *you*? After you called about your dad, I realised I hadn't asked you how you are. I'm worried about you, Kaitlin.'

'I'm OK, Mom. You don't need to worry about me. Just focus on Dad.'

'Kaitlin, why aren't you in school?'

Kaitlin sighed. She really didn't want to get into those kinds of questions. 'I'll be back soon, Mom.'

'You haven't called me in so long for one of our talks.'

'I texted.'

'It's not the same. I'm worried about you, Kaitlin. We both are. Your father, he misses you so much.'

'I was just there not long ago.'

'You know what I mean. He feels like he doesn't know you any more. First we lose Conor and now we're losing you too. I think . . . I think maybe your father knows you too well. You've always been like him.'

'You always say that.'

'You're both so stubborn. You don't give up. And that's a good thing. But this isn't good for you. You've seen what it's done to him. Don't let it do that to you, too.'

'I just want to know the truth. About the plane, about Conor. About everything.' Kaitlin furrowed her brow at the long silence on the other end. 'Mom?'

'I should have told you this before. Your father – I haven't told him.' Another silence. Then: 'Conor was on that plane because I told him to come back.'

Kaitlin reeled. 'You *told* him to come back?'

'He and Thomas were going to get married. Conor was going to tell Dad.'

'Conor never told *me* that.'

More silence.

'He was going to. You know, I liked Thomas. I thought he was a nice boy. He made Conor happy. He really loved him. Your father thinks . . . differently.'

Kaitlin felt hurt, not only that Conor had kept it from her, but her mother, too. Still, now wasn't the time.

'What do you think Dad would have done if he'd known?' she asked. Her father was a deeply conservative man. He'd never really come to terms with Conor's sexuality.

'I don't really know, my love. It was better not to tell him, I thought. But Conor wanted Dad to know.'

'I wish you'd have told me. I wish *he*'d have told me.'

'I don't know why he didn't. You and Conor were always so close.'

One thought was scrabbling at the back of her head. 'Mom, have you talked to Thomas?'

'We both loved Conor so much.'

'So, you have?'

'He gave me a number, just for me and him.'

'What do you talk about?'

'Everything. Sometimes nothing. It doesn't matter what, really. It just helps when I'm missing Conor badly. We call it the hotline. He says I can call anytime. Sometimes we talk for hours.'

And yet Thomas hadn't returned any of her calls. That feeling of hurt burned hotter. *Had she really upset Conor that much?*

Once her mother had gone, Kaitlin flopped back on the bed. She felt relieved that finally, she now knew why Conor was on the flight back home. After all of her digging, it was an answer that was somehow both mundane and momentous at the same time. He was getting engaged and he wanted his father's approval.

And yet he still hadn't been able to bring himself to tell her, his twin sister, and Thomas still refused to talk to her. That stupid argument, those hurtful words.

Kaitlin thought back to when they were kids, riding their bikes after school. They'd travel for miles, pretending to be detectives trying to crack some mystery or other, or just talking and talking about anything and everything. They weren't just brother and sister. They were best friends.

She felt a deep ache in her heart.

And now there was no way to put it right.

Somehow, any information she'd gleaned from Professor Marshal paled beside that. For the first time, the scale of what she was trying to do dawned on her. She could no longer do this on her own.

13

A strip of light leaked out from under the door at the storage unit. Kaitlin stared at it for a long moment, wondering if she should go in to see Agent Dennison. Her flight from Atlanta had landed an hour earlier and when she'd called Dennison again to update him, he'd sounded even more manic than when she'd left him.

The truth was, her mother's news about Conor still haunted her. She'd pulled together so much information about the passengers on Flight 702, but she still couldn't see how the pieces fit together, if at all. She wasn't sure if Dennison was helping or making it worse, either.

Before she could reach a decision, the door rattled up and light flooded out. Dennison loomed, silhouetted against the glow from the bare bulb. Kaitlin noticed an odd posture, one hand thrust into his jacket pocket. *Did he have a firearm tucked away?*

'Oh, it's you,' he said. He stepped out and looked up and down the line of darkened units. 'I heard something. Can't be too careful.'

Kaitlin froze. *Could he have shot her?*

'People are watching me,' he continued, beckoning her inside. 'Not sure which agency. NSA? Homeland Security? Maybe the CIA. That means we're getting close. But that means this is the point of greatest danger. They'll stop at nothing to prevent us from revealing the truth.'

'OK.' Kaitlin half wondered if she should run. Instead,

she stepped inside the unit and Dennison clanged down the door.

She couldn't do this on her own, that was true. But the knot in her stomach told her Dennison wasn't the right ally.

'I'm getting close to finding out where they are,' he said, spinning off to one of the piles of files.

'Where? Where who are?'

'My daughter! Your brother. The passengers. They're all still alive.'

'I don't think that's true. There's no evidence. It's just wishful thinking.' She couldn't let herself be led down that road. She'd drive herself mad.

'There's evidence. All right, not evidence. But enough to cause a strong suspicion. Don't lose heart now, Kaitlin.'

'I need to focus on the reason why the flight went down. Not get distracted by—'

'Wait. Hear me out.' Dennison crashed over to the pile of files and began riffling through them. 'There's just a few more details that I need to . . . OK, for example, I think there was a passenger travelling with a fake passport. The Bureau were cagey about it, so it might have just been a smokescreen.'

'You mean Dimo Dragov. Yeah, I already looked into him. He was a Bulgarian crime boss.'

'No, no, no. I'm not talking about him. It was a woman.' Dennison flipped through a file with frantic movements. 'Laura something. She seemed to be . . . She was definitely . . . They had something about her.'

'Agent Dennison . . .'

'Seemed really—'

'Agent Dennison!' Kaitlin snapped.

'Fishy.'

'Jim!'

Dennison snapped out of his manic state and stared at her.

'I'm sorry. I'm sorry for your daughter,' she began.

'No. No, no. No. Don't! Don't give up on this, Kaitlin. Don't let them get to you.'

'No one's getting to me. I don't want to believe it any more than you do, but—'

'No. My daughter's still alive.'

'Jim, this is—'

'And she's being held in a top-secret facility, along with your brother and . . . and . . . and the other 254 passengers of Flight 702. And I'm gonna find her.'

Dennison ranged around the unit, tearing open the drawers of filing cabinets, grabbing files and books.

'Jim, I'm leaving,' Kaitlin said in a gentle voice.

Dennison didn't seem to hear her. He continued to search and even when she was back out in the night, she could hear him crashing around his space like a wounded beast.

On the way back to the East Village, Kaitlin dialled Dylan's number again. The same voicemail message, the same futile wait for him to call her back. She wanted to fill him in on her visit to Atlanta and get his perspective on what she'd learned. But it looked like she'd have to keep it to herself.

As she climbed the steps to her apartment, Kaitlin felt the isolation close in around her. She'd forged this path on her own, but she'd always had Amelia and her other college friends around. Now she felt truly lonely.

In the dark of her bedroom, she stared out at the city lights. Who could she turn *to now?*

'Mr Murray, you have a visitor.'

Kaitlin looked around the cramped office. The reek of the garbage boats hung in the air. *Had she made the right decision? There was still time to get out.*

The lawyer jumped up from behind his desk when he saw her, rocking the take-out coffee from its coaster, splashing fresh brew over a pile of papers.

'Don't worry about that,' he said, hastily shaking the moisture off them. 'Come in. Take a seat. And thank you, Shana. Thank you. Hold all of my meetings until further notice.'

'But, Mr Murray,' his assistant began.

The lawyer held up his hand and gave the woman a firm stare.

'Thank you, Shana.'

She hesitated a moment, then she left, closing the door behind her.

'Mr Murray,' Kaitlin began.

'Rory,' he corrected. 'Please.'

Kaitlin sat. She felt bone-weary, like she'd been running a marathon for days. Hungry. Directionless. The solution to the mystery of Flight 702 hovered like a mirage on the horizon and she never seemed to get any closer.

'Tell me why I should trust you,' she said.

Rory held out both hands. 'A great start. Let's lay everything on the table. You know I'm putting together a class-action suit.'

'I'm not interested in winning any financial award. I just want the truth.'

'A noble pursuit. And of course, that lies at the heart of what I do.' Rory paused and stared into the corner of the room. 'OK. I'll be honest with you. When I started to pull this together, I saw an opportunity. I'm not proud to admit it. I understand the suffering and the pain. But this is the business. It's not a charity. And if I didn't step forwards, someone else would. It's easy to be dispassionate, treat it as just another legal conundrum, until you see the human face.'

Rory looked at Kaitlin and for the first time, she thought she saw some honesty in his features. The last time he'd cornered her, in the park, he came across like a performer. Good with words, a surfeit of charisma and a dollop of flamboyance. That might work with some people. Not her.

'Go on,' she said.

'I met with some of the families. I saw at first-hand what they're going through.'

'Grief does terrible things to people.'

He nodded. 'I want to help.'

'So, now it's about charity?'

'No, I've not had some Damascene conversion. You're a highly intelligent person, I could see that the first time we met, so I'm not going to try to give you the patter. You'll see right through it anyway. I need this case, for my business, and personally. But that doesn't mean that at the same time I can't do it for the best of reasons. To help people find answers. To champion those who don't have a voice, and to take a stand against the corporate cover-ups and the government lies.'

'A knight in shining armour.'

'I wouldn't go that far. But if you want to say that, who am I to argue?' Rory's eyes twinkled. 'And if I come out of this a better person, that's win–win, right?'

Kaitlin nodded. Maybe this was the right decision. 'So, how do we do this?'

'We have different areas of expertise – that's always good in a team. Let's exchange notes, see what we both know, and then we divide up the lines of inquiry.'

'OK,' Kaitlin said, holding out a hand. 'Partners.'

14

The gulls swooped against the blue sky, their hungry screeches ringing out as they circled the heaps of garbage. Rory tracked their passage as he stood at the fence looking out over the water. A chill wind blasted from the north, but he felt toasty in his thick overcoat.

He was worried about the woman standing beside him. She shivered from time to time in her thin hoodie and she had a hollow, hungry look to her face. He wanted to offer her his coat, but he didn't want to offend her with some patriarchal nonsense. She was tough, though, he could see that. She didn't complain. And more than anything, her investigation had dug far deeper than he'd ever imagined.

'Let's assess what we know,' he said. 'You think the people-trafficking gang is a dead end?'

'They're dangerous, no doubt about that. Hard. They're running a lucrative trade and they're linked to some extremely powerful people in DC who wouldn't be happy to see their names exposed, to say the very least. Would they have brought down a plane if they thought Maria Elian might still expose them? Absolutely.'

Rory nodded. 'And I'd say the lieutenants wouldn't have any qualms about taking out their leader, Dragov, under those circumstances. What about the evangelist woman?'

'Definitely sick. The experts don't think it was Ebola, but she'd travelled upriver. Who knows what she might have contracted.'

'OK. How about the psychic witch? She sounds like quite a character.'

'That's one way of describing her. A con artist with ties to a war criminal.'

Rory watched the gulls fight over some choice piece of garbage. 'Unless the spirits really were in touch with her, she had knowledge Flight 702 was in danger. I think you're right – she could have been tipped off by her friends in low places.

'Though why she got on board in the first place . . .' He turned over his thoughts. 'But the important thing to me is that her story, that knowledge, hints at a plot, a wider conspiracy, perhaps a terrorist threat. Something that was circulating among that fraternity.'

'And she mentioned the Syrian doctor, Mohammad Aziz, the immunologist. The FBI agent, Dennison, suggested he might have something to do with biological warfare. Maybe he was what set the alarm bells ringing for the psychic witch. Why she decided to get out of there.' Kaitlin gripped the chain-link fence. She was staring at the water, but she seemed to be a million miles away.

'What did you think about Aziz's colleague, the egghead you met at the conference in Atlanta?'

'He didn't put my mind at rest, let's say that.'

'OK. I'm moving Aziz right to the top of the list until we get some confirmation that he's innocent. No point speculating exactly what he did, but he's certainly a person of interest. But Dennison interests me, too. FBI. He could have access to information that's out of our reach. He thinks the plane is still in one piece, hidden by some government agency. Is that right?'

'Yeah. I'm not sure how much we should trust anything Dennison says, though. He's got some mental health issues. A lot of them.'

Rory nodded. 'Still, you've got a lot of important information. It's amazing you've done all this on your own.'

'What, for a girl?'

'Oh my Lord, you're hard work. OK. We've got a lot of pieces of the puzzle. Now we need to start fitting them together.'

That night, as Kaitlin tried to sleep, her phone buzzed and lit up the dark bedroom. It was Amelia.

'Hey. What's up?' she asked, rubbing her eyes and trying to hide the exhaustion in her voice.

'Mate, you need to get out of there, fast,' Amelia hissed, sounding tense. 'You need to run.'

'What? What are you talking about? Amelia, what's wrong?'

'I've just got back from a meeting with campus security.'

Kaitlin sat bolt upright. 'Is everything OK?'

'I'm fine. This isn't about me. Look, I don't know what you've been getting up to since you've been here, but you've pissed off some very bad people. Our dorm got trashed. At first, I thought it was just some frat boys playing a prank. But then there were some seriously low-rent thugs asking after you all over campus, all gold chains, tattoos and Eastern European accents.'

Dragov's gang. It had to be.

'I told campus security and they're doing regular sweeps,' Amelia continued. 'But those guys are still around, watching. Thought I ought to warn you.'

Kaitlin felt a rising tide of guilt. 'I'm so sorry you had to deal with that. The last thing I wanted was you getting dragged into this.'

'Don't worry about me. What are you getting yourself into, mate?'

'The less you know, the better. Thank you for warning me. Just . . . stay as far away from me as possible. I won't call you. Don't call me.'

'Kaitlin, you're meant to be my best mate. What the actual fuck is going on?'

'I can't say any more right now. You just have to trust me.'

All thoughts of sleep were now gone. Once she'd hung up, Kaitlin felt bad about pushing Amelia away, but she knew it was in her friend's best interests not to get dragged into her mess. And now she had another wave of paranoia washing over her. Not only was she trying to avoid the attention of government agencies, but it seemed she was going to have to stay one step ahead of a brutal criminal gang, too.

Kaitlin closed her eyes, but she knew sleep wasn't going to come easily.

News Recordings

British Newscaster

The three missing British schoolgirls believed to have travelled to Turkey as part of an attempt to join ISIS have likely reached Syria, British police have said. They're thought to be the victims of online grooming by a woman known as the White Matchmaker, because of her success recruiting jihadi brides from the West for ISIS fighters.

Terrorism Expert

If you look at Islamic terrorist organisations in the last fifteen years, many have tried to recruit girls and have been very unsuccessful. But ISIL has had a very aggressive social media campaign of deliberately targeting girls and they've had a great success.

British Newscaster

A British Islamic State recruiter known as the White Matchmaker and her twelve-year-old son are believed to have been killed in a US-led bombing raid on Aleppo in Syria. Sources say she died close to the border between Syria and Iraq, in a strike also thought to have killed her son.

15

Rory grabbed the falafels from the food truck just off Park Avenue and handed one to Kaitlin. She longed to tear off the foil and attack it, but she restrained herself. She couldn't remember the last time she'd eaten and she'd resorted to using a belt she'd found in one of the closets at the apartment to stop her jeans from slipping down.

'My investigator pulled up another lead on one of the names on the passenger list. Instantly raised a red flag or two.'

'Wish I had an investigator.'

'He's costing me a small fortune. Really, you're better off with your own shoe leather.' Rory unwrapped his falafel and wafted the aroma under his nose.

'If your investigator uncovered it, why are you handing it over to me?'

'Because this one requires a sensitive approach and I'm not someone known for my sensitivities. My guy spoke to a Brit, Gavin Jones. His wife was on Flight 702.'

'Laura Jones.'

'Right. Only, Mr Jones claims his wife didn't disappear with the plane. She's living in New Zealand with their daughter.'

'She survived the flight?'

Rory took a huge bite of his falafel. 'Mr Jones says she's "on holiday",' he said, munching. 'Told the police all this when they came round to question him about her name on the passenger manifest. He's not heard anything from them since. He refused to pass on a contact number for her.'

'Probably sick of being bothered.'

'Or maybe it's because she's staying in Karatanga Women's Refuge for domestic violence survivors.' Rory cocked an eyebrow. 'You want to give her a call and find out her side of the story?'

'I'm sorry to say you've got the wrong Laura Jones.'

The voice on the other end of the call had a musical lilt, which Kaitlin took to be a Welsh accent.

'Yeah, there was another Laura Jones on that flight. There are a fair few number of us in the world, you know,' the other woman continued.

'Was she a teacher, too?'

'I don't know. Why are you so interested?'

'My brother, Conor, was one of the passengers on Flight 702.'

'I see. I'm sorry. For your loss. But I don't think I can help you. I went through everything with the police at the time.'

'Why were the police involved?' Kaitlin stretched out on her bed, watching the shadows creep across her apartment.

'They thought I was on that flight, too. Everyone did. But I wasn't. I lost my passport some months before. Had to get a replacement. And the police said there are criminal gangs that buy and steal these things, so yeah, Laura Jones on the flight might well have been using my passport. The police wouldn't say. They said it was an ongoing investigation, couldn't tell me anything.'

A missing passport. Someone flying under an assumed identity. Kaitlin felt the familiar prickle. Maybe Rory was on to something here, after all.

'Can you talk me through how you found your passport was missing?' she asked.

A long silence hummed.

'This has been a difficult year,' Laura replied after a while. 'I was in the process of leaving my husband. It's been very messy, the whole thing, really. We had to get out, my daughter and me. We left in the middle of the night.' She swallowed. 'My friend – well, colleague, Chrissy. She gave us refuge for a few nights. I just . . . I needed to get away, for the sake of my daughter. My husband was violent.'

'I'm sorry.'

'He wasn't always. It started after our daughter was born. I just reached the point where I couldn't stay any more.'

Kaitlin listened to a siren whining in the distance. She felt like she was intruding in someone else's pain. But she had to do this. 'And you had the passport when you left?'

'Yes, initially. I must have lost it in transit. Maybe one of the refuges we stayed at. We moved around a lot. When you've got a violent, manipulative man on your trail, phoning you constantly, leaving messages, sending threatening texts . . . I was worried for our safety. We had to keep moving.'

'I understand. So, someone at one of these refuges might have taken it?'

'At the time I thought it was my husband. I thought he was trying to stop me from leaving.'

'I thought you said you had it with you when you left.'

Another silence, this one heavy. 'Look. This is really hard for me to talk about.' Laura began to sob.

Kaitlin clutched the phone, listening until the sound ebbed.

'Shit. Shit, shit,' Laura gasped. She took a deep breath and added, 'I agreed to see Gavin again. Don't judge me, please.'

'I'm not.'

'I thought it was the best thing to do. He was so persistent. He made so many promises. We met in a park in Cardiff, in Wales. And it started off all right, so I thought, OK, maybe we can work this out. Maybe things can change.

'When we first dated, he was the kindest, most considerate man you could ever hope to meet. We travelled the world together. Free spirits, you know? Maybe I thought we could go back to that.'

'When was this?'

'A week or so after I walked out. We were still staying at Chrissy's place. She was so supportive. I was depending on her totally. We were colleagues, both teachers, and she just took me under her wing.

'Anyway, Chrissy encouraged me not to see him under any circumstances. But I did. I let him come back with me to Chrissy's place. Chrissy wasn't there. How dumb was that?' A long pause. Then: 'Gavin tried to strangle me.'

'Oh my God.'

'All I could think about was what a mess we were making of Chrissy's place.' Another sob.

Kaitlin shifted at the raw emotion. She knew about things like this, of course she did, but it had all been so removed from the life she'd led.

'That's when I realised I just had to go, get out, disappear somewhere he couldn't find us. I felt a bit guilty because Chrissy supported me so much. I never even thanked her. I just left. I picked up my daughter from the nursery and I left.'

'So, you think it's possible your husband might have taken your passport when he came to see you at Chrissy's place?'

'If it wasn't Gavin, then who?' Laura choked on her words.

'Could Chrissy have taken your passport?'

'No. Why would she do that?'

'Have you been in contact with her since?'

This time, the silence seemed to go on for ever.

Finally: 'Oh my God! Do you think Chrissy might have been on the plane?'

Hunched in the glow of her laptop screen, Kaitlin scrolled through the digital files of the recordings of her interviews until she found the one she wanted. She hit Play and the voice of the psychic witch rolled out. Eventually, she dropped into the section she needed:

> The man becomes very icy. He shoots daggers at me – like I'm being inconsiderate for not moving. He calls out, 'I'm sorry, Chrissy, but we can't sit together.' Very passive–aggressive. I feel dread, coming over me like a thick fog. I know in that moment that the plane's heading to disaster. I try to warn them. They won't listen. They won't listen!

Kaitlin played it again, just to be sure. There was no doubt.

I'm sorry, Chrissy . . .

Kaitlin called Laura Jones' old school in some place she'd never heard of called Stanmore in the UK and tried to pick up a trail to Chrissy. No luck. Afterwards, she left several messages for Professor Marshal in Atlanta. Finally, he returned her calls.

'I appreciated the honesty in the messages you left, but the fact that your brother was on that plane doesn't change anything I told you in Atlanta,' he said.

'There was something you mentioned when we met, about Dr Aziz, that I wanted to follow up on.'

'You lied to me, Miss Le. You're not a Georgia Tech student, and you can't just go round pretending to be someone you're not. I understand your pain. I'm sorry for you, for your family. Otherwise I'd have had my lawyer—'

'There's . . . something else going on here,' Kaitlin interjected.

'You're trying to tarnish my colleague's name, his reputation. Think of Dr Aziz's family. They've lost someone, too.'

'One question, Professor Marshal. That's all.'

He paused. 'Go on.'

'Dr Aziz was travelling with someone. Can you at least confirm that? A woman, possibly a teacher, going under the name of Laura Jones.'

'I don't know anything about that.'

'It could have been Chrissy. I think he knew her as Chrissy.'

'Did you say Chrissy?'

'Yes. He – he wanted to sit with her, but they were seated separately.'

'Chrissy was his fiancée.'

'His fiancée?'

'I didn't know Chrissy was on the flight. Are you sure?'

'She was travelling on a stolen passport.'

'Stolen? No, I don't believe that. Dr Aziz talked about Chrissy all the time. But why would she join him on that flight?'

'That's what I'd like to find out.'

'He said he was planning to meet Chrissy in Florida, after the conference. I think they were going to visit his family in Miami.'

★

Kaitlin trailed through Tompkins Square Park, weaving round the kids on skateboards surfing through rolling amber waves of crisp leaves. Her lungs burned when she breathed in the cold air blasting in from the east. She'd tried to call Rory. No response. That worried her. Then she'd attempted to connect with Dylan, but the call went straight to voicemail. It had been a while since he'd been in touch and all of her calls to him had gone unanswered. That worried her even more.

But she needed to tell someone about her mounting suspicion that she'd finally uncovered the truth about the disappearance of Flight 702. Chrissy travelling under a stolen passport was the red flag. Dr Aziz was key, she was sure of it.

As she started to leave a message for Dylan, she glanced back in the direction of her apartment and saw four men walking towards her. Brutish, heavyset, the guys she'd seen outside the warehouse where the trafficked women were being held.

Since Amelia's worried phone call, paranoia had cranked up Kaitlin's instinct into the red zone. She'd kept one eye out for Dragov's gang, but a part of her had always felt they'd never be able to track her down to the East Village.

She leaped the low border fence and raced across the grass among the trees. Her breath seared in her throat as she ran. She was exhausted, but she knew what would happen if those men got their hands on her.

Footsteps thundered behind her, drawing nearer.

They'd have her in no time. Nobody would help.

As she burst out of the northern side of the park, she darted across the street. The wail of car horns and the screech of brakes echoed all around.

Just before she reached the other side, a sleek black sedan screamed in front of her and she slammed into the side of it. Wind rushed out of her lungs as she went down hard.

When her vision cleared, she was looking up into the eyes of a man and woman looming over her. They were holding out badges.

'FBI?' she gasped. She never thought she'd be so pleased to fall into the arms of the Feds.

'Homeland Security,' the man replied.

Kaitlin dived into the back of the sedan without any encouragement. The woman slid in next to her. She had dark features and a hard face. The man slipped behind the wheel. In the rear-view mirror, Kaitlin saw grey eyes in a tanned face.

'Kaitlin Le, right?' he said. 'I'm Agent Richards. This is Agent Fellowes. Just so you know, you're not in any trouble.'

'Yeah, that's what everybody keeps telling me. Just before I get into trouble.'

'What we mean is, you're not in any trouble unless you decide that's the route you want to take,' Agent Fellowes added. She had one of those faces that looked like it never smiled.

The sedan rumbled away.

'Who was chasing you?' Richards asked.

'I've made some enemies,' Kaitlin replied.

'Yeah? Those looked pretty violent enemies.'

'People traffickers,' Kaitlin muttered, glancing behind her to check they weren't being followed.

'Nothing to do with a guy called Dragov?' Richards' reflection locked eyes with Fellowes. A hint of a smile.

'What?' Kaitlin asked.

'We know his links to Flight 702. Can't tell you much, for obvious reasons,' Richards said. 'There's a cross-agency investigation under way. Some journalist at *New York* magazine is helping us with it before she publishes her exposé. You don't need to be worrying about those guys.'

'No, you've got other things to worry about,' Fellowes added.

Kaitlin sat behind the table at the Department of Homeland Security office downtown. One World Trade Center was framed in the window.

'I told the FBI everything I knew,' she said.

'We're a different agency. Different interests, different needs.' Richards blew on his coffee.

Her mind raced at that comment. *Was this about terrorism? Dr Aziz and an attack on Flight 702? Chrissy with the double life?*

I wish Rory was here.

'I need my lawyer,' she said.

'Your prerogative, of course,' Richards replied, 'but you really don't.'

'Yet,' Fellowes added.

'Do you want to tell me what this is about?' Kaitlin said. 'I've already spoken to the FBI.'

'Your name seems to be popping up on all sorts of radars,' Fellowes said. 'And that's never a good thing.'

'Is Murphy coming?' Richard asked his partner.

Fellowes nodded.

'OK, let's wait.'

Kaitlin stewed in silence until she heard footsteps approaching. The door swung open to reveal a woman in her mid-forties, short greying hair, no make-up.

'Are we all set?' she asked Richards.

'This is Kaitlin Le.'

'Good.' The woman pulled up a chair opposite. 'I'm Sarah Murphy. I head the task team here.'

Kaitlin nodded. Her heart thumped harder.

'Let's get down to it,' Murphy said. 'How long have you known a James Dennison?'

'Agent Dennison?'

'Just answer the question.'

'I don't know him, really. I mean, he contacted me after he heard about my investigation into 702. And he said he wanted to help.'

'And did he?'

'I don't know.'

'You don't know?' Murphy placed her palms flat on the table and fixed her gaze on Kaitlin. 'Did he give you anything?'

'Like what?'

'Did he hand you any files?'

'No.'

'We searched the apartment,' Richards said.

Kaitlin jerked round. 'You searched my apartment?'

'Where are the files, Kaitlin?' Murphy pressed.

'I don't know what you think you're doing—'

'Where are the files?'

'What files?' Kaitlin felt genuinely puzzled.

'Where are the files?' When Murphy saw she wasn't going to get an answer, she leaned back. 'You could go to jail, you know.'

Kaitlin showed a blank face. She'd been threatened too many times now to let this get to her. 'For what?'

'Handling and distributing official documents. Chelsea Manning got thirty-five years for less.'

'Then I want a lawyer. I'm not saying any more without a lawyer.' She folded her arms and leaned back.

'We're just asking questions, trying to clear things up,' Agent Richards said. He prowled around the edge of the room, no doubt a tactical attempt to unnerve her.

'Am I under arrest?' Kaitlin demanded.

Agent Fellowes crossed the room to stand behind Murphy. 'You broke the law. Aiding and abetting a known felon.'

'I didn't know Dennison was wanted.'

'What about impersonation?' Fellowes insisted. 'How many bereaved relatives have you contacted and lied about who you are? That's actually illegal.'

Kaitlin's mind raced ahead of the questions. She was turning over the chaotic jumble in the FBI agent's storage unit. All those piles of paper. *Did he actually have something there that was vital to understanding what happened with Flight 702?*

'You think Agent Dennison gave me some kind of top-secret files?' she asked.

Murphy leaned forwards again. 'Did he?'

'No! Did he say he gave me some files?'

Richards shook a creamer into his coffee. He was still playing it cool, unlike the other two.

'Dennison had privileged access. Before he went rogue, he did a clean sweep of sensitive information. Files that could compromise national security. We need to get them back.'

Kaitlin inwardly kicked herself. Maybe she'd been too harsh on Dennison, leaping to judgement based on how destabilised he'd seemed through grief and worry. *But hadn't other people done the same to her?*

'Where is he?' she asked.

'He's been committed to a psychiatric facility,' Murphy said in a bloodless voice. 'For observation.'

Kaitlin stared. She couldn't believe what she was hearing, what levels these people were prepared to go to. 'You mean you just put him there to stop him from asking questions?'

No one answered.

'What are you guys trying to hide?' she blazed. All the repressed emotion she'd been trying to control since being chased in the park came flooding out.

'Come on,' Richards said, trying to placate. 'You met him. You know he was in a fragile mental state. He lost his daughter, just like you lost your brother. Not only was he prejudicing the investigation, but he was also in danger of getting himself killed.'

'There are dangerous people out there, Kaitlin,' Murphy said.

Fellowes leaned forwards. 'You've found that out by yourself. The Dragov mob don't play nice with anyone.'

'That's why we're talking to you.' Richards sipped his coffee, winced. 'We don't want you to get hurt.'

Kaitlin laughed without humour. 'You lied. About the plane. You lied to the families who lost loved ones. And now you're saying you don't want me to—'

'We didn't lie about anything,' Murphy said. 'The Federal Aviation Administration came to its own conclusions about why the plane came down. In fairness, without the plane, they had nothing else to go on.'

'But now,' Fellowes began, 'we've been working behind the scenes because we believe there could have been other causes.'

Kaitlin felt a chill. There it was. The official confirmation she'd always wanted.

Other causes.

The rest of the conversation blurred into the background. As she rode the elevator down, Kaitlin felt a rush of exhilaration. All those long months of banging her head against every wall she came up against, all those lonely sleepless hours when she'd questioned everything she was doing.

Mostly, she'd secretly been worried that the pitying faces had been right, that she was deluding herself in displacement activity to prevent her from dealing with her grief.

As she walked out into the street, she felt renewed. She was ready for whatever lay ahead.

16

Light flooded out of the open storage unit door, casting a square across the night-dark walkway. Men and women in suits traipsed back and forth, heaving boxes of files into the back of an MPV.

Kaitlin peered through the windshield of the car, which was parked far enough away to be cloaked in shadow. 'There goes all of Dennison's work.'

'Don't beat yourself up about it. If he was as erratic as you said, there was no reason to think any of his information was valid.' Rory sucked on the straw of his Big Gulp as he watched the back and forth.

'Yeah. Now we know better. Dennison might have been our best shot.'

Kaitlin felt comforted that the lawyer was there. Dylan had seemingly disappeared as abruptly as he'd come into her life. Never before had she experienced feeling as isolated as she had during the last few days in the city. Rory had finally returned her calls as she'd walked out of the Homeland Security office. He'd been caught up in a long meeting with his investigator, which she'd started to realise had something to do with monies owed.

Homeland Security had reluctantly let her go. They knew they had nothing on her. Just an attempt to monster her to see if Dennison really had handed anything over. But they'd keep watching. As would the FBI. It was weird. All the agencies seemed to be acting independently. *What was going on?*

One thing was sure: everybody was watching her.

'So, now we know the authorities suspect it wasn't a bird-strike and they're still investigating,' Rory mused. 'Does that mean it's not a top-level cover-up, or does the left hand not know what the right is doing? These agencies keep as many secrets from each other as they do from the rest of us.'

'I wish I could remember what Dennison said. Something about a shadow on a satellite image or something.' She hammered the flat of her hand on the dash. 'Goddammit. Every time you get close to something, it throws up three more questions that need answering.'

'Don't blow a blood vessel. Eat your fries,' Rory prompted.

'I'm convinced this has something to do with Aziz,' she continued. 'His fiancée flying under an assumed name. That's got to mean something, right?'

'Maybe.'

'If a bioweapon had been released on board, that would explain everything.'

'So would a bomb.'

'That's your theory?'

'Seems more likely. Occam's Razor and all that. The simplest explanation is the most likely one.'

'But there's no wreckage.'

'That's the one gaping hole in my theory.' Rory drained the last of his drink with one long, noisy slurp and tossed the cup into the back seat. 'OK. Your virologist bought his ticket at the last minute. He needed to be on board that flight. He was travelling with a woman with a stolen passport. That does indeed suggest something shady. How about you travel down to Miami and talk to Aziz's relatives?'

'I don't have an address.'

'I do. Or rather, my investigator does, which he held over my head, rather irritatingly.'

She sighed. 'I don't have any—'

'I'll pay for your ticket.'

'You don't have to do that.'

'It'll come out of expenses. Do you want to solve this or not?'

Kaitlin grinned. 'OK. Thank you. What about you?'

'I'm going to talk to my deep throat informant. If anyone knows what Homeland Security is investigating, it's her.'

'When I described you as my deep throat informant, I didn't expect us to actually be skulking around in an underground parking lot.'

'Don't be an ass, Rory,' Renee said.

She stood behind a pillar so she could see the door to the stairwell but was hidden from any car driving down the ramp. She was dressed in a smart business suit and had her briefcase tight beside her.

'OK. Now you're worrying me.' Rory shifted from foot to foot.

'You should be worried. There are a lot of very top-level people interested in 702. The kind of people you don't want paying attention to you.'

Rory edged another step into the shadows. He'd never seen Renee like this. Nothing ever fazed her.

'What are you hearing, Renee?'

'It wasn't a bird-strike.'

'Well, put me in a dress and call me Nancy.'

'Current thinking is that it was a bomb.'

'I knew it!'

Renee lowered her voice until it was little more than a rasp. 'The woman you mentioned who was travelling on the passport of Laura Jones – there's intel to suggest she's someone known as the White Matchmaker.'

'The White what?'

'Also known as Uzma Griegen. She was a known terrorist and top recruiter for the Somali-based radical militant group Al-Shabaab. Recruited young girls from the West. Persuaded them to leave their homes to become brides of jihadi fighters.'

'Laura Jones?'

'The White Matchmaker was called that because she was a white British woman. Her real name was Samantha Griegen, who disappeared in 2015.'

A car rumbled down the ramp. Renee watched until it had parked and the driver had made his way into the stairwell. Rory felt his unease climb as he saw the worry etched in her face. There was even more here than she was saying, he was sure of it.

'The intelligence services believe she was radicalised and made her way back to the UK, where she took on a new identity. Disappeared back into some community.'

Rory edged closer. 'Do they think she planted the bomb? That it was a suicide attack?'

'She wasn't working alone, that's what I'm hearing. There was another terrorist on the plane.'

'Who?'

'That, I don't know.'

Rory chewed this over for a moment. 'OK. But I've got to say, you've always been straight with me, Renee. I'm sensing there's something you're not saying.'

'As you know me so well, you should realise that if I'm not telling you something, there's good reason,' she replied, her voice hardening. 'There are things floating around – whispers, rumours. I don't know what's true or not. But

I do know that if some are true, simply knowing about them puts your life in danger. I'm protecting you, Rory.'

Renee turned and strode away without looking back. Rory watched her go, hearing what she'd said, knowing it was too late to back out now.

Kaitlin adjusted the cheap sunglasses she'd picked up at the airport. They were good as a disguise, but they also protected her from the glare of the Miami sun. Still blasting out Afro-Cuban beats, the cab pulled away and she looked up at the neat suburban house. Rory had left her a message about all that he'd learned from his informant. Now, it was down to her.

Hassan Aziz answered the door. He was a short man, a little overweight, with a polite smile never far away.

'Thanks for agreeing to see me,' she said.

'Come in, please.'

Hassan led her into the lounge. The air was filled with the music of pet birds chirping in another room.

'You want to talk about my late brother.'

'I do. But I'm actually more interested in the woman he was travelling with.'

Hassan motioned for Kaitlin sit. 'Ah, yes, Chrissy. They were going to get married.'

'What did you know about her?'

'Not much. They hadn't been together very long. She was a teacher, I think.'

'She was travelling on a false passport. Did you know that?'

'No. I did not.'

Kaitlin weighed her words, trying to find an easy way to say it. There wasn't one. 'She was a suspected terrorist. The White Matchmaker.'

Hassan laughed. 'Oh, my goodness. That's quite a thing to say. Can I get you something to drink?'

'No, thank you. Did you know all this?'

Hassan looked to the ceiling fan, choosing his own words. 'There were rumours about such things, after the plane crashed. The press, the police, the FBI. There's nothing new here, Kaitlin. I didn't believe it then and I don't believe it now. My brother would never be a terrorist.'

'The authorities are looking for her accomplice. Someone she was travelling with.'

'Did Homeland Security send you? To make me panic and call my network of terrorist contacts?'

'No.'

Hassan stood and paced around the room, his face tightening. 'They've been watching me since the day the plane crashed. The whole apartment is bugged. Everything we say is being recorded. They know all there is to know about my brother, me, our family. And they have found nothing. They're using you.'

'No, they told me to stop.'

'Ah, reverse psychology. They knew you wouldn't. Kaitlin, my brother was a respected scientist. His life was dedicated to saving lives.'

'Maybe. Or maybe we never truly know other people. Even the people we're close to.'

Hassan looked out of the window on to the sun-bleached front lawn. 'You must be an unhappy young woman if you can never trust anyone. You said when you rang me up, you lost a brother. Could you think your brother was responsible? Who could do that?'

He glanced at her and Kaitlin squirmed uncomfortably, feeling her cheeks flush.

'And this White Matchmaker, is this really to be believed?' he continued. 'Maybe she was just a teacher from Wales who fell in love with a doctor from Syria. Last year, they said they had killed the White Matchmaker in a bombing raid in Aleppo. And she's magically alive again?'

'Maybe it wasn't the White Matchmaker. But an innocent person doesn't fly on a fake passport.'

'A woman may have many reasons to run away, Kaitlin.'

Hassan sat down, holding his head in his hands for a moment. Now, she could see the grief and the worry breaking through his polite exterior.

'Homeland Security have created a myth – a convenient myth – with which to scare people. A bogeyman. Maybe all this is to help ease the passing into law of even more repressive measures against people they don't like. You know what happened to the Japanese here during the war? They were interned in concentration camps.'

'Of course I know that.'

'You think that couldn't happen again? To Muslims? Surely you know what it's like, Kaitlin. To have people assume something about you because of who you are. Because of where you're from. I'm surprised you'd so easily do the same.'

Kaitlin flashed back to high school, the bully with the neck tattoo who'd reduced her to tears with slurs about her ethnicity. Conor had never been a fighter, but he'd waited for the bully after class and given him a pasting. He'd got beaten himself in retaliation, but he always said it was worth it.

'I'm just trying to find the truth,' she said.

'My dear girl, you have now moved into an area where there are no criteria, no measures, which you can apply that will tell you if you are in a world of truth or lies, the world where two plus two is four. You're no longer living in that world. You're living in one where two plus two is nine, or nothing at all. The only currency in this world is lies. It is a place where lies become truth. Lies are no longer lies. There are no truths any more.'

'There has to be a truth here.'

Hassan sighed. 'You need to go back to your family. You need to mourn your brother. And then live your life.'

Kaitlin munched on a slice of Joe's Pizza. Rory plucked his portion from the box and leaned back on his sofa, eyeing her. She felt drained after her travels and she was sure he could see her exhaustion.

'We tried, right?' he said. 'That's all we can do. So, Dr Aziz's brother didn't add much materially to what we already know, but we still had to follow the lead.'

'Do you think "Chrissy" is the White Matchmaker?'

'I don't know. I went to Homeland Security, tried to pass on what we had. They gave me the brush-off. Couldn't tell if it was because they didn't want this information made public, or because they've already discounted it.'

'Sometimes I feel like we're going round in circles.'

'You're tired, I get that. But don't lose hope.' Rory took a big bite, the mozzarella snaking down his chin.

'I'm not. Although sometimes I have my moments.'

'Understandable,' he said through a mouthful.

'There were so many people with secrets on this flight,' she sighed. 'I mean, it's crazy, right? Is it a coincidence? Or . . . I don't know what.'

Rory swallowed. 'Or maybe it's just normal. Everybody has secrets. Every flight is packed with people hiding something. Sometimes little things. Sometimes big things. We never know who's sitting beside us or across the aisle. The difference here is, you've shone a bright light on it and now we're starting to see the truth.'

'I can understand how people become crazy conspiracists. When you go down the rabbit hole, it just keeps going.'

Her phone buzzed on the carpet beside where she was sitting cross-legged. She stared at the incoming message for a long moment.

'Something interesting?' Rory wiped his mouth with the back of his hand.

'Yeah, it's Dylan.' She continued to stare at her phone, not quite believing what she was reading. 'He wants to meet.'

17

The hotel bar buzzed with conversation. The after-work crowd bustled around the counter, laughing and chinking their glasses. Kaitlin preferred it busier than the time she'd met Dennison here. Easier to blur into the background now that her paranoia had reached fever pitch.

As she headed towards the same corner table, a voice echoed behind her: 'Kaitlin?'

She turned, her mind already flashing up the image she'd created of Dylan. Instead, she reeled for a moment as she stared at a familiar face, good-looking, blond hair, nose ring, the faintest scar above the left eye.

'Thomas?' She choked on the name, trying to make sense of what was happening. Then she felt the rush of realisation. 'Thomas . . . you're Dylan?'

'Sorry,' he said with a sheepish lowering of his head. 'But the fake accent was good, right?'

Kaitlin hovered for an instant, not sure if she should be angry at the deceit, and then she buried her face in his shoulder, hugging him so tight it was as if she never wanted to let him go. She choked back a sob and shook. *How long since she'd had such human contact? How much had she missed it?*

'Hey,' he said in a soft voice, stroking her hair.

'I thought you might be dead,' she stuttered. 'I mean, Dylan . . . and you.'

'Shh. Come on, let's sit.'

Thomas led her to the table and they let the shadows swallow them.

'I'm sorry,' he murmured when they were both sure they weren't being observed. 'I had to get off the grid, fast.'

'It's so good to see you.'

'I really am so sorry for the deception. And it's good to see you, too.'

'Why would you lie to me about being Dylan? I told you things about me, and about Conor, that I haven't told anyone else.'

'I know, and I'm so sorry for lying. But believe me, it had to be that way. I needed to help you, but I couldn't risk you knowing it was me.'

Kaitlin leaned across the table and clutched his hand. 'Why would you have to hide? And why run away now? I mean, Thomas, you have to tell me what the fuck is going on.'

'It actually goes back to how I met Conor. That's what's so . . .' He paused, choosing his words. 'You know, I have this question in the back of my head: what if Conor's in the middle of this somehow? And I just needed to know. I'd been hoping you and I could maybe figure this out together if we went through the passenger list, but the long and short of it, I suppose, is that . . . I work for MI6.'

Kaitlin gaped. *Was this a joke?*

'Well, worked. Until two weeks ago, when I left.'

'How is that possible? You and Conor were hackers.'

'Yes, professional ones. Conor with a security firm and me with MI6. I'd been tasked with understanding the scope of the Elysians.'

'The . . . wait, the cyber-utopian group that Conor was a part of?'

'That's the one. It was my job to find out more about them. From the inside. That's how I met Conor.'

'So you were, what, undercover?'

'I've been working with MI6 for six years now, basically since I got out of uni. It was all very much like work until I met Conor and then I suddenly realised I could be putting him away. And that's when things started to get complicated faster than I could project.'

Kaitlin thought back over the last couple of years, seeing things in a new light. 'That explains why Conor never talked about your work.'

'Technically, he didn't even know.'

A waitress drifted over and they ordered a couple of gin and tonics.

Once she'd gone, Kaitlin said, 'Jesus. Thomas, is there anyone in your life you haven't been lying to?'

'Well, let's not put all the troublesome ethics on my shoulders. Conor was hacking for an international criminal syndicate, no matter how well-intentioned he may have been. But I told him, eventually, right when MI6 and the FBI were moving in on the Elysians. That's why Conor was able to cover his tracks to the degree that he did, otherwise he would have ended up in prison.'

'I can't believe he didn't tell me any of this.'

'He wanted to.'

'Obviously not enough.'

'As you said, things were strained.'

'Because he was stealing! Was I supposed to pretend to be OK with that?'

'Believe me, I know how you feel. It nearly destroyed our relationship, too.'

'It wasn't even the stealing that was the real problem. I mean, obviously, that was bad, but taking money from a bank to give it to what he thought was a good cause? That's Conor all over.'

'Using malware someone else gave him – Conor should have been too smart for that.'

'Do you think he knew how out of hand it would get?'

Thomas looked into the crowd, reflecting. 'No. I think he was serious about just skimming off the top, taking pennies from the largest accounts, from people who wouldn't even miss it.'

'But then the Koschei almost collapsed the entire bank. I mean, millions of people could have lost everything if Conor hadn't stopped it.'

'But he did.'

Kaitlin felt all those old emotions come surging back. 'Yeah, and he didn't even care! That's why I was so mad at him. He put so many people at risk and he treated it like some big adventure.'

She bit her tongue as the waitress dropped off the drinks. The bar was getting even busier and she enjoyed the anonymity that it brought.

Thomas swirled his drink in his glass. 'To defend my fiancé for a moment, at that point he didn't know what the money he was stealing was really going to. He thought he was funding an activist group. People who thought technology could make the world a better place.'

'Right. The Elysians.'

'Yes.'

'Why was MI6 investigating them? What were you trying to find out?'

'For starters, all the illegal activity that was going through them. Conor isn't the first Robin Hood hacker they've had.'

'You were investigating your own boyfriend?'

Thomas shook his head. 'Absolutely not. Conor wasn't involved in anything illegal when we first met as far as I know. But then we both got deeper into the group and they weren't what they appeared. All groups on the internet have their dark spots, but the Elysians have a black hole at their centre. That's what Conor was funding. When he found that out, trust me, he wasn't treating it as a great adventure any more.'

Kaitlin felt her thoughts racing to catch up. 'So, you think the plane going down . . . you think it could have something to do with Conor?'

'I wondered. A lot. A couple of days after 702 went missing, I started using my access to find out as much as I could. But it was hard. I couldn't very well start asking questions of the recently bereaved just to find out more about who was on that plane. So, when I saw what you were doing, I thought, well, maybe this is perfect. Maybe this is the universe telling us how to move forwards.'

'How the hell do I trust you now?' she demanded. 'The last thing I need is some MI6 agent manipulating me.'

'I told you. I left MI6. I hid out in Moscow for a while. Easy to disappear there.'

'Oh, great! Now I could be the pawn of a Russian agent!'

Thomas grinned over the lip of his glass. 'The US, British and European governments are all looking for me. If I were a Russian agent, do you think I ever would have left Russia?'

Kaitlin bowed her head. 'I don't know what to think any more. Or who to trust.'

'When you and I started poking around, I installed an alert on the MI6 intelligence hubs I'd been using so that I'd be warned if anyone started following my tracks. The alarms went off a few times over the past couple of months.

But then two weeks ago, they all started going off at once. So I knew my bosses were on to me.

'They knew I'd been investigating, far outside my lane. It's one thing to go rogue, it's another to start hacking your own agency. The false logins I'd been using, and the workarounds, they're the kind of things that get people like me renditioned. Not to mention, I'd started to suspect there was something that wasn't even stored on the top-secret classified servers.'

'Something about the flight?'

Thomas' eyes darted around the bar. 'All I know is there are as many different accounts of when the plane went missing as there are intelligence and avionics agencies in the North Atlantic. And I'm not sure half those agencies even know what they're talking about.

'From what you've told me about the FBI, it definitely sounds like there's a hell of a lot of misinformation out there. To be honest, though, I've been wondering if, maybe, there *is* no cover-up. Maybe it's just that no one knows exactly what happened.'

Kaitlin stared into her glass. She didn't want to hear that. A mystery that would never be answered. No closure. The rest of her life stretching out in this murky twilight.

She pushed those thoughts aside and said, 'Why show yourself to me now?'

'I came to the States to get some supplies and make a plan, but I can't stay here. There are way too many eyes and ears. It felt wrong not to see you before I go away, for good.'

'You're going to walk away from all this?' She felt a pang of desperation.

'I can't be running at full speed on our little arrangement any more.'

'Because you're scared, or because you aren't sure we'll find an answer?'

'I'm just being honest with you.'

'I don't know if I can move forwards on this without you.'

Thomas dropped his chin. 'I'm so sorry any of this happened to us in the first place. And I'm sorry I encouraged you to go down this path. If Conor were here, he'd . . . Maybe it's time to move on.'

'I'm just not there yet. Are you?'

He sighed. 'I don't know. These days, though, I keep wondering whether or not this whole investigation isn't just our way of coping instead of accepting that Conor's gone.'

Kaitlin winced. How many times had she heard that, in one form or another, from people whose path she'd crossed?

'I know there's something real here,' she said, as much to herself as to Thomas. 'Can I still count on you?'

He tapped on his phone and held the screen up to her. 'The number of my new burner. I'll be harder to reach, but if you need me, I'll try to be there.'

Her instinct prickled. Something in his words, in the flicker of his eyes. 'What aren't you telling me, Thomas?'

Thomas weighed her question and for a moment, she thought he wasn't going to answer. Then: 'I'd advise you to walk away, but I know you won't listen. But you've got to be careful. Really careful. There's more at play here than you could imagine.'

'What do you mean? Tell me!'

He shook his head. Kaitlin couldn't understand why he'd been so helpful before and now he was obfuscating. *What had he discovered?*

'All I'll say is that it's not just the CIA and British intelligence agencies you should watch out for.'

He seemed to feel he'd already said too much, for he stood without warning, looked around the bar and stepped away from the table. One last smile for her, and Kaitlin thought she saw pity in it.

'You look after yourself,' he said. And then he walked away into the crowd.

18

'Have you seen the news?' Rory's voice blared from the phone as Kaitlin stepped out of the hotel bar into the night.

'What's wrong?' Her heart thumped at the urgency of his words, but she couldn't read any emotion in his voice beyond passion.

'Just get over to my place, fast as you can.'

Half an hour later, Rory swung open the door to his apartment and Kaitlin all but tumbled in, breathless. He was wearing a monogrammed silk dressing gown and pyjamas, but his mood was electric. He spun away from her to the TV, where CNN droned.

'What is it?' Kaitlin gasped. The words died in her mouth when she stood beside him. All was clear.

The screen showed moving images of waves breaking on pebbles under a grey sky, a line of snowy hills in the distance. On the beach, people in heavy coats moved around a twisted slab of grey metal.

The headline underneath said: Wreckage from Flight 702 Found off the Coast of Nova Scotia, Canada.

Kaitlin felt ice water flood through her. 'Is this for real?' she breathed.

'They've already done tests on what they pulled from the water. Said they found traces of explosive on it.'

The newscaster's voice hummed from the TV, but Kaitlin flipped into her own grey world where none of the words reached her. She felt the stew of long-suppressed emotions bubble. Since the news of the flight, Conor had been caught in some in-between world, not alive or dead. Lost and waiting to be found. She'd never really allowed herself to hope, but despite her best intentions, a small flame had flickered somewhere in the depths of her mind.

Now, though, it was all over. An ending. Only the explanations remained to be found.

This shouldn't be hitting her so hard. But there it was. She felt hot tears burn and she scrubbed them away with the back of her hand before Rory could see. He was wagging a finger at the TV screen, running away at the mouth about something or other.

'What are you saying?' she said, pulling herself back.

Rory looked round and from the way his face softened, he clearly understood what was churning away inside.

'Hey, are you OK?' he breathed. 'Sorry. I've been a total dick. Got myself carried away with the detail.' He dipped in his dressing gown pocket and pulled out a handkerchief bearing his initials. 'Here.'

She smiled and took it, dabbing at her eyes. 'Thanks. Don't worry about me. I just had a moment. Tell me again what you were saying.'

'OK. That trace of explosives. Looks like the terrorism theory is the most likely.'

'So, not a virus released on board, or people getting sick from something the evangelists picked up in the Congo. You're thinking the White Matchmaker?'

'I could construct a case for Drago's mob trying to eliminate their boss and his wife, maybe. Or . . . Well, no point speculating. We need something solid. Though this could be the point where the authorities start doing something instead of trying to cover it up.'

Kaitlin thought back to the warning that Thomas had given. She mentioned his cryptic comments to Rory and his involvement with the intelligence fraternity and the investigation into the Elysians.

'OK, there's some meat there,' Rory said. 'Something to chew over. I think we need a night to sleep on this. Come back fresh tomorrow and decide on the way forwards.' He hesitated. 'You going to be all right?'

'I'll be fine. Probably good to get some alone time with my thoughts.'

Kaitlin traipsed back through the streets, dwelling on that image of twisted wreckage on the beach, trying not to imagine the point that had left it that way. Leaving the lights in the apartment turned off, she slumped cross-legged on her bed and looked out across the park to the illuminated skyline.

That was the moment she saw the notification for a new voicemail on her original cell.

Absently, she picked it up and called. The message played.

Kaitlin?

She felt the blood drain from her and for an instant, she thought she was going mad.

Kaitlin? It's me.

Haunted, her hands trembled and she almost dropped the phone.

It's Conor.

The grief, she told herself. *You can't really be hearing this.*

The message fizzed with some kind of interference. What sounded like ghost voices babbled, fading in and out, the words incomprehensible. After another jolt of static, it cleared and the voice came through loud and clear.

Definitely, definitely Conor's voice.

I'm OK. We're all OK. I can't get . . .

The call faded again and Kaitlin strangled a cry of frustration. His message faded back in:

We're alive. We're all alive. Listen, we need your help. Help us. Help us.

The message ended abruptly.

PART TWO

News Recordings

NEWSCASTER 1: Breaking news. Wreckage believed to have come from the missing Atlantic Flight 702 has been found in the North Atlantic just west of . . .

NEWSCASTER 2: Atlantic Flight 702, from London Heathrow, was expected in New York at . . .

FISHERMAN: We were pulling up the nets and I saw what I thought was a whale caught up there. But . . .

REPORTER 1: Other objects found drifting in the ocean currents suggest a crash site just south of Greenland, close to the . . .

REPORTER 2: . . . including this, a child's water bottle, a poignant reminder of the lives lost that night on Flight 702 . . .

EXPERT 1: The indications of burning along the tail fin suggest a catastrophic event of some kind like . . .

NEWSCASTER 1: . . . appears to confirm that Atlantic Flight 702 was brought down by an explosion or fire on board . . .

EXPERT 2: . . . six months of being pushed along by the currents and it should be possible to pinpoint the approximate site of the crash fairly accurately.

NEWSCASTER 2: The focus of the inquiry now is to pin down the exact location . . .

REPORTER 3: What we know is that radio contact was broken off at . . .

NEWSCASTER 3: Newly released satellite images show the plane changing course dramatically . . .

NEWSCASTER 4: . . . altered course before descending rapidly to 20,000 feet . . .

REPORTER 4: Some relatives of missing passengers were forcefully removed from a news conference . . .

EXPERT 3: But what doesn't make any sense is that we have a tail fin found just south of the Faro Islands, with seats and other objects found off the coast of Newfoundland – the North Atlantic currents don't work in that way . . .

EXPERT 4: The problem is, the more time that passes, the harder it is to know what happened . . .

EXPERT 5: If there was terrorism or criminal intent, the sea has effectively aided and abetted to hide the crime.

MAYOR OF NEW YORK [at press conference]: We have to move on. Life is a fragile thing. Maybe this is a time for all of us to pause and turn to those we love and hold them close, because life . . . well, life is . . . fragile.

19

'That is definitely Conor's voice? One hundred per cent?'

Rory paced around Kaitlin's darkened apartment, illuminated by the street light outside. The shadows swooped across the walls as he moved. He'd now listened to the message five times in a row.

'I know what my own brother sounds like.' Kaitlin's hand was still shaking. She felt queasy to the pit of her stomach and her thoughts spun so wildly she could barely think straight.

In one instant, the world around her had collapsed.

'Of course you do,' Rory soothed. 'I'm not questioning you. But if someone wants to screw with you – and God knows we've discovered there are a lot of strange psychologies out there – there are plenty of ways they can achieve something like this. Cutting together old recordings, maybe, if they have access to them. Mimicking him with one of those voice modulation apps.'

'It's him, Rory. Trust me.'

Kaitlin stuffed her cell away. There was no need to listen to it any more. She watched Rory continue to pace as he tried to make sense of this new development. She was glad he was here. He'd raced round the moment she called him and after so long walking this road alone, it was comforting to have someone who was prepared to do that.

'What does this all mean?' she wondered aloud.

Rory paused at the window and looked back at her. Kaitlin watched his silhouette for a long moment as he gathered his thoughts.

'We have two pieces of conflicting evidence,' he began. 'Wreckage found off the coast of Nova Scotia, with trace elements of explosives, implying Flight 702 was lost at sea after a terrorist attack. And a voice message from your brother, Conor, who was on that plane. They can't both be right.

'If you're certain that really is Conor, and you are, then the wreckage is a cover-up, probably at the highest level, one of the biggest cover-ups in history.' He breathed in for a moment, letting those words sink in for both of them. 'And that means Conor – and, by the sounds of it, perhaps all of the passengers – are still alive somewhere.'

Kaitlin felt a surge of euphoria. It was the conclusion she'd come to herself, but it was good to hear it from someone else.

Conor was alive.

She couldn't believe it. So much time spent hoping, longing for some shred of proof that Conor wasn't really gone. Even now she barely dared allow herself to accept it. But it was the only logical explanation for that voice message.

Rory stepped forwards, his voice softening. 'You're focusing on Conor. That's understandable. Take a moment to enjoy that feeling.'

'Tell me what's on your mind. You're going to get there soon enough anyway.'

'A cover-up that big, a conspiracy, can you imagine how high it must go? The agencies involved? All that planting of evidence, reports, signing off? Are we . . . Are we getting into Watergate territory here? Who ordered this? *Why* did they order it? I mean, if we can crack this, the payout is going to be immense. Immense. But . . .'

Rory was babbling, as he tended to do from time to time when his thoughts came too fast for his mouth. Kaitlin watched him, feeling her euphoria ebb away as she started to comprehend what he was saying.

'The thing about powerful people is that they have so much to lose when they're caught out on the wrong side of the law,' he continued. 'And when the stakes are that high, those people will go to any lengths to make sure they aren't found out. I think you're in danger. I think we both are. I mean, I thought we were in danger before. But this is a whole other level.'

He let that hang for a moment.

'This explains all the surveillance,' Kaitlin said. 'That constant feeling of being watched and followed – that wasn't paranoia at all.'

'Exactly. And look what happened to Dennison. They've got him locked up in a rubber room now. You've had two agencies activated against you so far. Unusual? Yes. But you had a high profile what with the hotline and all the families you contacted. You were bound to fall on the official radar.

'But they were trying to frighten you off, right? That's how it seemed. I'm not saying Homeland Security and the FBI are in on this conspiracy, but they were activated by someone higher up who may well have been. Now, though, you have direct proof that all is not as it's purported to be. Before, you were just a grief-stricken amateur, however dogged. Someone who could easily be downplayed. This makes you a direct threat.'

Kaitlin pulled out her cell. 'Should I delete the voice-mail? I don't want to, but . . .'

She really didn't. Just hearing Conor's voice again after so long filled her with a feeling of warmth. She wanted to be able to play it back whenever she felt low.

'No point. The NSA will already know. They've probably been monitoring your original cell for a long time now.' That final word died in Rory's throat and he looked around the dark room.

'What?'

'I wonder if this place is bugged,' he whispered. 'I could get one of those devices to sweep for it, but we should presume it probably is.'

'How?' Kaitlin felt her spine prickle.

'Easy enough for someone to gain access. They can be in and out in maybe fifteen minutes.' He marched across the lounge and pressed his ear to the front door. Once he'd heard enough, he strode back. 'Starting to think this paranoia is driving me crazy. You ever see that movie *The Conversation*? No, no, before your time, obviously. Gene Hackman caught up in this kind of surveillance world and the paranoia finally does for him. Anyway, I digress. I think we need to get you out of here.'

'And go where?'

'Not back to Vassar, or your folks' place in Kansas. They'll have those covered. Just away somewhere. Off the grid, until we figure out what the next step is.'

'On the run?'

'Let's say lying low. You've got your burner. You need to change it regularly.'

'I'm just about out of funds.'

Rory dipped in his jacket pocket and pulled out his wallet. 'Here,' he said, holding out a wad of notes.

'I know money's tight for you, too.'

'I see this as an investment. Once we break this open, dollars are going to be raining down all around me.'

Kaitlin knew Rory was being kind. For all his bluster, he had a big heart. But she took his donation and folded it away. 'Thank you.'

'OK. Now, I'd better get out of here. I don't know how much they know of my involvement with you and with my mercenary reputation. I'm pretty sure they won't be taking me too seriously, but I need to be on the outside, able to operate freely. I can be your anchor. You contact me any time, Kaitlin, OK?'

Kaitlin stared into the shadows. For the first time, she felt frightened, adrift.

Rory turned back at the doorway. 'You gonna be OK?'

'I'll be fine.' She felt her determination harden as she said those words and she knew it was true. 'We're in a new place. There were times when I was wavering before, I admit that. But I know Conor is alive now and I'm going to do everything in my power to bring him back home.'

Kaitlin's cell buzzed in the lonely silence of her room and she jumped. From the glow on the screen, she could see it was her mother. She'd been frantically stuffing possessions into her backpack and her thoughts were racing far away from a pleasant domestic conversation. But she could never ignore her mom.

'Hi,' she said.

'Kaitlin, what is wrong with you?' her mother blurted.

'What do you mean?'

'You've still not been attending classes. At all. I spoke to your room-mate and she attempted to cover for you. Only to be expected, of course. Are you throwing away your life on this wild goose chase?'

'Mom, this isn't the time.'

'And when is the time? You never call any more. Your poor father is desperate to hear from you. He's afraid – we're both afraid – that you're destroying your future.'

'How is Dad?'

Silence. Then: 'Well. As well as can be expected.'

Kaitlin swallowed. What could she say? She desperately wanted to tell her mom that Conor was still alive, but at this stage it would only cause more heartache and she didn't want that. She needed to find out more first.

'Please don't worry about me.'

'I do worry! How can I not? You're my daughter, Kaitlin. You're . . . You're my only child now.'

Kaitlin felt a rush of pain as she heard the break in her mom's voice. When she spoke again, her mother was quieter.

'You saw the report? About the wreckage?'

'Of course.'

'It's time to give up this . . . search. This quest. It's dominated your life for so long.'

Now, the pity in her mom's voice was just as heartbreaking.

'You're free to return to your life now, my little girl.'

'Mom—'

'Please. For me. You need to get back to class, Kaitlin. Vassar won't keep your place open much longer.'

'I will. Please trust me. I have a few more things to sort out. If you can just give me a little more time. Look, I've got to go, Mom.'

'Kaitlin—'

'I've got to go.'

She hung up. She hated being so abrupt – she knew it would have hurt her mother's feelings – but she wasn't in the position to face more of her incisive questions and she didn't want to lie.

But that call had driven one thing home: she wasn't just doing this for herself any more. She had to find Conor for the sake of her parents. She was their only hope.

Kaitlin stuffed the last of her possessions in her backpack and looked around the apartment one last time. She had no idea where she'd be going next or what the future held. But at that moment, it seemed that every aspect of the life she'd built for herself since she was a girl was being systematically stripped away.

If Conor was here, he'd tell her to be positive. She was being reborn. A butterfly emerging from its chrysalis. Instead, she felt as though she were being whittled away until there would be nothing left.

Her shadow dancing from the sodium glow from the street lights around the park, she eased to the open door of her bedroom. The block was uncharacteristically still. No throb of music from the students having an impromptu party on the roof. No rumble of voices from the young parents who always seemed to be arguing, or the incessant cries of their toddler.

Quiet.

As she looked out into the sparsely furnished lounge, the sole lamp winked out.

Kaitlin stiffened. Just a bulb dying, but in this paranoid existence, everything seemed weighted with meaning.

She pulled out her cell to light her way to the door and as the screen illuminated, she noticed she had no signal. That was weird. There had never been a problem there before. Checking, she unlocked it to call Rory, but there was only a strange humming.

Trust your instinct.

Kaitlin reached out and flicked the main light switch. Nothing. The power was out. She hurried back to her bedroom window and peered out into the night. Only her block was in darkness. Something else jarred – there was no traffic rumbling along the street outside. That never happened in New York.

Now, her heart was starting to patter. Rory's warning about danger echoed in her mind. The silence seemed to get deeper with every moment, but inside, her instincts were screaming at her to get out.

Scrambling to the door, she squinted through the spyhole, but the darkness rendered the action futile. Taking a deep breath, she prepared herself to run, then wrenched it open, hurling herself along the hall to the top of the stairs. There, the suffocating blanket of stillness was even more noticeable. Her sneakers whispered down the steps.

The glass front door looked out on a deserted Avenue A. Kaitlin ground to a halt and watched, her blood thumping in her head.

She had a clear run to Tompkins Square Park. She could lose herself among the trees and head to . . . where? Out to the East Side? Head up to Midtown? Her thoughts whirled.

Kaitlin took a step towards the door and paused. A shadow across the sidewalk moved, almost imperceptibly, but to her heightened senses that flicker was like a lightning strike.

Somebody was waiting beside the door, out of sight.

Kaitlin spun round and crept back along the hall. She had two choices. Head up to the roof and move from building to building until she could drop to a fire escape and make her way down. But if there were any drones, she'd be clearly visible. If she'd said that to anyone, they'd have thought she was paranoid. That was how crazy her world had become.

That left out of the back, across the yard and over the high security fence into the neighbouring property. There should be enough shadows out there to give her cover, if only she could make it over the fence.

As she eased forwards, the click of the front door lock echoed through the stillness.

Kaitlin sprinted forwards. No time for subterfuge. They'd be on her in an instant. She slammed through the door into the dark backyard. Her breath clouded in the chill air.

Footsteps rang out behind like the cracks of a gun. They knew she was running.

The chain-link security fence soared up four times her height. Daunting, but she could do it.

She had no choice.

As Kaitlin launched herself towards the towering barrier, two shadows separated from the wider darkness, one on each side of her.

She cried out in shock, but there was no time to turn away.

A bag rammed down over head, and then she was choking to catch her breath as her arms were yanked behind her back and plastic cuffs burned into her wrists.

20

Light flooded into Kaitlin's vision as the bag was yanked off her head. She screwed up her eyes until they'd adjusted to the glare, straining at the cuffs that bound her hands behind the chair on which she was sitting.

'You can't do this to me,' she snarled.

'I'm not doing anything.' A voice with a hint of Texan wide open spaces rolled out at her back.

'You can't snatch me from my home.'

'You weren't snatched.'

'How did I get here, then?'

'You're not here.'

At that, Kaitlin felt a chill. She understood the implication. This was outside the law. She was a nobody, nowhere, with no voice, and if she wasn't careful, she might never find her way back to the world she knew.

A man wandered round into her frame of vision. He was heavyset, bearded, with a Hawaiian shirt open to reveal tufts of chest hair. He slumped down and rocked back on the rear two legs.

'Is this how the government acts now?' she asked. 'What are you, CIA?'

He shrugged. *Definitely CIA.*

'Lucky me. I got the trifecta. Don't any of you government agencies ever talk to each other?'

'That implies we're all working to the same end,' he drawled.

'Conspiracies everywhere.'

'Yup.'

'What's your name?'

He looked up at the ceiling fan for a moment. 'You can call me Grady.'

'Am I under arrest?'

'Course not. Just wanted to make sure you're OK.'

'Well, I'm just fine.' Her expression was stony.

'That's good to know.' Grady rocked back and forth, staring at her and grinning.

Kaitlin held his gaze. After a moment, he picked up a plastic file from the table and flicked through the contents.

'You visited the brother of one of the passengers on Flight 702, one Dr Aziz.'

'Not against the law.'

'It's the kind of thing that sets those old alarm bells jangling. Your parents are pretty worried about you, I hear.'

'Leave my parents out of it.'

'I'm afraid I can't do that, Kaitlin. Sorry. They're a part of this. One step removed, maybe. But they made Conor Le and Conor Le is . . .' He wafted a hand in the air. 'A person of interest, shall we say.'

'Get to the point.'

'Feisty. I like that. Well, now, just like you, I'm investigating Flight 702 – 'cept I'm doing it legitimately.'

'And I'm illegitimate?'

'Hanging round with shady characters like Rory Murray? That's not a good look, Kaitlin.'

'What's he got to do with anything?'

'Just seems like a strange choice of ally. You shouldn't be so sure you can trust him.'

'Well, I'm pretty sure I can't trust you.'

Grady examined his file again. 'You know he was involved with a plane crash before, right? Helped to cover up the cause, in fact. He protected his client, the airline, and as a result, more people died.'

Kaitlin flinched. *Surely that couldn't be true? Was this another layer to the smokescreen of lies?*

'He knew there was a fault in their planes. But if he'd revealed that information, his clients would have lost a pretty big lawsuit.'

'I don't believe you.'

'That's neither here nor there. The point is, there are official investigations under way, and yours and Mr Murray's are not among them.'

Kaitlin strained against the cuffs again. Futile. But the pain where they cut into her wrists cleared her head from the hurt she felt at Rory having potentially lied to her. Suddenly, it clicked.

'This is about my brother.'

'It is, indeed. The guy you think called you.'

'He did call me.'

'Impossible. Conor's dead. You know that.'

His voice was edged with humour. She couldn't read him at all.

'Why are you interested in Conor?'

'You mean with all those skills as a hacker?'

'You think my brother brought the plane down?'

'Now that really would upset your parents, wouldn't it? After everything they've already gone through.'

'I told you to leave my parents out of this,' she snapped. 'Conor had nothing to do with it.'

'We never truly know the people close to us, Kaitlin. There's a life lesson for you. Take it or leave it.' Grady tossed the file back on the table. 'However, you know more about Conor than most. That little secret life he had going on.'

'I don't know what you're talking about.'

'OK.' Grady pulled out his phone, swiped through the apps, then opened one.

To her astonishment, it was her own voice rolling out of the speaker, taking her back to that awful night

'Do you know who these people even are?'

'What business is it of yours?'

That was Conor.

She felt a rush of shock. That was when he'd dropped round to her place, basking in the glory of cracking the bank hack. *Why had the CIA been spying on her back then, long before Flight 702 disappeared?*

She was yelling, her phone distorting through the phone's speaker.

'You always do this! You just soak up all the admiration and assume it's deserved. That you're always right, that every choice you make is OK. You never stop to question things.'

'You don't get a say in this any more, Kait. It's my life, it's my job,'

'Who are you even working for! I'm worried about you!'

'For God's sake, I'm not a kid! This kind of thing is exactly why I moved out.'

'What's that supposed to mean?'

Kaitlin remembered the hurt she'd felt at that moment.

'I don't need this kind of scrutiny.'

At the time, he'd rolled his eyes like a teenager.

'No, you do. I know you, Conor. You just don't want
anyone around who can tell when you're doing something wrong.'

'I'm not doing anything wrong. It's a broken system –
I'm just trying to fix it.'

'And the people you work for? Are you sure that's what
they're doing?'

'Leave me alone, Kait. Just get off my back.'

She heard the sound of a door slamming and in that instant,
she was back there, remembering her anger, knowing with
the benefit of hindsight that it would soon fade into guilt
and regret.

Grady clicked off the recording.

'You were right to be worried about what your brother
was involved in. Is it surprising that other people were
worried, too?'

'How did you get this recording?' Kaitlin caught herself.
'You were monitoring him because of his hacking activity.'

'Correctomundo.'

'Did you have him under observation, right up to . . .
right up to Flight 702?'

'Of course not. He was in the UK. Not our jurisdiction.
What did you think he was doing?'

'I don't know.'

'You were that upset over "I don't know"?'

'I just thought he had some unreliable friends.'

'If you're aware of criminal activity and you don't report it, that makes you an accomplice. You know that, right?'

Kaitlin didn't answer.

'You should talk to me, you know.'

'I have no reason to talk to you.'

'What about your parents?'

'I told you—'

'They're happy in Kansas, aren't they. Settled?' Grady pushed himself up and sauntered across the room. 'I understand there might be some problems with their immigration status.'

'They've been here since 1986. They have green cards. They're not illegal.'

He leaned against the wall and folded his arms. 'Yeah. There's so much paperwork involved in immigration. So easy to make a mistake. And if someone spots a mistake now, the wrong box ticked, maybe, or a spelling error, then we'd have no choice but to get our buddies at immigration to follow up. Maybe Homeland Security, too.'

'You're threatening to kick out legal immigrants?' Half of her was simmering with rage at this threat, the other half was terrified.

'The last administration was concerned about how easy it is to enter this country illegally. We're a bit behind the times here, still operating on old ways of behaviour, you get me? We're trying to be a bit more diligent from here on out in making sure everyone is here legally. That's all.'

'Oh my God.'

'Of course, if we were confident that you and your family were loyal to the United States, we wouldn't have any reason to look into your paperwork at all. Would we? So, why was Conor on that flight?'

Kaitlin clenched her teeth. 'I don't know.'

'That's your final word on the matter?'

'I don't have any other words. I just don't know.'

Grady studied her. After a moment, he nodded. 'OK. Seems to me you know now what's at stake. So, let's set you back on your way.'

'That's it?'

'Like you said, you don't have any other words. But I'm sure we'll see each other again. Or rather, I'll see you.'

Kaitlin raced through the night. She still had no idea where she was going, but now she was truly scared witless for the first time since she'd started her investigation. She pressed her burner tight to her ear as she ran.

'You want to come here?' Rory was saying.

'No. God, no. I've got to disappear. They threatened to deport my parents, Rory.'

'They can't do that. There's no legal basis for deporting immigrants who haven't committed a felony.'

'If you believe they'll stick to the rules, you've not been paying attention.'

'What did they want?'

'They were asking me about Conor.'

'I know this doesn't help right now, but at least now we know for sure that we're on the right track. If the CIA are going to these lengths—'

'You're right, it doesn't help. Rory, they told me you were involved in hiding some information about problems with an airline's planes that cost lives.'

A long silence. *So, it was true.*

Kaitlin felt sick.

'We need to have a conversation,' he began.

'I can't believe you hid that from me!'

'I've got my flaws, Kaitlin. I'm not going to try to hide that. I've not been a good guy. I've let my family down, let myself down. But I'm trying to do the right thing here, believe me.'

'I don't know if I can trust you, Rory. Look, I've got to go.'

'Where are you going?'

'If we need to speak again, I'll be in touch.'

She hung up.

21

Kaitlin scrambled out of the dumpster at the back of the convenience store in the dark of the night. Her breath clouded in the cold air as she choked on the reek of rotting food. Her prize for rooting through the refuse for fifteen minutes: one still-wrapped burrito. Her stomach was growling so hard it could have been a feast from the best restaurant in Manhattan.

'Hey! Who's there?'

The voice barked away in the dark. A torch beam carved through the gloom.

Kaitlin threw herself into the shadows. This was the third time she'd nearly been caught by some bleary-eyed security guard. Sooner or later, her luck would probably run out, she knew that.

As she vanished into the trees, the angry cries faded away, and soon there was only the sound of her ragged breathing and the hoot of a hunting owl. Slumping down at the foot of a pine, she tore open the burrito and stuffed it into her mouth. Once her hunger was assuaged, she felt a grey mood settle on her. Survival had been confirmed for one more day, but the grim reality of her existence continually gnawed at her.

Going off-grid had been harder than she'd ever imagined. Here she was in some godforsaken part of Jersey, trying to keep moving while she tried to formulate some kind of plan, on foot most of the time, risking hitching a ride whenever she got desperate. She couldn't use her card – not that she had any cash in her account anyway. Dumpster-diving was her go-to for feeding herself. Occasionally, she opted for the five-finger discount. That was how low she'd fallen. She washed in restrooms, begged for glasses of water in bars. She steered clear of drinking from streams, aware that she'd likely come down with some microbial infection.

Now, the nights were getting colder and it was harder to find somewhere to sleep. She wasn't sure she could survive the winter.

Her head sagged onto her chest and she shuddered with a few brief sobs before she huddled into her thin jacket, her head on her rucksack.

Shivering in the thin light of dawn, she thumbed the call button on her burner and listened as it went to voicemail. Thomas' brief message rolled out.

'It's me,' she said. 'I need your help. Please call me.'

For the next three hours, she traipsed back and forth on some nature trail. Thomas didn't return her call. *Was that by choice, or had they got to him?* She had no idea.

But away from the lonely depths of the night, her determination burned brighter again. She couldn't just drift, not while there were still answers to find. It didn't matter what powers were ranged against her. She had to be tough, for Conor's sake, for the sake of all the families who were still suffering.

Steeling herself, she called Rory.

'Oh, thank the Lord,' he said when he heard her voice. 'Kaitlin, why haven't you answered any of my calls? I thought you were, well, you know – not with us any more.'

'We still have work to do and as much as I have doubts about you, we need to work together.'

'That's fair. Completely fair. I have some explaining to do. And some amends to be made. I know I'm going to need to earn your trust again. But we were a great team, right?'

Kaitlin felt surprised at the flood of warmth from hearing a friendly voice. 'I'm heading back to the city,' she said. 'I'll hitch a ride. Here's what we need to do . . .'

The CIA may well be waiting for her along with any one of the other powers hiding in the shadows. But it was time to roll the dice and hope she came out a winner.

The psychic witch looked from Kaitlin to Rory, her eyes narrowing. 'I'm not sure why you've brought your legal representation. I told you everything I know.'

Rory folded his hands on the circular table. 'I represent the families of 702 and we really need your help.'

'What exactly do you want from me?' The shadows cast by the flickering candles danced across Mia's face.

'It's my belief that you have information that could help my clients get to the truth. I'm offering you a chance to do the right thing here.'

'If your clients want my help then they're welcome to make an appointment to see me.' She turned to Kaitlin. 'There's nothing I can tell you that you don't already know.'

'Let's start with what you said about my brother and the other passengers,' Kaitlin said.

'I told you the truth. That they're not present. In this realm or the next.'

'Tell me, Mia, have you been calling the passengers' families, pretending to be their loved ones?' Rory clicked open his briefcase and pulled out a thick file.

'How dare you! Why on earth would I do that?'

'To lay the groundwork for a psychic coup? Hit them up for cash?'

'I'd never do such a thing!'

'Because you're a woman of such integrity?' Rory flicked open the file. 'My investigator dug up a real treasure trove of your disgruntled clients.'

Mia blanched.

'Which leads me onto Slobodan Begovic. Your poison-quaffing warlord client. The one you consulted with before you got on the plane.'

Mia's face hardened in the pale light.

'I will not discuss my clients with you.'

'Did he know something was going to happen to the plane? Did he warn you? Is that the real reason you got off the plane?'

'Subscribe to my YouTube channel, Mr Murray. There are countless interviews on it regarding why I left that plane.'

'I've seen them. They're what we in the legal profession term "horse pucky".'

'You con your way into my place of business and now you insult me? I will *not* tolerate this. I must ask you both to leave.'

'We both know I'm not the con artist here.'

'Do I need to call the police?'

Rory tapped the file. 'You could do that. Just like I could put together a class action against you for emotional distress. It won't be hard to round up your disgruntled clients, seeing as they have their own Facebook group.'

Kaitlin watched Mia's face sag. Her instinct had been right. There was leverage here. She glanced over at Rory. A ghost of a smile flickered on his lips.

'I'm really not interested in taking you down, Mia,' he continued. 'Give me a dollar and anything you say to me will remain confidential. The families deserve the truth, don't they? Please, Ms Risal. Tell me what you know and you'll never see me again.'

Mia hesitated, then she wagged a finger at him.

'You won't go to the media with anything I tell you?'

'Anything you say will stay strictly between us. You have my word.'

Mia slumped back in her chair. 'Slobodan – he didn't warn me exactly. He suggested that I keep my eyes and ears open. Especially when flying.'

'Did he have reason to believe the plane would be targeted?' Kaitlin demanded.

'That was all he said. He was a complicated man, with many demons.'

'But if he told you that, he must have had some kind of insider knowledge. You didn't question him about it?' Kaitlin pressed.

'He was a man who had been on the run for many years. He could be paranoid.'

'Yet you took his warning seriously.'

'Coupled with my intuition that something was very wrong, yes.'

'You told Kaitlin you had a bad feeling about some of the passengers on board,' Rory said. 'Most notably, the man sitting next to you, Dr Aziz, the immunologist. You said he became frosty when you refused to move to let him sit with his wife.'

'That woman wasn't his wife.'

'We know that now.'

'Yes, but I knew it then.'

'How?' Rory said.

'I'm psychic, Mr Murray.'

'Oh, come on, Mia, drop the act.'

She waved a hand in the air dismissively. 'Fine. It was the way they were with each other. Her body language especially. It was guarded. Tense. On edge. I'm intuitive about these things. I have to be.'

'And you said there was also a woman who was unwell on the plane?'

'Yes. She was in some distress.'

Rory leaned forwards. 'There's something else as well, isn't there? You're not the only one who's intuitive. Comes in handy in my job, too. It'll stay between us, I promise.'

Mia paused for a moment, as though weighing up her words, then she nodded.

'Slobodan warned me that at some point a transatlantic flight would be targeted by a terrorist group. He didn't specify which one. But he said I should take care travelling.

'When we were going through the pre-flight checks, that woman was having a heated argument with the man pretending to be her husband. A confrontation. He was uncomfortable. She was threatening. I couldn't hear exactly what was being said. But I had a feeling from the tone, the half-heard words, that something bad was going to happen.'

'Anything else you can add?' Rory asked.

She shook her head. 'I've told you everything I know.'

'Then thank you for your time,' he said, pushing back his chair and standing.

As he turned to go, Mia looked him up and down.

'There's a darkness to your aura, Mr Murray. The signs of a troubled soul. What is it that's poisoning you?'

Rory smiled. 'You really don't have to keep your routine running for our sake, Mia.'

'Is it shame? Is the manner in which you conduct your business poisoning your conscience? Or is it something more personal?'

Rory continued to smile as he strode to the door, but Kaitlin could see his expression had tightened. A nerve had clearly been touched.

'Come back any time,' Mia continued. 'I can help you, Mr Murray. Help you to exorcise the darkness that surrounds you. Guilt is not a healthy emotion to carry around. It will eat you up and spit you out.'

Outside, Kaitlin felt a wave of compassion for Rory. Whatever he'd done in the past, it was clearly something that burdened him. She didn't feel right punishing him any further.

'Thanks for coming along,' she said. 'You were the big stick I needed to beat the truth out of her.'

'That's me,' Rory replied with a broad grin. 'Just a big old chunk of wood. And now we know for sure the word was out about a terrorist attack. And we know—'

'That we must be looking at the White Matchmaker.' Kaitlin swallowed her relief that this new line didn't point to Conor's involvement.

'And now,' Rory said with a flourish, 'I think it's time we went public.'

22

The *New York Chronicle* building thrust up from the sprawl on the east side of Midtown. In gleaming glass and steel, with windows looking out across all parts of the city it served, the skyscraper was a monument to the principles of campaigning journalism.

'If this is all true, it's dynamite material, Mr Murray.'

Rachel Cohen stared down at the notes she'd scrawled on the yellow legal pad in the compact interview office overlooking the bustling newsroom. Rachel was one of the more seasoned hacks in this media empire, with several awards to her name and a resumé that saw her covering almost every major event of the last fifteen years. Rory had used all of his communication skills to get Rachel on board. This story needed the weight that she could offer, not some spotty-faced kid straight out of journalism college.

'It's all true, believe me. As much as I wish it weren't.' Rory showed a well-practised concerned expression. 'Where do we go from here?'

'I'm going to type up my notes and get the story into the morning news conference.' She checked the time on her phone. 'Which I can just about do if I'm fast. I'm confident the editor will give it the green light. Once we have that approval, I think we'll get you in for our daily news podcast so you can talk through your investigation. It's hugely popular; global reach.

'We'll run the story in the paper and online alongside that, backed up by our social media channels. Maybe a profile of you for our weekend magazine. How does that suit you?'

'That sounds perfect.'

'OK. If I could ask you to keep your phone on at all times. We'll need to move quickly on a story of this magnitude. We'll need plenty of fact-checking and we won't want any of the agencies you mentioned trying to shut this down. If everything stands up, we'll be ready to run.'

'Hot off the presses!' Rory stood up and gave the faintest of bows. 'And I have to say, big fan of your work. Let's shine the light of truth into the murky corners of the entire Flight 702 cover-up.'

Rory eased through the queues in the coffee shop and the cloud of fragrant steam to the small room at the back. There, Kaitlin sat in the corner in her shapeless hoodie with her Jets cap pulled so low it was impossible to tell even her gender.

He watched her for a moment, feeling a rare sense of warmth and protectiveness over her, which made him think of his daughter, Zara. Kaitlin looked so fragile and insignificant, yet she'd been a relentless force, single-handedly driving this entire investigation with courage and determination.

She was scared now, he could see that. Her encounter with the CIA and her nights spent God only knew where had rattled her. But here she was still, risking it all to do the right thing.

'How did it go?' she asked when he pulled up a chair opposite her.

'Just waiting for final approval, then we're good to go.'

'You still think this is the right thing to do?'

'Conspiracies thrive in the dark, and so do threats. Once this is out there, the CIA won't have to concern themselves with you exposing their shortcomings. They'll have bigger things to worry about.'

'Or so you hope.'

'OK, it's a gamble. But once the story is in the public sphere, we can get real government oversight of any investigation – here and in the UK.'

'Unless both governments are involved.'

'Then you and I are both spending the rest of our lives hanging out in the wilds of Nebraska.' Rory watched her weary face as her eyes darted around the coffee shop. This clearly wasn't the moment for his light-hearted humour. 'We're near the endgame now,' he told her gently, reaching out to squeeze her hand. 'We've identified the major players. We're just putting the final pieces in the puzzle, but we can see the big picture forming. We've just got to hold firm for a little bit longer.'

Kaitlin nodded. 'You're right. I know.'

'Don't forget – you don't have to do this on your own. Not any more.'

She forced a pale smile. After the darkness and misery he'd seen in her face, it seemed like a lamp coming on.

His phone buzzed and as he glanced down at it and saw a familiar photo, he felt his blood run cold. Oblivious to Kaitlin's curious expression, he scanned the accompanying message and then said, 'I've gotta take this. I'll be back in a minute.'

He hurried out before she had the chance to say a word.

Rory glanced up and down the street, searching every face that passed. Finally, he heard a name muttered just behind his ear and he turned to see a woman with dyed blue hair, shaved on the right side and a nose ring.

'Walk with me,' she said and stepped away.

Rory skipped to catch up. 'Who are you?' he demanded.

'You saw the photo?'

'Who are you?' he insisted again.

'There's a lot more material where that came from. You've really dug deep in some holes. There's a *lot* more material.'

'CIA? S-some underground group?'

'You visited the *New York Chronicle* office.' She paused by her reflection in a window and ran fingers through her hair. 'If you're thinking of going public with any of the information you have, I'd definitely think again.'

They were watching him, whoever 'they' were. He'd suspected it, of course he had. But he'd never thought they'd take this route. That was stupid of him. He really should have known better.

'You're going to blackmail me?' he said.

Finishing her grooming, the woman set off again, not even deigning to throw Rory a glance. 'That photo. Rose Greer. You remember her? Of course you do. Wow, that was a messy affair. And with a client, too. That must have thrown up a few ethical issues. I mean, I'm no attorney, but I'm guessing sleeping with a client and *then* screwing up her case might raise a conflict or two with the American Bar Association's Model Rules of Professional Conduct? Yes? No?'

Rory stared at the sidewalk. That had been a difficult time in his life. He had thought it was dead and buried.

'I don't know how much your wife knew about it. Remind me, which wife was it at the time? I'll have to check. You did a great job keeping that out of the public eye. But if it hit now? With a daughter locked up in a foreign clinic?'

'She's not locked up,' he snapped.

'And the bills not getting paid, like you don't really care for her.' The woman shrugged. 'Wow. What a dick. That's what people will be thinking, right? Could be career ending. Oh, if only that was the end of it.'

Rory swallowed. He could see where this was going.

'I took a look at a pretty big file,' she continued. 'Some quite detailed accusations of bribery and corruption.'

'Accusations!' Rory stressed. He could feel the sweat trickling down his back. 'Nothing proven.'

'Because none of them, as yet, have been investigated.' This time, she did glance at him. A tight smile, twitching at the corners. 'So, here's the deal, Mr Murray. You go public. We go public. You decide to walk away from this, so do we.'

Rory stared into her eyes, but he was looking right through her, into his past and deep into his future. He could see how this would unfold. The scandal. The shame. Everything he'd worked so hard for, destroyed. He was a pragmatic man. He could weigh the opposing outcomes and it wasn't even close. Besides, he wasn't a brave man. He was clear-eyed about his flaws. He'd rather run and hide and live to fight another day.

No, he couldn't see his whole life brought down, just for Flight 702.

There would be other fights. He'd have a chance to redeem himself.

'OK,' he said, feeling his stomach churn. 'You have a deal.'

'You're a wise man, Mr Murray. Hopefully, we'll never have to meet again.'

She turned round and walked away into the flow of passers-by. Rory watched her blue hair bobbing away.

In that instant, he realised his hands were trembling. And not just that. His entire body was shuddering as if he were gripped by an awful sickness. He staggered to one side and crashed against the wall, propping himself up before he slumped down to the sidewalk.

Get a grip. You're falling apart. What's wrong with you?

A moment later, he understood what this terrible, unfamiliar feeling was: his conscience.

God, he hated it.

Gritting his teeth, Rory hurled himself along the sidewalk, throwing cursing strangers this way and that. Finally, he caught up with the blue-haired woman and grabbed her shoulder. She whirled.

'I take it back,' he gasped. 'I take it all back.'

Those eyes, like steel, carving him up.

'Do your worst,' he said.

The woman raised an eyebrow, then she nodded. 'Oh, don't worry. We will.'

She marched away without a backwards glance.

Still shaking, Rory staggered back inside and slipped into the seat opposite Kaitlin.

'Rory! What's happened?' she asked, looking shocked.

After pouring out his experience, he sucked in a few deep breaths to calm himself and said, 'Let me tell you what a horrible human being I am.'

And for the next half-hour, Rory detailed every failing, every flaw, every line crossed for whatever reason, in both his business and personal life. He spoke about all of his ex-wives and the stupid things he'd done to crash every marriage. The affairs he'd had and the ones he'd seemed incapable of avoiding, even when he was happy with his partner at the time. He admitted to his emotional weaknesses – and for the first time admitted them to himself

– and described how he felt he'd failed his daughter and had never done enough to help with her addiction. He'd even let down some of his clients, and his business was where his focus had always been.

Rory watched Kaitlin's eyes widen as the seemingly endless list continued and he gripped himself for the moment when she'd get up and walk out. But to her credit, she stuck it out.

'You deserve to know who you're working with,' he said, 'and I apologise for not being straight with you from the start. I guess I didn't want you to judge me. To be honest, I've spent so long avoiding even thinking about any of this to refrain from judging myself.'

'So why now?'

'Someone just tried to blackmail me. Said they'd make all this public if I didn't walk away from the investigation, or if I made any attempt to go public with what we know.'

Kaitlin tapped her straw on the edge of the table. 'This will pretty much destroy you.'

'I know.'

'So?'

Rory sucked in a steadying breath. 'I told them to get back on their horse and ride out of town.'

Kaitlin nodded. She had a good poker face, he thought.

'I'm pretty horrified. I mean, anyone would be, hearing all that.'

'I understand.'

'But, taking a stand like that, I suppose it shows some integrity.'

'I thank you for that, however grudging it might be.'

They both grinned at one another and the tension broke. A brief moment of relief among all the sweat and doubt and fear.

'On a positive note, they must be worried,' Kaitlin added. 'We're getting closer to the truth.'

Rory cracked his knuckles. 'Time to let the world know all about Flight 702 and the White Matchmaker.'

23

Kaitlin watched through the window of the recording booth as Rory hunched over the microphone. He was a natural performer, she had to give him that. For the *New York Chronicle* podcast, he weaved all the complex information into a gripping tale. She could see from the light in Rachel Cohen's eyes that this was going even better than expected.

When they walked out, Rachel and Rory were laughing as if they were old friends.

'How does this work?' Rory asked Rachel.

'Once we've edited the podcast, we're going to release it immediately,' she said. 'Flood social media. This is too big to sit on. The editor's clearing the front page so we can go big on this in today's print final. Looks like you're going to become something of a celebrity. I'd brace yourself.'

Rory held his arms wide. 'In my mind, Rachel, I've always been a celebrity.'

'I'm serious. You don't realise how these things take off.'

As they took the elevator down, having bid Rachel farewell, Kaitlin asked, 'Are you sure this was the right thing to do?'

Rory licked a fingertip and smoothed an eyebrow in his reflection in the brass plate around the floor buttons. He actually seemed to be relishing what was lying ahead.

'No going back now.'

'If they go for your reputation—'

He chuckled. '"What reputation?" many might say. My calculation: they'll be too busy scrambling to control the public fallout. All those questions about who knew what, when. Why it wasn't made public. How high did the cover-up go.'

So many risks, though. How this developed was now out of their hands.

Rory seemed to see her doubts. 'We'd got as far as we could with our investigation. All of the passengers we've got on our list, all of the agencies trying to block us at every turn. We needed something spectacular to reset the rules. It's a new game now and maybe when the dust has cleared, we can see the road ahead.'

'To finding Conor and the others?'

He nodded. 'We do that, it was all worth it, right? All the dangers, the threats. A better tomorrow. That's my reasoning for what some might say is a reckless roll of the dice. This is the moment of our greatest success – or greatest danger.'

Cameras flashed. Rory's eyes flared as he stood behind the forest of microphones at the podium. The pack of journalists swelled around the front of the low stage, desperate to catch his attention. As Kaitlin scanned the crowd from the back of the room, it seemed to her as though every major publication from anywhere in the world was represented here. This was big news.

She felt a rush of joy that the families of the passengers of Flight 702 were finally getting their concerns heard and, hopefully, the answers they deserved after so long in the dark. But behind it all she was still afraid. That seemed to be the mood music for her life these days.

The media event had been called at short notice owing to the burgeoning public interest. The *New York Chronicle* was keen to publicise its exclusive and had offered the use of its boardroom. Turned out it was barely big enough.

As Rory fielded the questions with all his usual panache, Kaitlin zoned out the incessant shouting of journalists and Rory's smooth answers while skimming social media. The *Chronicle* account had gone viral. Retweets piling up. Facebook groups burning with conspiracy theories. Rory's face was everywhere: The Man Who Blew the Lid Off the Flight 702 Cover-up.

She was glad it wasn't her.

As Rory slipped off the stage, Rachel Cohen wrapped up the event, telling the hacks that there would be more revelations to come. The airline was to hold a media conference, and soon there would be a response from the US and UK governments.

Rory nodded to the rear door and Kaitlin darted out with him. They headed straight to the elevators before they could be pursued.

'My cell's buzzing with messages from the families,' Rory said. 'All those folks who rejected me out of hand. They now want to be a part of this. We're going to get this class action off the ground.'

'You did a great job there. I'm so proud of you.'

Rory clamped his mouth shut for a moment. Then, his voice a little hoarse: 'It's been a while since anyone's said that to me.'

He was still quiet as they crossed the lobby, but once they were out in the chill morning, his natural exuberance flourished once more.

'We need to lie low while this plays out,' he said. 'My investigator has booked us an Airbnb in Williamsburg under an assumed name. Wait here while I hail a cab.'

While Rory dived off the kerb, waving his arm, Kaitlin

pressed herself back against the wall of the *Chronicle* building. She kept her head down, trying to look inconspicuous.

She jolted when a hand grabbed her arm. Trying to wrench herself free, she glanced round. Into the face of Agent Dennison.

'You made a big mistake,' he growled. 'And there's going to be a price to pay.'

Kaitlin could hear Rory calling her name and sounding increasingly panicked, but Dennison had dragged her a little way down the street and round the side of the building out of sight. Though he wasn't rough with her as she struggled, he was insistent and his eyes burned with a light that worried her.

'Let me go,' she gasped.

'I'm not going to hurt you. Quite the opposite. I want to make sure you're safe.'

'This isn't the way to do it.'

'Who's that guy you're with?'

'My friend.'

'You trust him?'

'Yes!'

Dennison peered round the edge of the building, watching Rory as he searched back and forth.

'How did you get out?' she demanded.

'That doesn't matter now.' Dennison seemed to weigh the situation, then he dragged Kaitlin out into view. 'We're over here,' he bellowed.

Rory raced down the street when he saw them. 'Leave her alone,' he demanded, 'or so help me—'

'Don't pick a fight with me,' Dennison snarled. 'I'm on your side.'

'Rory, it's OK. This is Agent Dennison,' Kaitlin said with haste.

'Not agent any more,' Dennison said. 'The FBI are done with me. Just Jim.'

Rory scrutinised him, no doubt trying to see what kind of trouble lay ahead. 'What the hell is this?'

'You made a mistake identifying the White Matchmaker as the key to this. My contacts tell me the truth about her is going to come out soon. Then you two will be out in the open, no cover, and ripe for being taken down.' He looked around. 'We need to get out of sight.'

Kaitlin hesitated for a moment, then she made a decision. 'Let's take him with us to Williamsburg.'

'You sure?' Rory asked.

'Yes. I-I trust him.'

'Thanks,' Dennison said. 'And you're right to. I admit I got a little . . . erratic . . . before. Desperation does that to you. But you know that, right?' he said to Kaitlin.

She nodded.

Minutes later, they were in a yellow cab, heading away from Delancey and across the Williamsburg Bridge.

No one spoke.

'This is what I meant,' Dennison said when he was standing in front of the TV in the apartment. CNN played a picture of Rory followed by a media conference hosted by the UK foreign minister.

'Allegations made this morning that Flight 702 was brought down by the terrorist known as the White Matchmaker have already started to unravel,' the newscaster was saying. 'At a briefing at the Foreign, Commonwealth & Development Office in London, an intelligence report was revealed that showed the White Matchmaker is currently incarcerated in Kabul, Afghanistan. Real name Samantha Griegen, also known as Uzma Griegen, she gained her title because she was a white Westerner who recruited young girls for the Somali-based radical militant group Al-Shabaab . . .'

Dennison muted the TV and turned to Rory and Kaitlin. 'That wasn't the White Matchmaker on Flight 702.'

'Who was it, then?' Kaitlin asked, bewildered. She'd been so sure. She turned to Rory. 'Your contact said—'

'I know.' Rory rubbed his chin. 'She'd been Fed intel.'

'This is one smokescreen after another,' Dennison interrupted. 'This is how these people work. You can't trust anything. The lies and the half-truths pile up until you can't tell what's real and what's not.'

'Laura Jones – Chrissy – was on the flight,' Kaitlin pressed. 'She was posing as the wife of Aziz. You're telling me there's nothing in that?'

'Not at all.' Dennison tossed the remote aside. 'The news is going to come out later. A leak, but a true one. The teacher, Laura Jones, was an MI6 agent investigating the virologist's connections to Iranian intelligence. That's why there was so much secrecy surrounding her identity.'

Kaitlin flopped on the sofa. Rory buried his face in his hands.

'OK, so I'm now the public face of a debunked conspiracy theory, plastered across all media,' he began. 'Nobody's going to trust a word I say any more. So, when all my past indiscretions are rolled out, I won't stand a chance at defending myself. Completely, utterly discredited.'

Kaitlin felt her heart go out to Rory, but when he took his hands away, she was relieved to see that he didn't look too dispirited.

'The details were wrong, but the thrust of the argument is correct,' Rory continued. He was staring into the middle distance, speaking as his mind turned over the evidence.

'MI6 was investigating Aziz. They were clearly worried about him. There's something there.'

'You're damn right,' Dennison said. 'The problem is that now you've played your cards, you've got nothing. And all of those people who want to stop the truth about Flight 702 from being brought into the light are going to come for you.'

Kaitlin sagged. She really didn't want to go off-grid again. The thought of running and hiding crushed her.

As they all bounced ideas around, Rory's cell buzzed and his eyes lit up when he checked it. He glanced at her before answering, grinning.

'Maybe I've found our lifeline.'

'We've got to stop meeting like this, Renee.' The underground parking lot reeked of car fumes.

'Trust me, I want that way more than you.'

She sounded weary, Rory thought, and, if anything, she looked even more worried than the last time they'd met. Her eyes darted around the parked cars, searching for any sign of movement.

'I didn't think I'd be hearing from you again,' he said.

'As much as I hate it, I felt I owed you. The false information about the White Matchmaker was on me.'

'You didn't know it was false.'

'I'm trying to do the right thing here, Rory, so why don't you keep your mouth shut?'

'OK. Carry on.'

'I saw your face all over the media. Getting torn apart. You deserve a lot of things, but you don't deserve that, not when it was clear you were taking a risk for the sake of the families. If it was just about the class action, you wouldn't have gone to those lengths. So . . .' She took a deep breath. 'I have some new information. This, I'm sure, is correct because it's so fragmentary and it's only been circulated in the highest circles of the industry. Suppressed. I could be putting myself at risk even mentioning it to you.'

Rory felt his intuition tingle. 'Go on.'

'You could call it a rumour. It could be nothing. But we have an eyewitness report of an aircraft flying too low near Thule Air Base on the north-western coast of Greenland, followed by the sound of an explosion. That's our northernmost air base and the only one in the Arctic Circle, and—'

'It's on the flight path 702 was taking when it swung north from its transatlantic route.' Rory felt a rush of excitement. 'That's a coincidence too far.'

'You're going to Greenland, aren't you?' Renee asked in an even wearier tone.

Rory grinned.

24

A square of light from the Rosewood Art Gallery flooded across the sidewalk. Inside, a well-heeled but dressed-down crowd swilled back champagne as they drifted around the private viewing. The wintry night air was sharp, but it was warmed with the spicy scents from the curry house two blocks over.

Kaitlin eased away from the light and the activity to a gated entryway, where she nestled in the shadows. She didn't have to wait long.

The figure walked up from the direction of Bed-Stuy, hunched in a thick coat, head kept well down. Back at the apartment, Dennison was monitoring events and making calls to his contacts. Rory wasn't back from his assignation yet, but when he'd called, he was buzzing with anticipation. Funny how things turned out. Only a few hours ago, the decision to go public had seemed like a disaster. But Rory's deep throat wouldn't have stepped forwards to help them if they hadn't gone so spectacularly off course. Humiliation could be a positive force.

'You came,' she said. 'I thought I might have seen the last of you.'

Thomas slipped into the shadows beside her. His gaze flickered around the street. 'You really expected me to stay away when you leave a message saying Conor is still alive?'

'I didn't want to tell you until I'd found out more, but you weren't responding and I was getting desperate.'

Kaitlin watched Thomas' face as she played back the voicemail. A tremor crossed his features when he heard Conor's voice. She knew what he was feeling, how he'd struggled keeping all those emotions locked down tight for so long for fear they could only be released in a deluge.

'It's him. You know it is,' she said.

He nodded.

'What do you think?'

For a long moment, Thomas said nothing. He seemed to be wrestling with himself, she thought. She reached out and touched his arm, prompting him.

'There's something I didn't tell you. I wanted to protect you, but . . .' He shook his head. 'Just after the plane took off, Conor sent me a message: something's going down. That was what he said. That was all he said. All those hackers and activists and psychos and whatever in that utilitarian group he loved. Conor was a keen part of that.'

Kaitlin gaped. 'He was with them?'

'They all had different agendas. Some were more dangerous than others. Some were just crazy. But they all shared one aim: to disrupt the global status quo. I persuaded Conor to spy on them and inform on any who were likely to be a threat to life. Then I could channel it up the chain of command.

'Conor got word that they were planning something big. Something to do with a biological weapon that involved the airline industry. The intel was strong enough to be true but vague enough that we had nothing solid enough to go on. We didn't know where or when. MI6, the CIA, all the agencies on both sides of the Atlantic were working on it.'

'What else are you keeping from me?' She heard her voice crack.

'Nothing, honestly.'

'All those agencies. They have to know what happened. Where Conor is.'

'Maybe they do. But I don't. I was cut out of the loop the minute Flight 702 vanished. Any intel after that was purely on a need-to-know basis. That's when I started pulling away from the security services. At first, I thought I was locked out because of my relationship with Conor, but whatever went down it seems like a lot of the agencies have stopped talking about it.' Thomas shuddered, pressed his hand across his eyes.

'What is it?' Kaitlin breathed.

'The guilt's been eating me up since that night.' He swallowed, fighting to control his emotions. 'What if . . . What if I'm responsible? By passing on Conor's last message. What if I'm responsible for his death? The death of all those passengers? The grief those families felt. You . . . your mom and dad . . .'

'How could you be responsible?'

Thomas stared at her with glistening eyes. 'Governments have to take hard choices. If someone on Flight 702 was suspected of harbouring a biological weapon, the decision might have been taken to shoot the plane down.'

'But Conor's alive, Thomas!' Kaitlin gripped his arm, willing him to believe her. 'He's alive.'

'Is he, though? How do we know that for sure?'

'You heard the message!'

'I heard Conor's voice. What it means, I don't know. You don't know. An old recording? A trick to flush you out? More disinformation? That's how intelligence agencies work. They don't need to deny. They only need to confuse. The more confusion the better. Until everyone's wandering around in a fog, not able to tell what's truth or lie. Lost for good.'

Kaitlin slumped. 'Conor's alive, Thomas, I know he is.'

Thomas squeezed her shoulder. 'I can help you disappear,' he murmured. 'A new identity. A new life. So you don't have the government breathing down your neck for the rest of your days.'

'No.' Kaitlin felt her defiance burn. 'I'm not running away. I'm seeing this through to the end. You walk away if you want, that's down to you. But not me.'

Thomas flinched as if she'd slapped him.

'My friend has a lead. A big one. If this is where the answers lie, then I know the risks are going to be huge. But I have to do this, Thomas, for Conor. And I'm not sure I can do it on my own.' She bit her lip. 'Will you help me?'

Thomas and Dennison eyed each other over the coffee table like two competing species. They didn't trust anyone. In their business, that was probably a healthy response, Kaitlin thought. She set a Diet Coke down in front of Thomas and a Jack Daniels in front of Dennison, then cupped her hands round her matcha tea. Even her generous hospitality didn't thaw the atmosphere.

A key rattled in the door and they all turned. Rory whirled in, beaming and excited. Kaitlin felt her spirits lift instantly.

He looked stunned to find yet another new addition to the team sitting in the apartment, but once he'd been introduced to Thomas, he said, 'This could be the big one. My contact heard about a lawsuit over in Greenland that's being handled by a colleague. The day Flight 702 went missing, someone was hit by a piece of flying debris. This person said they saw a plane flying close to Thule Air Base. Too close. And then a piece of metal shattered their windshield.'

Dennison slammed his glass on the table. 'Damn.'

'Thule would fit the new flight path,' Thomas mused.

'The eyewitness think it crashed,' Rory continued. 'They heard an explosion, or what they think was an explosion. A loud boom.'

'Could anyone survive that?' Kaitlin asked.

'Maybe,' Dennison said.

'Possibly,' Thomas said.

'Yes, absolutely,' Rory insisted. 'If it was flying low enough, yes. Trust me, I have old case files about this clogging up my office. But here's the thing. Even if the plane did crash, it wasn't in the sea.'

'So the wreckage was planted,' Dennison interjected. 'A cover-up.' He snatched up his bourbon and threw it back in one gulp.

Rory nodded, grinning. 'Something's going on at that air base.'

25

The last of the few hours of sunlight glinted off the frozen landscape. As the twin-prop descended, Kaitlin looked out of the window and marvelled at the loneliness of this part of the world. Just a few scattered villages dotted the tundra and one small town nestled close to the fjord. Below, Qaanaaq Airport was little more than one airstrip and a low-level arrivals and departure building with sapphire-painted walls and a white roof.

The juddering plane bounced down and rumbled to a halt. As the door was thrown open, Kaitlin winced at the bite of the wind.

'Minus seven out there,' Thomas said as he pulled on his parka. 'Could drop as low as minus twenty when the sun goes down.'

Rory yanked his fur-edged hood so tight only a small circle of pink face showed. 'Sooner we're in, sooner we're out.'

Kaitlin admired his optimism.

At the foot of the steps, she felt a hand tug her sleeve. Dennison leaned in.

'Kaitlin, I need to apologise again. When we first met, I was in a very dark place. And I worry that I scared you.'

'You didn't scare me.'

'All that talk about shadows and biological weapons.'

'You were right, though. I think you were right about all of it.'

He nodded, seemingly relieved by what she'd said. He was a good man. They all were.

As they traipsed through the departures door into the glaring light and warmth, Kaitlin threw back her hood.

'Our papers are ready,' Thomas muttered. 'Any problem, let me do the talking.'

Kaitlin felt relieved Thomas and Dennison had come along. She didn't know how she'd have made it through otherwise. Between them, they'd sourced new passports under fake identities, tickets and enough cash to book passage with a change at Copenhagen in Denmark to throw off their trail for whoever might be tracking them. If they'd gone directly to Thule Air Base, they'd have needed a permit from the Danish Foreign Ministry, but Thomas had persuaded them it was better to scope out the lie of the land before making a direct approach.

They eased through immigration, with Thomas claiming he and Kaitlin were eloping; one week here in the Arctic Circle and then off to Europe for a honeymoon. Whatever lies Rory and Dennison spun, it seemed to do the trick.

Out in the car park, Kaitlin stamped her feet and rubbed her hands for warmth. Only a sliver of red sun edged the horizon.

'Now what?' she said.

'Now, we split up,' Thomas replied. 'I've got a guide waiting so we can check out the area where Flight 702 was supposed to have come down.'

'Jim's coming with me,' Rory said. 'Got a meeting with the lawyer acting for the eyewitness. Old friend. We'll see what we can pick up and then check in at the hotel. When you get back there, we can discuss the next step.'

While Rory and Dennison headed towards their rental car, Thomas slipped behind the wheel of a jeep. A few minutes later, they were rumbling along frozen roads, swathed in the heat blasting out of the vents.

'Only another twenty minutes or so,' Thomas said.

Maybe he could sense her anxiety. So close now to knowing the truth.

'You're sure this guide is on the up and up?'

'He's an old contact. Been a few years since I've seen him, but we can trust him.' He snaked his hand down into his bag and pulled out a GoPro. 'Before I forget.'

'What's this for?'

'Clip it to your jacket.'

'I'm already recording. I'm always recording.'

'We're heading deep into the tundra. There won't be any cell service. It's going to be bitter cold, probably very windy and, overall, incredibly harsh.'

'Sounds like fun,' Kaitlin said, clipping on the GoPro.

'That camera is made to withstand harsh conditions. Your iPhone isn't. You need to think ahead.'

Kaitlin eyed him, feeling a rush of irritation. 'Patronising much? You've been gone the past few months and I've been doing just fine without you. I told you all along that Conor was still alive and I was right.'

'Maybe.'

'Would it kill you to give me some credit?'

'I just want us to keep our heads. Think before we act.'

Kaitlin softened her tone. There was no point getting into a fight. 'I know we still have to get in and a lot of things could go wrong, but it's OK to be hopeful.'

'What if Conor isn't there? What if that's an old recording?'

'It doesn't matter,' she replied, looking out into the white landscape. 'This is the closest we've got and we have to keep going.'

'If we don't do this right – if we don't do this perfectly – and something happens to Conor . . . I can't fail him again.'

'You're not going to fail him. You haven't failed him. You never stopped looking, just like me.'

The road rumbled beneath them. With every mile that passed, Kaitlin felt her chest grow tighter.

The office was cramped, with a computer on the desk from a brand that Rory didn't recognise. It looked like it came from the last century. But at least it was warm. Probably too warm. He fanned himself.

Dennison sat beside him like an Easter Island statue, giving nothing away. They both watched the lawyer moving around her den, putting files into cabinets as if that were a far more important task. Malina Jensen was blonde and slim. Danish stock. God knows why she was out here on the edge of nowhere.

'So good to see you again, Rory,' she said as if it wasn't even remotely good to see him.

Dennison eyed him.

'Good to see you, too, Malina. Been a few years since we worked on the Kangerlussuaq Airport case.'

'Oh, you remember that? You forgot my phone number quickly enough.'

Now Dennison was glaring at him.

'Life got on top of me, Malina, and I'm truly sorry for that. But let's not dwell on the past.'

She tucked the final file away and slipped into her chair. 'If you want to go after GreelandAir, you can—'

'No, no, it's not that,' Rory stressed.

'We're here about Flight 702,' Dennison growled.

Malina smiled. 'Of course. That's just the sort of case you'd go for. So, you're suing Atlantic Airlines, I take it?' She turned to Dennison. 'And who are you, exactly? Forgive me, but you seem rather too old to be his intern.'

'I used to work for the American government,' Dennison said in that voice that made everything sound like a potential threat.

Malina took notice, though.

'I heard that you were working an injury case,' Rory began.

'I work a lot of injury cases.'

'Of someone who got hit by flying debris from a plane crash.'

'My clients' cases are confidential, you know that.'

'People don't get hit by falling debris very often. Especially from flights that disappeared without a trace.'

Malina cocked her head. 'Flight 702 was found in the Atlantic.'

'Parts of it were,' Dennison said. 'Which is why it's odd you have a client who was hit by flying debris while driving a car. On land. Miles away from the Atlantic.' He shrugged. 'I'm not an aviation expert, but two plus two isn't adding up to four for me here.'

'I think you'll find that no part of this equation bears out the way you think it will.'

Dennison folded his hands together. 'My daughter was on Flight 702.'

Malina flinched. 'I'm very sorry for your loss.'

'So, you think the plane crashed, then?' Rory said, seizing the moment.

'It's not my job to determine what happened to Flight 702. The only thing I care about is getting someone to pay for my client's medical bills and car repairs.'

'Malina, please. Just give us the nod that we're not on a wild goose chase,' Rory pressed.

Malina thought for a moment. 'OK. I will tell you this. My client is opposed to the US presence in Greenland and has been very vocal on the matter. I recognise this could be a potential obstacle if a case were to be made that he's simply trying to use it as another way to make his political point.'

'You wouldn't have taken it this far if you thought he was making it up, Malina,' Rory said, smiling wryly.

'I've interviewed him in detail. His story never changes. He's adamant he saw a passenger plane in trouble that day, not a military aircraft.'

Rory eased back in his chair. 'That's good enough for me.'

'What exactly is your plan, if you don't mind me asking?' Malina said. 'You've come all the way to Greenland in the hope of drumming up more evidence that they're not telling us everything about 702? Looking to find definitively what happened? Because trust me, I've been doing this for many months and I can't find my way through the tangle of information. You are two men, far from home. I can't help you and you can't go up against this alone.'

Dennison leaned forwards. 'But we're not alone.'

The full moon glowed and stars sprayed across the vault of the heavens. Under the majestic sky, the two snowmobiles trundled across the frozen wastes.

Despite multiple layers, Kaitlin shivered in the wind blasting from the north. She couldn't feel her face. Both her arms were wrapped around Thomas, who was steering. The guide drove the other vehicle. He was a short man, heavyset, with a thick beard.

'How much further?' she shouted over the drone of the engines.

'It's just up here,' the guide bellowed back.

Thomas craned his neck back. 'You all right?'

'Fine. When did you learn to drive one of these things?'

'My parents used to take me to the Alps for the holidays.'

'Well, la-di-da.'

'Just up here,' the guide shouted again. He killed his engine and jumped off.

Thomas eased his snowmobile alongside and cut the power. Now they were stationary, the wind didn't feel quite so harsh. Kaitlin looked out across a vast stretch of billowing snow. A stillness hung over everything.

'Where are we?' she asked as she climbed off.

The guide pointed into the distance. 'Just over four miles from Thule Air Base.'

'And this is where everyone saw it?' Thomas asked.

'Clear as day. A passenger plane, fire and smoke coming from its tail, falling out of the sky.'

'You're sure it was a passenger plane?'

'I know a military plane when I see one. You know how many fly across here? My whole life, your government has been treating our land like it's theirs.'

'You live near here?' Kaitlin asked.

'About two miles south.'

'Whose land are we on?'

'Greenland's.'

'This is public land?'

'All of Greenland is for everyone. No one owns private property here. We share.'

'Except Thule.'

'Except Thule. That day, I followed the plane as far as I could on my snowmobile.'

Kaitlin stamped her feet again to try to revive her frozen toes. 'What were you doing out here?'

'Hunting. At least until all the animals got scared away by the noise.'

'Did you see where the plane landed?'

'It didn't land. It crashed.'

'No, it didn't,' she insisted. 'Because some of the passengers survived.'

The guide said nothing for a moment. Then: 'Maybe they did. But there was an explosion. I could hear it, even miles behind.'

'Did you hear anything else?' Thomas said. 'Before you saw the plane, was there an explosion? Gunfire? Another plane?'

The guide shook his head. Thomas took a deep breath. Relief, Kaitlin guessed.

'Can you take us to the crash site?' Thomas asked.

'No. This is as far as I can go.'

'OK. Tell us where it is. We'll go on our own.'

'I can't. Not with any certainty.'

'I thought you said you followed it.' Kaitlin's breath clouded.

'As far as I could,' the guide replied. 'The explosion had barely stopped ringing when the helicopter noises started.'

Thomas paced forwards a few steps and peered away into the night. 'The military.'

'Like I said, the air base is very close. They responded quickly.'

'So, if there were any survivors of the initial crash—'

'The military would have gotten them out quickly,' Kaitlin interrupted. 'I told you. He's alive.'

Thomas ignored her. All right, if you can't take us to the crash site, then we'll go to the air base.'

'You crazy?'

'This is a huge, empty place. There has to be a spot we could sneak in unnoticed.'

'They patrol the perimeter.'

'We'll wait for a gap in the patrol.'

The guide was looking at Thomas as if he were insane. Maybe he was. Maybe they both were.

'In sub-zero temperatures?' He turned to Kaitlin. 'Can you talk some sense into him?'

'Just point us in the right direction,' she said. 'We'll pay you for the snowmobile.'

'You're both crazy. If the military doesn't get you, you'll die of exposure.'

Kaitlin knew he could be right. But all she could think of was Conor and she was sure it was the same for Thomas.

'Which way is the base?'

Rory and Dennison strode from the hotel check-in desk to the elevator. After the bitter chill of the night, Rory felt relief to be back in the warmth. He wasn't a man cut out for cold weather, that's for sure.

'Pity Malina couldn't be more helpful. But at least we're confident there *are* witnesses to the plane crashing,' he said as the door slid open.

'And the government is doing its damnedest to keep those witnesses quiet.'

Rory eyed Dennison. He was a hard man to read. His daughter's disappearance must have hit him hard, but he kept those emotions locked away.

'The more cracks in the armour, the better. Now, though, time for a hot shower,' Rory said.

From the elevator, they walked along the corridor, checking the room numbers. Dennison was a few paces ahead of him and when the ex-FBI man reached a corner, he lurched back, throwing out an arm to pin Rory to the wall. Dennison pressed a finger to his lips before Rory could call out.

He peeked round the corner again and then whispered, 'Two men in military uniforms standing outside my room.'

'Did they see you?' Rory breathed.

'Don't think so.'

'We need to get out of here.'

Dennison shook his head. 'We need to warn Kaitlin and Thomas.'

Before they could move, the sound of footsteps echoed along the corridor, moving towards them.

The rumble of the snowmobile died and then there was only the whine of the wind. Kaitlin eased off the seat and stared at the lights glowing in the distance. Thule Air Base. The approach road, the security fence and the landing strips were all illuminated. Several buildings were scattered around the hangars.

'Let's leave the snowmobiles here. Go the rest of the way on foot,' Thomas said.

'Can we have a little hope yet?' she replied.

'When I look Conor in the eye. Only then.' Thomas crunched across the snow to get a better look. 'It's bigger than I expected.'

'Should be somewhere we can sneak in,' she said. 'I bet they don't expect many prying eyes out here.'

'OK. Let's go.'

They strode out across the crisp snow. After a few steps, Kaitlin felt a prickle of unease.

'Look,' she said, pointing. 'One of those lights is moving.'

Not just moving, but rising.

'Fuck,' Thomas muttered. 'Run.'

Kaitlin spun on her heel and lurched back towards the snowmobile. But now the icy silence shattered as the helicopter swept towards them. Her heart pounded, but that thunder roared up faster than she could run.

Lights blazed on, sweeping the white waste all around.

We were too confident, she thought.

A voice boomed out of the chopper's speakers: 'Stop where you are and get on the ground.'

'Keep running,' Thomas gasped.

'You are trespassing on US government property. Stop where you are or we are authorised to shoot.'

Thomas ground to a halt. Kaitlin threw herself down, the snow burning her face as she clasped her hands on her head.

We've failed. So close, but we failed.

The roar of the helicopter rushed down and the gale blasted them.

26

In a white windowless room under a glaring strip light, Kaitlin stared at her two captors across the table. One was a sergeant: buzz cut, blue eyes, solid muscle. She didn't catch his name. The other was a woman, blonde hair pulled back in a ponytail, charcoal suit. She didn't have that military rigidity about her, so Kaitlin assumed she was probably a civilian of some kind. Kaitlin remembered, during the flurry of activity when she was dragged in, that this woman's name was Marianne.

Her mind was racing ahead, as it always did in times of high stress. *What were the possible outcomes for her here? None of them good, that was for sure.*

Marianne flicked on a recording device. 'Interview with Kaitlin Le—'

'My name's Sophie Nguyen.'

'Did you say something, Miss Le?' the sergeant growled.

'I'm Sophie Nguyen. I'm here with my fiancé. I'm sorry if we've strayed onto . . . I don't know what this place is. We were trying to see the Northern Lights. We didn't realise we were on . . . What *is* this place?'

'What are you doing here?' The sergeant fixed those cold blue eyes on her.

'I told you, we were . . . We were looking for the Northern Lights,' she stuttered. 'But everything looks the same here. I guess we got lost and . . .'

The sergeant tossed the GoPro on the table. Kaitlin stared at it for a moment.

'I wasn't filming you guys,' she began. 'I was trying to film the landscape, maybe even the aurora. I don't know if you've noticed, but it's pretty picturesque out there.' She glanced to the door, desperately thinking of ways to gain the upper hand. 'Where's my fiancé? Why are you holding us? We just got lost.'

Marianne smiled. 'Kaitlin, we need to ask you about the man you were with.'

'My fiancé?'

'The man you were with,' the sergeant stressed. 'Do you know who he is?'

'You need to be open with us,' Marianne stressed. 'We're giving you a chance to save yourself. You were led into this, right? The fake passport. He persuaded you.'

'That's not true.'

'Listen to me, Kaitlin. You're in big trouble. We're trying to help you.'

'Help me?'

'Do you know what happens to spies?' Marianne said in a calm voice that disguised the menace in the statement.

Kaitlin felt a rush of cold. They were threatening to go in hard: jail time, years of it, disgrace, the devastation of her parents. *Were they really that scared of what she was doing?* She jumped to her feet. 'I want a lawyer.'

'Sit down, please,' the sergeant said.

'Is there a lawyer here?'

The sergeant's eyes blazed and he roared, 'I said, sit down.'

Kaitlin slumped back to her seat, but she wasn't going to be cowed.

'I want a lawyer. Before I utter another word.'

Marianne smiled again. That was getting as menacing as the sergeant's toxic masculinity.

'We're not on US soil,' she said. 'You don't have any rights here.'

'What does that mean?'

'Tell us about the man you were with. You might as well. You've come to the end of it all now. There's nowhere to hide here, no one you can hide behind.'

'I don't know what to say. He's British. He works for—'

'The British Government? MI6?'

Kaitlin feigned a frown. 'No, of course not.'

'Did you know he's a Russian agent?'

Kaitlin stared. *Shit, Thomas. What have you gotten us into?*

'The British authorities have been looking for him ever since he disappeared. He's a spy. And this is a US base,' Marianne continued.

'What kind of base?'

'Just your regular satellite communications and intelligence base. We have bases like this all over the world. Nothing unusual about it being here.'

'Then am I free to go?'

The sergeant hammered the flat of his hand on the table. 'No, you are not free to go. You were in the company of a Russian agent.'

'I haven't done anything wrong.' Kaitlin heaved a deep breath. 'OK, maybe travelling on a false passport, I admit, that wasn't . . . But, look, I don't have anything to hide. I'm just trying to find the truth about Flight 702. Is that a crime?

'My brother was on that plane. I've given up everything. My studies, my family. All to find out what happened. I've followed every lead. I've done everything humanly possible to get to the bottom of what happened and I've ended up here.' She looked from the sergeant to Marianne. 'Is my brother . . . ? Is Conor here?'

'Flight 702 crashed into the sea, Kaitlin,' Marianne said.

'I know that's what's been said. But there was a crash near here. I have proof. There are witnesses, satellite images. It happened at exactly the same time Flight 702 went missing. Were there any survivors? Is Conor here?'

Marianne shook her head with a note of sadness.

'I'm sorry. You've been wasting your time. We don't know anything about what you're saying.'

They weren't going to give anything away. *Did she expect any less?*

'Where's Thomas? Can I see him?'

'He's not here. He's been handed back to the British government,' the sergeant said.

'What's going to happen to me?'

'You'll be repatriated and processed back to the US.'

'Processed?'

The sergeant stood up. 'OK. Time to go.'

Kaitlin felt her stomach knot. 'Where?'

'You'll be kept in custody until we can arrange transport.' He swung open the door and called for the guards.

As he walked out into the corridor, Marianne leaned across the table and whispered, 'Don't eat the food.'

'What?'

'Don't eat the—'

Marianne clamped her mouth shut when the sergeant stepped back in. She stood up and walked away as if nothing had happened.

The sergeant flexed his fingers for Kaitlin to stand. 'You can go with the officers here.'

Kaitlin watched Marianne vanish through the door, but her mind was racing once again: *what had just happened?*

After what seemed like an age in a holding cell, more guards came and escorted Kaitlin to another room, this one painted in yellow. A couch sat against one wall and a chair next to it. A large mirror occupied the wall opposite the couch. A balding man with glasses smiled at her as she entered. He introduced himself as Dr Hallin from the Army Research Laboratory, a military psychologist.

He swept a hand towards the couch and Kaitlin sat. She felt her body clench as she tried to guess what was coming next.

'I have a few questions for you,' Hallin began. He was softly-spoken, kindly at first glance, although she couldn't tell if that was a front. 'General ones – at first, anyway. Some names, dates, who your contacts are here, who brought you to the base. You didn't find your own way here.'

'Where are the people who interviewed me before? The sergeant, and the woman – Marianne? I told them everything.'

'I'm sure you did. I'm here to assist them in their inquiries. Marianne – Dr Hawkins – in fact used to be a student of mine. She has an extremely perceptive mind. Razor-sharp focus. Very good at her job.'

'So, where is she?'

'Behind the glass, assisting me with this process.'

'I don't know what all this is about. I've been sitting in a cell for God knows how long and no one is telling me anything.'

'You want some answers, right? I understand how you're feeling.' Hallin picked up his iPad and turned his back on Kaitlin as he scrolled through it. 'Did they give you anything to eat?' he asked.

The comment sounded disinterested, but after Marianne's warning, she knew better. 'Yes,' she said. They'd brought her food, but she'd scraped it into the toilet and flushed it away.

'Want to go home?' Hallin asked, turning back to her.

'Yes . . . No, I want my brother.'

'Isn't your brother dead?'

'No. I spoke to him.'

'You spoke to him? How can that be? He was on Flight 702.'

Kaitlin clamped her mouth shut. She was sick of this charade.

'Kaitlin, if you're having trouble remembering, we have aids that can help,' Hallin said with a gentle smile.

'What do you mean, aids?'

Hallin leaned back in his chair and folded his arms. 'Years ago, when I was a student, I was involved in a study by Harvard Medical. In those days, they used to pay students to take part in these kinds of experiments. I don't know if they still do now. I was young, fit, poor. Taking part in a medical programme seemed like . . . well, easy money.'

Kaitlin nodded. *Why was he telling her this?* She didn't trust any of them.

'The experiment was about shock treatment. They wanted to see what the mind would do when the subject was shown various patterns of complex words that led to a specific keyword, like, say "truth". Each time they ran a series of words, you were sitting alone in a dark room. And each time the word "truth" came up, they put a sound through your head. A very loud, sharp sound. Did I mention you'd be wearing headphones and your hands would be secured to the table in front of you with cable ties, so you couldn't remove the headphones?'

'That sounds like torture.'

Hallin shrugged. 'A loud sound would come. Very loud. Jarring. I can tell you, Kaitlin, it was every bit as painful as shock treatment. But it worked. As the pattern of the words moved towards the keyword, my heart rate would go up, I'd start to sweat, I'd feel a growing sense of panic.

'And after they'd gone through the pattern a few times, they didn't have to put a sound through your head every time that word, or word pattern of words, came up. Just seeing the word, after a while, caused your heart rate to increase, your sweat glands, your entire body to respond. And soon, you'd tell them whatever it was they wanted to know.'

Brainwashing. That's what he was talking about.

'All they'd have to do is show you the word pattern. You see, your body learns to be obedient and it teaches your mind to be obedient.'

Kaitlin stifled a shudder. Just like Marianne, the calmness of his voice was terrifying.

'I don't know anything.'

'I think, Kaitlin, such a process might help you to remember.'

'No!' Her voice cracked.

Hallin beckoned to a guard watching through the glass in the door. Kaitlin jerked round as the guard marched in and grabbed her by the wrists. Crying, she wrenched away, but the grip was too hard.

'Leave me alone,' she yelled.

'Kaitlin, this doesn't work if you have the ability to take the headphones off,' Hallin said. 'You need to be restrained.'

'I'm not going to do this!'

'You really don't have a choice.'

The guard pinned her arms behind her back. Barbs of fire lanced into her joints.

Hallin hovered over her. 'Just relax. Breathe. You're going to need all your strength.'

The guard pushed her forwards, then snapped cable ties around her wrists.

'Try to calm yourself,' Hallin said. 'When the procedure is over, the restraints will be removed.'

Gritting her teeth, Kaitlin sagged, letting her arms go slack. She wasn't strong enough. She'd only hurt herself by struggling.

Hallin snatched up a pair of headphones and slipped them over Kaitlin's ears. 'How's that? Comfortable?' he asked as if she were preparing to relax. He nodded to the guard, who walked out and closed the door.

Hallin pulled up his chair and sat in front of her. 'I want you to be open and honest with me. We have the time. And everything will be fine – you can go back home, see your parents and all will be good. OK?'

Kaitlin screwed her eyes shut, listening to the thump of blood in her head.

'Let's begin,' he murmured before calling out, 'Dr Hawkins, are you ready?'

Kaitlin snapped open her eyes as she heard Marianne's voice both on an intercom and in the headphones: 'Ready, Doctor.'

Hallin loomed over her. 'We need to know, Kaitlin, why you think Flight 702 didn't come down in the Atlantic. We need to know everything about that. All the things you haven't shared. All the things you've kept to yourself. Everything. Doesn't matter how crazy any of them are. Even the things you've allowed yourself to forget. We want to help remind you. This is what all this is about, Kaitlin.'

Kaitlin stared at him, sensing the mesmeric beat he'd placed on his speech.

'We're going to ease into this with a few simple words,' he continued. 'It'll go on for a minute or two, so close your eyes and relax.' He waved a hand towards the glass.

A calm, robotic voice droned through the headphones. 'Desert . . . Tortoise . . . Mother . . . Home . . . America . . . Friends . . . Thomas . . . White . . . Matchmaker . . . Rabbit . . . White . . .'

Kaitlin screwed up her eyes again, trying not to listen, but the words slipped in like stiletto blades.

Then, like a jolt of electricity, Marianne's voice cut in. 'Kaitlin, I've got about forty-five seconds to talk. Hallin can't hear me. I'm taking a huge risk to help you. Don't answer, grit your teeth, keep your eyes shut and listen to me. I hope you didn't eat anything.'

'Relax,' Hallin's voice intruded. 'Let the words soak over you.'

'Jungle . . . Disease . . . Religion . . .'

'We're in very grave danger,' Marianne continued in her head. 'All of us – you, me, Conor, the other survivors.'

Kaitlin felt a rush of elation that almost made her cry out loud.

Conor was alive!

'Say you're feeling sick. Pretend to be drowsy. Do it,' Marianne urged.

Kaitlin snapped her eyes open and stared deep into Hallin's face. 'I feel sick. I really need to sleep.'

He smiled back. 'Oh dear, dear, dear. You'll feel better in a moment. This is when it starts to work.'

'Terror . . . Virus . . . Biology . . . Iran.'

A buzzing was running behind the words, growing louder with each few beats, Kaitlin noticed.

'Agent . . . Survivors . . . Truth . . .'

'Stay focused,' Marianne pleaded, deep in her skull. 'Try. After the session, you'll be taken back to a holding cell. They'll expect you to sleep for twelve hours because of the drugs. I'll come and get you. Trust me.'

Trust her?

Trust no one.

Trust . . .

The buzzing whirled up until her whole head was throbbing and she could no longer hear the words.

Kaitlin screamed.

27

'Kaitlin?'

Her eyes fluttered open when she heard her name. She was lying on her back on the bench in her holding cell. Her head thundered as if she'd been clouted with a mallet. Swinging her legs down, she sat up and clutched her forehead.

Marianne crouched beside her.

'Come on. We need to be quick,' she whispered.

Shaking off the wooziness, Kaitlin pushed herself up and felt her strength return as she followed Marianne out into the corridor.

'Where are we going?' she asked.

'I want to show you something.'

Marianne weaved a mazy path through the building, clearly avoiding any areas where they might encounter resistance. Slipping out of a side door into the bitter night, she crunched through snow in an area of deep shadow away from the floodlights. Ahead, the silhouette of a huge building obscured the stars.

Another side door led into a cathedral-like space – a hangar by the looks of it. Lights glimmered around the edge, but the distant roof was lost to darkness.

It was empty. The concrete floor burned cold through the soles of her boots. She hugged her arms around her.

'Go into the middle. It's the only place we can talk,' Marianne whispered.

As they walked, Kaitlin asked, 'What is this place?'

'The final resting place of Flight 702.'

Kaitlin stiffened, looking at their surroundings with new eyes.

'They took me to see it when I first arrived,' Marianne continued. 'They reconstructed it from all the wreckage. Every bolt, every wire.'

'Where is it now?' Kaitlin turned in a slow arc, imagining the plane that she'd studied in such intricate detail.

'They've taken it away. They don't need it any more. It's all gone, like it never even existed. These people, they're not jailers, they're cleaners. That's what they do, they clean it up. Are you OK?'

Kaitlin rubbed a hand over her eyes. 'Just feeling dizzy.'

'Did you eat the food?'

'No, of course not.'

'Here.' Marianne handed over a chocolate bar. 'From the vending machine. Eat. You'll have low blood sugar. We're safe here for a while. They're doing maintenance on the software, so the live feed is down.'

'The live feed?'

'To the cells. They've stopped monitoring the captives through the night, anyway.'

Kaitlin shook her head, bewildered. 'What's going on here?'

'I know, it's a lot to take in. But we need to be fast. This is our only chance to stop them. Through here.'

Marianne strode off, leading Kaitlin through to a side room taken up by multiple screens and keyboards.

'This was the control centre. It's what the engineers used when they were reconstructing the plane. They're in the process of decommissioning it.'

Marianne tapped on a keyboard.

'Only they haven't yet.'

The monitors flickered on.

'See, there he is. That's your "fiancé" right now in his cell.'

Kaitlin watched Thomas pacing around his confined space like a caged beast.

'Oh my God. Thomas. I thought they gave him back to the British?'

'Why would they do that?'

'They said—'

'It was a lie. Like everything else.'

Kaitlin shook her head, trying to calm her whirling mind. One by one, the important questions surfaced.

'Where are the passengers?'

'They're here.'

'And Conor?' She felt her heart patter. 'I need to see him.'

'You will, shortly.'

'I don't understand why they're being held here.'

'The authorities say they're sick.'

'What do you mean?'

'Contagious. That's why they're being kept in isolation. No one goes in among them except with protective equipment. But it's been six months, Kaitlin. Look . . .'

Marianne tapped more keys. More monitors burned into life. Men and women hunched in cells or pacing like Thomas.

'This is the live feed to the cells. Do these people look sick to you?'

Kaitlin searched those faces, seeing the despair, the suffering. All of them as familiar as old friends from the images she'd attached to her files. None of them appeared ill.

'The plane was diverted here because intel suggested there was a terrorist on board planning an attack on the

US mainland,' Marianne continued. 'A biological attack with a manufactured virus stolen from a lab in Iran. Think of it – millions of people dead, the economy, the country, devastated.'

Kaitlin scanned the monitors. 'This can't be everyone, though? Where are the rest of them?'

'No one who was seated in the front ten rows of the plane made it.'

In the long moment of silence, Kaitlin cast her thoughts back over the seating plan, trying to recall those who had been lost.

'The crash complicated things,' Marianne said. 'It made it impossible to gather all the facts. That's why they brought me here. I'm a forensic psychologist. My job was to interview the surviving passengers to see if I could identify which one could be the terrorist.'

'Wait a minute. They don't know who it is?'

'They have suspicions. Nothing concrete. The intel was gathered from many sources. They were expecting an attack. Waiting for it. There was a huge operation. Different agencies were involved. Multinational. And then there was intelligence that a terrorist was on board. The plane was already in the air by then. Fortunately, we had an agent among the passengers.'

Kaitlin nodded. 'Chrissy. We were convinced she was the White Matchmaker.'

'That was a smokescreen to confuse the other side. Chrissy had been working undercover tracking a suspect.'

'Dr Aziz, the doctor from Syria. He was the suspected terrorist.'

'He died in the crash, so we can't confirm his involvement.'

'And Chrissy?'

'She didn't survive the crash, either. She was in the cockpit with the pilot.'

Kaitlin bit her lip. Now she could understand the paranoia of all those agencies, the desperate lengths they'd gone to, snatching her from her home, interrogating her, lying to her.

'When I arrived here, it was a mess,' Marianne said. 'Such a huge amount of intelligence, all pointing to different scenarios, different possibilities. And twenty-two traumatised survivors of a plane crash, all of whom could have been infected with a deadly virus.'

'The virus was released on the plane?'

'That was the working assumption. Someone died during the flight. A woman called Wendy LaPeer.'

Kaitlin's thoughts flew back to her meeting with the evangelists' daughter on that chill, bright day just off Long Island Sound. 'The missionary travelling back from the Congo with her husband.'

'She had a fever and died. Passengers got concerned something was spreading. Everybody's so paranoid after the Ebola pandemic. It only took a few people to start coughing and there was panic. Chrissy scrambled up to the cockpit and got a message out to say the attack had begun.'

'And that was when everything went wrong? All because of people leaping to assumptions.'

'You've got to understand the threat level, the fear of an attack.'

'But Wendy LaPeer had nothing to do with it.'

'No. After Chrissy's message went out, Homeland Security thought the virus had been released. A decision had to be made fast. They couldn't risk landing the plane on the US mainland. So, it was diverted here. They had to dump fuel because the runway was too short. It crashed on landing.'

Kaitlin weighed up what she was hearing, watching the misery in those faces on the monitors. She could now see how the parts of the puzzle she'd uncovered with Rory fit into place. Conor had known for some time that the hacker group was planning a 'spectacular', possibly biological, attack. When he'd seen the sick evangelist on board, he'd put two and two together and he'd alerted Thomas, who passed the intel on to his connections. They in turn would have alerted Chrissy, who would have confirmed the virologist was on board and the details of the sick evangelist.

'Why is this a secret?' she said. 'Why haven't the survivors been released?'

'Because it's such a massive fuck-up. None of the agencies trust each other. Everyone is protecting their backs. That's why we've had so many cover-ups, some of them, frankly, half-assed. And that totally misjudged decision to plant the evidence of the wreckage.' She took a deep breath to steady herself. 'No one will tell the world what happened until we know for sure what happened and that it's safe.

'The problem is that so many of the passengers died when the plane crashed, including the pilot, Susan Klemant. None of the survivors got ill. They couldn't find the virus. They examined every inch of the plane. Took it apart. Every bolt, fixture, even the catering trolleys. Nothing.'

'Maybe there was nothing.'

Marianne shook her head. 'There was definitely something. The intel was clear. A biological weapon had been identified.'

Kaitlin felt the weight of that statement settle on her.

'Do you know why they chose me?' Marianne said.

Kaitlin glanced at her and in the pale light of the monitors thought that she looked years older.

'I'm very good at my job. I interviewed the Unabomber, got him to talk. I was an intern with the Bureau of Alcohol, Tobacco, Firearms and Explosives during the Waco siege. I discovered then that I could talk to people and that I was able to get people to talk to me. I got them to remember the things they'd even forgotten. I seemed to know these people. To understand them. But here . . .' She shook her head. 'So far, I've failed. That's why I need you.'

Kaitlin whirled. 'Wait – you arranged for Conor to call me?'

'Arrange isn't the right word. But I knew that if I presented him an opportunity, if I turned my back for a moment, he'd take it.'

'What do you want from me?'

'We need to approach this from a different perspective. As the plane was about to take off, someone hacked into the entertainment system. We think a Russian hacking group was behind this and may be connected.'

'Connected to what? If there was no virus on board . . . ?'

'There's something we're not seeing. Some connection. We have to find the truth because the stakes are so high. The virus exists, but . . .' She held out her hands. 'I want you to help me to get Conor to talk.

'We know there was a terrorist on the flight and Conor knows who it is, I'm sure. Dr Hallin just wants to tear people's brains apart. That's what he was trying to do to you. But not only do I think that's unethical, but it's also evil. I don't like to use that word, but I can't think of another way to describe it. It's not how I work.

'The authorities would never have sanctioned bringing you in. They've spent the last few months shutting down any connection with the outside world. So, I took matters into my own hands.'

'Why should I believe you?'

'Because it's your only chance to save your brother and get out of here.'

Kaitlin bristled. 'I've been lied to, I've been arrested, tortured. They've threatened to deport my parents. And you're one of them.'

'I'm not. You have to believe me.' Marianne grabbed Kaitlin's shoulders, the passion crackling through her. 'Because I'm going to take you to Conor.'

28

The door slid open and Marianne and Kaitlin stepped inside.

'Where is he?' Kaitlin demanded.

Her heart was hammering and she felt a rush of desperate excitement. All those months when she thought her brother was dead. All the pain, the tearing herself apart over their last meeting. And now, finally, she could reclaim her life.

Marianne flicked a switch and lights flashed on in an adjoining cell visible through a large window. One of those one-way observation panels, she guessed.

All of her thoughts crashed away when she saw the figure hunched on the edge of the bed, head in hands. Tears seared her eyes and she slammed against the glass, pressing her face against it as the sobs wracked her.

'Conor. Oh my God. Oh my God.'

'He can't hear you,' Marianne said and flicked another switch. 'Now try.'

Kaitlin pulled back from the window and tried to wipe away the tears and snot with the back of her hand. She breathed in, long and hard, steadying herself. Conor was the one who had really suffered here and he deserved more than the gush of her emotions.

'Conor, can you hear me?' she said in as calm a manner as she could muster.

Her brother's head jerked up and surprise burned in his features.

'Kaitlin?' That look shifted to confusion, then terror. 'Please, no more. I can't take this any more. Please. I beg you, no more.'

Kaitlin turned to Marianne. 'What have they done to him?'

'I can't do this any more,' Conor babbled. 'I've told you everything I know. I've told you. Please, please.' His body juddered as he began to weep.

Kaitlin felt her heart break. 'I've got to go to him.'

'That's impossible. They're all in quarantine. We can't go in without full biohazard suits. It's too risky.'

'You said there wasn't a virus.'

'We don't know—'

'Look at him – he's fine. Surely something would have manifested after all these months?' Kaitlin pressed her hands against the glass. 'Conor. It's me, Kaitlin. It's not Dr Hallin.'

Conor gaped. 'Kaitlin? They got you, too?'

'I'm fine. Listen to me. You have to talk. To end all this.'

'I've told them everything. It wasn't me. I was investigating the hacking attempt, that was all. I've told them all that. And I don't know anything about a biological attack. How many times do I have to say it?'

'It's all right, Conor. I'm here. I'm not going to let anyone hurt you. But you have to tell them.'

'There is no virus, Kaitlin. They're keeping us all here, but there is no virus, and I don't know why they keep asking me over and over.'

Kaitlin hated to hear the anguish in his voice. Beside her, Marianne silently urged her to keep pressing.

'Listen to me, Conor. We can go home, all of us. We can save the other passengers. They can all go home, if you tell them everything.'

Conor reached out a pleading hand, though he couldn't see her.

'Why would I get on a plane if I thought someone was going to bring it down? It wasn't about that. It was spyware, that's what the hackers wanted to install. They were going to infiltrate the whole airport network. The entertainment system was the doorway.'

Kaitlin pulled back from the glass. 'I believe you, Conor. It's OK.' She turned back to Marianne. 'He's telling the truth.'

'How do you know?'

'We've never been able to lie to each other. We always know. Always. He's telling the truth.'

Marianne frowned. 'Unless you're both lying. Maybe you're part of this, too. Why not? Maybe you always were. Perhaps everything you've done, your search, was just an elaborate game.'

Kaitlin snorted. 'Not you, too. That paranoia is corrosive.'

'The only way you're getting out of here is to do what I want. Otherwise, they're going to shut this down like it never happened. All of these people are dead already. That's what the world believes.'

Kaitlin gasped. 'You're saying they'd kill them? No, I don't believe it.'

'If you don't help . . .' The words died on her lips as she looked towards the door.

Kaitlin spun round.

Dennison was standing there, that granite face peering out from the hood of a parka. 'Don't believe anything she says. She's part of the clean-up operation. She can't be trusted.'

'Who the hell are you?' Marianne spat.

'Jim Dennison. Formerly a government shill, just like you.' He turned to Kaitlin. 'We need to get out of here. Fast.'

Marianne lunged towards the door, yelling, 'Guards! I need help.'

Dennison blocked her with an outstretched arm. 'You're wasting your breath. There are no guards around.'

'Guards!' she cried again.

'They're all investigating an intrusion on the perimeter fence on the westward side. A building on fire.' He smiled without humour. 'It's just us here.'

Kaitlin pushed her way past Marianne and looked up at the ex-FBI agent. 'Emily's alive, Jim. Your daughter is alive! You were right all along. She's here.'

For an instant his face shimmered with emotion, transforming those cold features, and Kaitlin could see the man he used to be before the grief settled on him. But he swallowed it just as quickly. This was not the time.

'We can't get her now.'

Kaitlin couldn't believe his self-control. 'But—'

'There's no time. Our only option is to get away and blow this open. Otherwise, we'll see out our days in one of these cells.' He levelled a scathing stare at Marianne. 'Open that door.'

'No,' she cried. 'He might be infected.'

'You'd do well to heed me.' His voice throbbed with menace.

Whatever Marianne saw in his face, it did the trick. She turned round, hit a button, then pressed herself in the farthest corner of the room as the door slid open. Kaitlin darted through the widening gap and threw her arms around Conor, burying her face in his chest. She breathed in his musk, an aroma she never thought she'd smell again.

Conor pressed his hands on her cheeks and raised her head. 'God,' he croaked. 'I never thought I'd see you again.'

Kaitlin blinked away her tears. 'We're not safe until we're out of here. You've got to come now.'

She grabbed his hand and led him out of his cell. Ignoring Marianne, who was cowering in the corner, she whispered to Dennison, 'Thomas?'

He shook his head. 'Later. Has to be.'

Still bewildered from his imprisonment, Conor didn't seem to understand what they were saying. Kaitlin was thankful for that.

Dennison flexed his fingers towards Marianne. 'Get in the cell.'

She scurried inside without another word and he slammed his hand on the button to close the door.

'How did you get in here?' Kaitlin asked Dennison.

'Special forces skills. Been doing this since I was eighteen. Snipped through the fence on the eastern side on a blind spot between the cameras.' He clapped a hand on Conor's shoulder. 'Good to meet you, buddy. Heard a lot about you.'

Conor blinked, then nodded. Kaitlin felt her heart leap when she saw the ghost of a familiar smile. He was going to be all right.

'How long have we got?' she asked as they hurried out into the corridor.

'A few minutes – five max.'

A siren screamed out, rising and falling.

Dennison shrugged. 'Maybe less.'

29

Flames licked up towards the stars. In the orange glow, men swarmed around, shouting at each other as they tried to fight the blaze. The siren whined across the entire base, only adding to the air of chaos.

Keeping low, Dennison raced away from the activity towards the eastern perimeter fence. Kaitlin clutched Conor around his waist, urging him on.

At the fence, Dennison yanked back a rip in the chain-link so that Kaitlin and Conor could scramble through, then he eased behind them.

Further out across the snowy landscape, two snow-mobiles gleamed under the light of the moon. A figure paced around them, keeping warm. As they neared, the waiting individual threw up their arms and ran towards them. It was Rory, bundled up in the thickest Arctic-wear Kaitlin had ever seen.

'I thought you were dead,' he gasped, throwing his arms around her and lifting her off the ground.

Kaitlin prised herself free and said, 'This is Conor.'

Rory stared for a moment, then threw his arms around her brother, too.

'Sorry,' he blustered. 'I get emotional at times like this. I'd convinced myself I'd never see you again. We were at the hotel and the military were searching for us, so we knew they'd be on to you, too. We slipped out by the skin of our teeth, hired these things'—he waved a gloved hand at the snowmobiles— 'and got out here as quick as we could. Thank the Lord for Jim. I'd probably be halfway to the North Pole by now if it was down to me.'

'Enough jibber-jabber,' Dennison snapped. 'We need to put this godforsaken frozen waste of a country behind us.'

The icy landscape blurred past. Kaitlin clung onto Dennison as the snowmobile roared towards civilisation. It wasn't long before they were on the flight out that Rory had booked for them, heading towards Montreal, where they'd change for JFK.

Dennison nursed a bourbon, his gaze fixed somewhere ahead, lost to his thoughts. Kaitlin prayed he'd find some relief now he had the news that his daughter was still alive. But he'd proved himself many times over. He'd even somehow sourced a fake passport for Conor.

Conor sat between Rory and her. He was staring into space, still trying to come to terms with freedom after so long in captivity. Most of the time he seemed dazed, as if he were emerging from being drugged. His skin was pale and he was far thinner than the last time she had seen him. His dark hair was thick and overgrown, and his eyes carried a haunted look that made her heart ache for him.

More than anything, she'd wanted to call her parents to tell them Conor was alive – it seemed cruel not to do it immediately. But they had to get away fast. And she knew her mom and dad would want to talk to Conor, but in his current state, he wasn't up to it. It would only worry them.

'We need to get Conor in front of the media as soon as we can,' Rory was saying. 'That's the only way we're going to save our necks. Because if we thought they were coming after us hard before, we ain't seen nothing yet.'

Conor jolted from his stupor. 'I don't want to answer any more questions. Please, Kaitlin.'

She grabbed his hand. 'Look at me, Conor. Look into my eyes. Remember when we were on holiday in Louisiana with Mom and Dad when we were kids and we weren't supposed to go into the swimming hole. Neither of us could swim yet, but we snuck out anyway, and then I fell in. And we thought there was an alligator in there, but it was just a tree trunk.

'We were afraid to scream for help because we knew Mom and Dad would be angry. And we had to work together, you and me, to get out of that pool. We did it together. Do you remember, Kait and Conor, that we could always—'

'Finish each other's sentences?'

'We're going to get through this together, too. Do you trust me?'

Conor hesitated for a moment and Kaitlin's heart broke at the thought of all he'd endured. Then he smiled at her weakly and nodded.

Rory leaned back in his seat and sighed. 'Well, that's the first bridge crossed. Getting the media to take this seriously may be a tad daunting, what with the whole White Matchmaker debacle and me being a ludicrously unreliable informant, mocked from sea to shining sea.'

'Leave that to me,' Kaitlin said.

Rory cocked an eyebrow, but he didn't question her. It seemed he trusted her, too.

Closing her eyes, Kaitlin pushed her head back and drifted with her thoughts. As the tension and fear ebbed away, she felt an unfocused anger begin to burn. After months of study, no evidence of a biological weapon had been found. The survivors all professed their innocence and hadn't shown any signs of sickness, yet their freedom had been taken away with no recourse to any justice. Their loved ones had been denied any knowledge of them, left to suffer in grief.

And in the end, it all seemed to have spun off from a series of coincidences. An ailing evangelist. The kind of people who had chosen to be on that flight. Random events that suggested meaning, connections.

Worried people had put two and two together and got five – and all of those on Flight 702 and their families had paid the price.

The flames of that anger fanned higher. The injustice. The unnecessary suffering. She'd fought so hard and for so long to uncover the truth. She wasn't going to turn away now, whatever the risks that lay ahead.

The moment they were back on American soil, that crippling tension returned. Kaitlin found herself peering into every face she passed, weighing up whether they were a potential threat.

'We don't have much time,' Dennison said when they emerged from JFK into the chill morning air. 'There will be red flags going up across numerous systems. They'll be coming for us soon enough.'

They split up in three Ubers to try to throw off any pursuit: Dennison in one, Rory in another, and Kaitlin and Conor in the third. It wasn't long before they were heading into Downtown Manhattan. At a building on Vesey Street, just east of Rockefeller Park, Dennison waited in the lobby to keep watch while the rest of them travelled up to the twenty-first floor and a bright modern office with clear views of Jersey across the water.

They were ushered into a side office, where Rory paced relentlessly. Kaitlin clutched Conor's hand, giving it a squeeze. When the door swung open, Kaitlin jumped to her feet.

'So, it is you,' Valarie Vennix said as she walked in. The *New York Magazine* investigations reporter looked around at the people waiting to meet her, bemused.

'I need your help,' Kaitlin blurted. 'I've got a big story, bigger than the human trafficking one.'

'And that was huge. That whole ring is staring at serious jail time.'

'We're in a lot of danger. This one has to be done quickly or you probably won't see us again.'

'I can move quickly.' Valarie eyed Rory. 'Hang on a second, don't I know you?'

Rory held up his hands. 'Just pretend I'm not here. This is all Kaitlin – and Conor.'

Valarie's eyes narrowed. She was starting to make the right connections, Kaitlin could see.

'That's right. This is about Flight 702,' Kaitlin said. 'My brother was on board. As you can see, he's alive. So are many of the other passengers.'

'It didn't crash in the ocean?' Valarie said.

Kaitlin rested a hand on her brother's shoulder. 'Everything you've been told about Flight 702 is a lie.'

The *New York Magazine* photographer moved around the studio, snapping Kaitlin and Conor as they perched on chairs opposite Valarie. The sound recordist checked the levels while the cameramen adjusted the focus ready for the broadcast to begin.

'A live stream is definitely the way to go,' Valarie said. 'We can reach a global audience instantly. Much harder for anyone to shut it down.' She smiled at Conor. 'You ready to be our cover boy for this weekend's magazine?'

'Not really.' He looked exhausted as he shifted in his seat, his mouth twisted as if he'd swallowed sour milk. 'But Kaitlin says it's got to be done. So . . .' He shrugged.

'You'll be fine,' Valarie comforted. She turned to Kaitlin. 'Before we start, I just want to say you've done an amazing thing here. The courage. The diligence. That relentless pursuit of justice. Ever thought about being an investigative journalist?'

'Not really.'

'You should. After this, you can write your own ticket.'

'I didn't think about anything big. I just wanted to find out about Conor. That's all.

'That's all?' Valarie grinned. She turned back to the technicians. 'OK, guys, you ready? Let's do this.'

Kaitlin felt a weight lift from her shoulders. After so long, it was almost over.

'Hello, I'm Valarie Vennix and I'm here reporting live from New York City with Kaitlin Le and her brother, Conor. In this exclusive story, we're going to reveal to you a shocking tale of corruption and cover-up that implicates some of the most important people involved in the defence of the US.

'This is the story of Flight 702, the lost flight that vanished somewhere over the Atlantic. A devastating tragedy with a mystery at its heart. One that was supposed to have been solved when wreckage was found in the ocean.

'But it was all a lie. Many of the passengers are still alive. And Conor Le is living proof of that. Conor, tell me your story.'

30

News Report

NEWSCASTER: Though many in the defence and security establishment described the Kaitlin and Conor Le revelations as so-called fake news, we're now receiving reports of a whistle-blower from the ranks of the military coming forwards to confirm the story. More witnesses are expected to break rank in coming days . . .

News Report

NEWSCASTER: . . . scenes of heightened emotion as the surviving passengers of Atlantic Flight 702 were reunited with their families at the airport terminal building they were supposed to have arrived at six months earlier . . .

News Report

NEWS ANCHOR: Kaitlin Le, the college student who busted the Flight 702 case wide open, gave evidence today at the formal inquiry.
REPORTER: Also at the court was former FBI Agent Jim Dennison with his daughter, Emily, one of the surviving passengers, and Maria Elian, who was aboard Flight 702, who was today reunited with the son she was forced to leave behind at Heathrow Airport. The court heard explosive

revelations, which the judge summed up as 'malfeasance that goes to the very top of government'.

Allegations were made of the systematic use of torture on innocent citizens, those passengers of Flight 702, and psychological techniques similar to those used during the Iraq War and at Guantanamo Bay.

MARIA ELIAN: There were times when I wished I had died in the crash. I'm being given counselling, along with many of the other passengers. But this trauma will not go away easily. All of us will take a long time to recover.

New York Magazine Podcast

VALARIE VENNIX: It's very difficult to see how heads are not going to roll for this, General Myers.

GENERAL MYERS: We did nothing wrong. Every decision we made was in the national interest, to protect the American people. I'm afraid in the end, national security must always trump personal freedoms.

VALARIE VENNIX: We're talking about US citizens here, General. Not all of them were US citizens, admittedly. But these were people who had done nothing wrong and who were effectively imprisoned and tortured – and then potentially murdered – by our own government.

News Report

NEW ANCHOR: The wedding of the British spy at the centre of the Flight 702 scandal took place today at the Episcopal Church in Topeka, Kansas.

REPORTER: It was a simple service between a former spy and the computer expert who managed to live-stream to the world the truth behind what had happened to the passengers of Flight 702. Thomas Rider had earlier been cleared of involvement with a Russian hacktivist group.

THOMAS: I'm so glad this is all over and that the truth has come out. The people responsible are going to pay for this.

News Report

NEWS ANCHOR: The FBI agent at the centre of the Flight 702 scandal received an official apology from the Bureau and was awarded a special commendation for his investigation into the missing plane. His daughter was by his side to receive it.

SENATOR TOM HACKETT: What can we learn from this? We're living in a new age of truth, where it's getting increasingly difficult to tell the difference between what's really there and what is illusion. We all need to adapt, and fast.

31

The Big Apple's streets sparkled with the lights of the holiday season. Kaitlin eased through the throngs inspecting the window displays in the crisp late afternoon, half hearing the laughter and chatter. She still found it hard to be merry, as if a shadow were always a few steps behind her. It would pass, she'd been told. Soon, her life would be back to normal.

'I know, Mom,' she said, pressing her cell closer to her ear to stifle the festive din.

'Because if you want, I can come to New York to be with you,' her mother was saying.

'No, Mom, Dad needs you there. Besides, I'm heading back to Vassar soon. I've got an interview with the dean's office on the last day of semester, to make sure they're letting me back in the spring.'

'Of course, of course. You've got a lot of catching up to do.'

'Yeah. Thanks for reminding me.'

'So, you *are* working hard to catch up on all that work you missed, I take it? Because you've been given a second chance, you know. You don't want to waste it. The college has been very reasonable.'

'I know, Mom. And don't worry. I won't fuck it up again.'

'Kaitlin! You know I hate it when you use those words.'

'Yeah, sorry. Anyway, gotta go. I'm meeting up with an old friend.'

When the crossing blazed green, she hurried across the street and weaved her way to Rockefeller Plaza. The Christmas tree towered in a blaze of light and skaters whirled around the ice rink in front of it.

Rory was waiting near the stall selling mulled cider, his hands shoved in the pockets of a camel-hair coat. He was growing a moustache, for some reason. His face lit up and he threw his arms wide when he saw her.

He's going to hug me, isn't he? Kaitlin thought.

He did, lifting her off the ground.

'It's so good to see you!' he said, setting her back down. 'The woman who everybody's talking about! Magazine covers, newspaper articles, podcasts, blogs by the thousand. You're an inspiration to many.'

Kaitlin shrugged. 'I'd happily settle for being invisible. So, how have you been doing, Rory? How's the case going?'

'Good. Probably be resolved in about . . . I don't know – seven years.'

Kaitlin laughed.

'The wheels of the law grind slow but hard. But with any luck, I may be moving to a new office – one with a more fragrant atmosphere.'

Rory's face softened and Kaitlin felt surprised to see some real warmth there.

'And my daughter's home, staying with me, which is probably the best Christmas present I could have asked for.'

'And how's your wife?'

'Ugh, which one? Oh, and congratulations on your brother's wedding. I saw the pictures on the news. How are they?'

'Thomas has got out without being charged. I mean, he was dismissed from MI6, but he's relieved to be out of the intelligence business. They just want to put all this behind them.'

Rory bought a couple of plastic cups of the mulled cider and handed one to her.

'Your parents OK? I know there were some tensions there.'

'I think they're beginning to accept Conor for who he is. They might not be there yet, but they will. In the end. Maybe in about seven years.'

This time, Rory laughed.

As they sipped their drinks and watched the skaters spin, they chatted like old friends. At one point, Kaitlin looked along the cross street and glimpsed the red lights of a passenger jet in the distance, beyond the water. For the first time, she didn't ache with memories of her brother.

32

The smell of freshly baked cookies drifted through the dorm as Kaitlin pushed open the door. The apartment had been decorated with fairy lights and tinsel and a tiny silver Christmas tree glimmered in one corner.

Amelia stepped forwards with a tray of the cookies balanced on one hand and said, 'Ta-da! I bear festive treats to celebrate the return of the prodigal room-mate.'

Kaitlin grinned. 'Crazy.'

'It's not been the same without you, babe. Although I did enjoy being able to take a shower whenever I wanted.' Her grin faded. 'So, you're back?'

'Yep.'

'For good?'

'For good. Just got the all-clear from the dean's office. Need to tidy up one final thing and then I'll never have to think about Flight 702 again. Hello to the future.'

Amelia set the cookies down. 'OK, give me a yell when you're done. I have wine. Lots of wine.' She slipped on her headphones and lounged on her bed.

Kaitlin jumped on her own bed and pulled out her laptop. *One last thing: shut down the Flight 702 hotline. No more conspiracy theorists, no more attention-seekers. Finally.*

But when she tapped in her password and the mailbox popped up, she saw one unplayed message waiting there. She stared at it, feeling the unease rise, remembering when her life had been haunted by mystery and when all she'd had was a desperate hope.

Her finger hovered over the key and then she smiled to herself and closed the laptop. She didn't need to listen to it now. She didn't need to listen to it ever again if she didn't want.

She'd got her life back.

'OK,' she called, waving so Amelia would see her. 'Let's get moving. We've got a lot to catch up on and I'm in the mood for the best night of my life.'

CREDITS

J.S. Dryden and Trapeze would like to thank everyone at Orion who worked on the publication of *Passenger List:*

Agent
Euan Thorneycroft

Editor
Marleigh Price

Copy-editor
Claire Dean

Proofreader
Clare Wallis

Editorial Management
Charlie Panayitou
Jane Hughes

Audio
Paul Stark
Amber Bates

Contracts
Anne Goddard
Jake Alderson

Design
Debbie Holmes
Rabab Adams
Joanna Ridley
Nick May

Finance
Jasdip Nandra
Tom Costello
Ibukun Ademefun

Marketing
Lucy Cameron

Production
Claire Keep
Fiona McIntosh

Publicity
Will O'Mullane

Sales
Jennifer Wilson

Victoria Laws
Esther Waters
Lucy Brem
Frances Doyle
Ben Goddard
Georgina Cutler
Jack Hallam
Ellie Kyrke-Smith
Inês Figuiera
Barbara Ronan
Andrew Hally
Dominic Smith
Deborah Deyong
Lauren Buck
Maggy Park
Linda McGregor
Sinead White
Jemimah James
Rachael Jones
Jack Dennison
Nigel Andrews

Ian Williamson
Julia Benson
Declan Kyle
Robert Mackenzie
Imogen Clarke
Megan Smith
Charlotte Clay
Rebecca Cobbold

Operations
Jo Jacobs
Sharon Willis
Lisa Pryde

Rights
Susan Howe
Richard King
Krystyna Kujawinska
Jessica Purdue
Louise Henderson

Help us make the next generation of readers

We – both author and publisher – hope you enjoyed this book. We believe that you can become a reader at any time in your life, but we'd love your help to give the next generation a head start.

Did you know that 9 per cent of children don't have a book of their own in their home, rising to 13 per cent in disadvantaged families*? We'd like to try to change that by asking you to consider the role you could play in helping to build readers of the future.

We'd love you to think of sharing, borrowing, reading, buying or talking about a book with a child in your life and spreading the love of reading. We want to make sure the next generation continue to have access to books, wherever they come from.

And if you would like to consider donating to charities that help fund literacy projects, find out more at **www.literacytrust.org.uk** and **www.booktrust.org.uk**.

THANK YOU

*As reported by the National Literacy Trust